Prologue

H e knew they'd come for him, deep down. It was inevitable really, despite his precautions.

"We'll be safe at sea," he'd assured her.

Yet somewhere at the back of his mind he'd been waiting for it — perhaps even willing it.

As soon as the movement woke him, he knew he hadn't been careful enough.

All the planning, all the thinking, all the precautions, and still they'd been found.

His initial thought was that he'd underestimated them.

In actual fact, he'd misidentified them.

CHARLIE

FINN ÓG

VINCI
BOOKS

Also by Finn Óg

"One crowded hour of glorious life, is worth an age without a name."
Mordaunt
For wee Lachlan, never forgotten.

Vinci Books

vinci-books.com

Published by Vinci Books Ltd in 2024

1

A CIP catalogue record for this book is available from the British Library.
Paperback ISBN: 9781036700003

Printed and bound in Great Britain by Clays Ltd, Elcograf S.p.A.

Chapter 1

S am sat on the afterdeck and watched the light fall from the lough. He thought of the contentment he'd once drawn from the rise and set of the sun. The down and the dawn over a calm sea had brought peace, prospect, hope, excitement. Now they crept upon him as a menacing reminder of all that remained undone. The red and orange retreat before him was the most peaceful he'd seen since his return, but it was hopeless. No quiet, no touch, no gentle benevolence or sympathy would settle him. He knew he'd succumb.

He thought of how he'd tried to stick to what he knew when he got home, but therein lay the problem: there was little call for his questionable talents in the real world. It had been twenty years since he'd known anything else. Back then it had been boat work, so that was where he began. But he felt that notion slipping away, like the ashes he'd shaken into a gentle sea breeze.

The only thing that that had held him back thus far was Isla. Their daughter. He stiffened, correcting himself. His daughter. For three days his little girl had suffered without him as some half-a-head from logistics thrashed around to get him replaced and repatriated from Bastion. He turned instead to imagining what had happened, outlines flickering like a slide show in the fresh darkness. Isla had been placed with his parents which was as good as it could possibly have been, but as soon as the news broke, he knew he'd never wear webbing again.

His mind inclined to the practical during moments of extreme stress – a protection measure of sorts, an escape from emotion. For those three days he kept his grief at bay, slowly working through what he would do and how he would do it. He'd caught the whispers of others, most convinced he was in shock. He knew that not to be true but said nothing. Perhaps he'd been conditioned, perhaps it was just his nature. Either way, he'd just worked towards securing a way forward.

His endgame was to wrap Isla in certainty – to assure her that nobody could harm her, or him, and that she was safe. He knew how obsessed she could become with little things – he recalled being similar himself when he was small. Because of what had happened to her mam she would be terrified of every noise at home, every opening of the front door, every coming and going. The solution presented itself in a straightforward fashion: they wouldn't live in a house. But then the problems crowded in as the head-banging judder of the transport flight rattled him all the way home.

Nobody would buy their house. Not after what had happened.

Occasionally he allowed himself the distraction and musings of retribution, before admonishing himself for such indulgences. If he was to be a single father, such plans could never be fulfilled. He tried, half-heartedly, to spurn such urges but his planning was frequently overcome by them. In between such blistering impulses he carved out their future.

His only smiles came with thoughts of Isla, her nature. He suspected that one day she would follow in her mammy's footsteps. A frightening prospect. Isla had inherited her mam's kindness – he could see it in every subtle gesture she made. She was programmed to be as gentle as he was brutal. She deserved a beautiful life; to be sheltered from the type of conflict that had brought her mother and him together. Their meeting amid horror as she worked to preserve life, and he to extinguish it.

Her mam had managed to coax some dormant empathy from deep within him, but he knew that keeping it at the surface would be a constant challenge now that she was gone. He thought of her then, his wife, of the progress she'd made. He sat in the gentle, lapping darkness and knew that he was about to place it all at risk.

Chapter 2

The call had come as Sam and his team were training at their home port of Poole, in the south of England. He'd hand-picked the three that would go with him, his sergeant and two specialists. From there the selected men were flown to Faslane Naval Base in Scotland, a place they were all familiar with. Then Sam was summoned to attend the operational, where he was but one among many. Three rows of three doubled, a space down the middle. Eighteen in all, gathered to spread the risk and cover the asses in what had the potential to be a politically problematic deployment. He was the most junior officer present. Although he was to lead the ground team, the briefing confirmed to him, if any confirmation was needed, that his troop represented the oily rags and overalls of special operations. Within the military they might be considered the elite, but as soon as he sat down in a briefing room with the soft-shoe brigade Sam felt himself being coated with distaste. It was reflected in the brevity of information they'd been offered.

"The target vessel is more accustomed to ferrying cattle feed but has been adapted with the rather grand ambition of delivering sanitary products to the women of Gaza," an older man, undoubtedly from the intelligence service, told the small group assembled before him. "On board is a minuscule amount of Semtex. Are we all familiar with the characteristics of Semtex?"

All nodded except for Sam, which caught the attention of the spook.

"Does the lieutenant need educated?" The man ignored Sam and looked instead to his commanding officer in the chair in front.

"Mr Ireland is," the major paused without so much as looking around at Sam, "Irish."

"Then surely he doesn't need a lesson on Semtex?" the spook said, his sneer poorly shielded behind a snigger.

Sam shook his head slowly. "No more than I need a lesson in manners," he said, prompting his own major to turn to him with a glare: insubordination, not to be tolerated. Sam didn't give a rat's ass. It was their choice to send him; they could deploy someone else if they preferred.

"There are obvious issues with the proposed incursion," the spook ignored the quip and assumed a clipped tone. "Israel cannot, under any circumstances, become aware of our presence."

Sam watched the spook's gaze wander to his own before darting away. If their intelligence was so good, he thought, why had they allowed the Semtex to get aboard the boat in the first place?

"Boarding the ship in transit would be much too obvious for our purposes, fun as you people might find it," the spook continued. "In the event of failure, such overt action would suggest prior knowledge of the presence of said Semtex. Therefore a covert operation in allied territory is the only option, albeit far from ideal."

Sam's major rose and took to the front of the room. He walked as if carrying two basketballs under his arms, nodded to the spook in deference and puffed out his chest like a pigeon.

"We do not know the whereabouts of the explosive on board, but the ship has a skeleton crew and aside from the captain and three hands they are all rather crustie leftie volunteers – students of one kind or another. My men will board the ship at night, conduct a thorough search and remove the offending substance."

Sam sat silent and expressionless. He was but one of *my men*, spoken of as if not present. He knew the briefing was for the optics, providing cover for the intelligence services. Because of how the operation would play out, there could be no comeback on whatever intelligence agency soft shoes belonged to. Maps were produced but the real detail would be for Sam and his sergeant to interrogate on passage. Sam knew what would happen next. Soft shoes would ask if special forces had any reservations and the major would say, "No, none at all. We are ready and trained and able." Because that was what he had to say. The major would never pipe up and question the sanity of sending specialist troops into an ally's territory unannounced. If the whole thing went tits up, Sam's team would take the blame because their major had agreed to take the job. Because that was what they existed to do. The major couldn't be seen to raise any worries – to do so would suggest that *his men* weren't up to the job. No queries, no qualms. If things went bad, the spooks could say they weren't warned of any misgivings. Any mess would fall at the feet of special forces.

"RIGHT, HERE'S THE SCORE." Sam stood in their cramped quarters.

From Faslane they'd been flown to Gibraltar where they boarded the submarine that would ferry them towards their target. He wasn't supposed to tell his small team what little he knew, but he'd always hated when that had been done to him. "Who likes Battenberg?"

The two specialists looked at one another in confusion. Sam's sergeant, Min, a burly little Glaswegian and Sam's closest friend – chuckled. He was the only one who didn't have to stoop in the space they'd been allocated. "So we're after a drop Semtex, then?"

"Yes."

"Nae bloody wonder they chose us."

The two other men looked blankly at them. They knew that Sam and Min shared a long history, but little of the detail.

"Why?" asked the dive expert, a tall man and seasoned operator at the age of twenty-six.

"Battenberg is Semtex," Min explained. "You know the cake wrapped in marzipan with different coloured squares?"

The diver looked baffled.

"Semtex smells of marzipan – almonds, at least it should."

"Ok?"

"It was the explosive of choice where the boss grew up." Min nodded at Sam. "We did a bit of time over there looking for the stuff. Blow your bloody heed aff."

Sam gently altered course. "We're to board a campaign

ship bringing aid to the Middle East. The ship will be in Gaza. You all get what that means?"

"Gaza?" Min's face creased in incredulity.

"Gaza," Sam repeated.

"Why don't they send the Israeli Defence Force?" the fourth man asked. As a former Army Technical Officer, he'd been nicknamed Sparky. Sam had chosen him specifically for his bomb disposal expertise.

"Good question," Sam replied.

"So we're going in without the Israeli's knowing we're there?" Min's countenance hadn't changed.

Sam nodded.

"That's mad," the diver said shaking his head. "They know everything that happens on their turf."

"Well, they can't know about this," Sam hardened his tone. "We get caught, we get denied."

"Who will they say we are?"

"Mercenaries, probably. But that's got nothing to do with anything because we won't get caught cos we can't get caught. Clear enough?"

"Clear," the two more junior men replied.

"They're calling it a mercy mission," Sam explained. "The ship's bringing medical kit, sanitary stuff and food to the Palestinians. Don't ask me the details cos I don't know, but my guess is some IRA head is doing a swap with someone in Hamas."

"Semtex for what?" the diver probed.

"Who knows. The IRA has a habit of helping other groups, so maybe it's just out of the goodness of their hearts. Anyway, there's explosives smuggled on board and that's a problem. If it gets used and the Israelis trace it to Northern Ireland, they'll be asking the Brits how that managed to happen. So we've got to get it off as if it was never there in the first place."

"But why did they let it get on board?" Sparky asked.

Min shook his head. "You're wasting your time trying to work that one out, kiddo. When we worked in Ireland there were sources and agents doing things that made nae bloody sense at all."

"It's not for us to worry about," Sam said. "We just need to get the stuff. You already packed the kit you need, so read the briefing packs, get your heads down and we'll go through any outstanding detail in two hours."

The two men nodded and moved into the next compartment.

Min threw his papers onto the bunk above Sam's then grabbed an overhead pipe and chinned himself up, swinging his thick little legs in. For a short, stubby man he could move like a gymnast. Sam lay beneath and heard Min peeling through the pages, absorbing the detail. It wasn't long before his head appeared over the edge. Sam had been waiting for it.

"This is mad, pal. Israeli-controlled territory in the middle of an upsurge?"

Sam didn't even look up. He simply mimicked the major's plummy voice. "Leave the politics to those better equipped. An exchange of materials has been arranged. Your *function* is *simply* to prevent one element of that from occurring."

Min snorted and rolled back. He shared Sam's distaste for their boss, who was convinced he did all the thinking while his grunts obeyed orders and performed menial tasks. Few in the service behaved like that; it was just their bad luck that the major was their commanding officer and that he viewed Sam and Min as a challenging, if effective, pairing. "So when we're far enough into the Med, we'll pop up, take a Zodiac close and swim in. That's the plan, Sam?"

"Yep."

"That's the mad, daft plan," he muttered.

"It might be ok," Sam said.

"Why would the IRA be bothered? It's years since peace broke out in Belfast. Seems like a risk for them."

"You know the score. Remember the Palestinian flags in Belfast?"

"Course I do. I get that. I know the Provos like Palestine and think Israel's like the Brits – occupying force and all that, but what I don't get is why the intelligence folks didn't swap out the Semtex before it got on the ship. If they knew it was happening, it would save all this risk."

"Must be someone worth protecting."

"An agent?"

"They mustn't have wanted to compromise a good CHIS. You know as well as I do, covert human intelligence sources—"

"Better than eavesdropping," Min finished. "I haven't forgotten the tripe we were told. But still."

"Maybe only two people knew it was happening. If the stuff got seized before it was stowed on board, one of them would be for the knacker's."

Sam could hear Min flicking through the pages of the pack.

"That ship's one rickety rust bucket," he said. "How was that not condemned by the MCA?"

Sam looked at the images. Getting a ship through Belfast without inspection by the Maritime and Coastguard Agency was unusual, which suggested it had been allowed to sail without official scrutiny, which was no mean feat. Pulling the wool over the eyes of the MCA was tricky.

"They're really going daft again in Gaza," Min sighed, leafing pages. "The boys are right. Sending special forces into the middle of it is mental. I still don't see why they didn't swap the Semtex for something inert."

"You're overthinking it."

"What'll happen if the Israelis lift us?"

"They won't."

"Aye."

"My guess is they thought it through and decided that if the Israelis ever found out their British allies knew Semtex was on the way from Britain and did nothing, it would be very bad."

"So they should just tell the Israelis and get them to raid it."

"Yeah," was all Sam could manage.

The two men had trained together, gone through selection together and served together in a unit under the dusky direction of spooks before. They both knew there'd be some convoluted reason for the covert deployment.

"And what's Hamas gonnae send to Ireland in return? I mean, it's no' like the IRA needs weapons or money."

"That's not for us to worry about."

"Aye, well, it's no' me that's from Northern Ireland, so you can not worry all you like."

"It's straightforward. Our esteemed leader says so and we are the men to do it." Sam began the voice again. "We are like the SAS but wetter and better." Min snorted at the impression. "We must simply swim, land, locate the ship, take the stuff, extract," Sam trotted out the orders as if fired in short bursts.

"Aye," muttered Min, "just like that. Hell of a risk."

"That's why we can't get lifted," Sam said.

"Well, we are slippery when wet."

"Get some kip. I've a notion we'll be needing it."

Chapter 3

I t was her smile that had disarmed him as he
squelched up a beach in Gaza.

The sub had dived mid-Med. One hundred
nautical miles off the shore of Egypt, following check and
re-check from the dive specialist, they were launched to the
surface. In the swell they inflated the boat, climbed aboard
and ripped the outboard engine from its waterproof bag,
before motoring further east. The risk increased as they got
closer to Israeli territorial waters and the boat had to
meander at a snail's pace to avoid radar interest. Ten miles
from the coast they attached fins over lightweight boots and
returned to the sea. The coxswain, a marine attached to
their SBS unit, turned tail and left the four of them to kick
ashore.

Then, as they used to say when a plan fell apart, it went
shit shape.

Two miles from the sand and on top of a rolling sea
they watched as missiles lit the night sky. Sam knew they
must have come from an Israeli helicopter gunship, and that

they'd struck right where his team had intended to land. He watched their chances of a successful mission narrow with each explosion. The nature of the operation meant they had virtually no comms. Not, he thought, that it would have mattered. Israeli action so close to the coast meant that the sub captain wouldn't be able to send an assault craft to collect them. The search would take too long meaning the Israelis would probably spot the boat, sparking a diplomatic inquiry and a shit fight with an ally. So they swam and beached in hell.

Two of his team fanned right, the other left as Sam made his way up the middle of the beach, tired and restricted by his clingy kit. The night was as black as they'd predicted, and while wary of any impact the gunship attack might have had, Sam hadn't expected to find it so quickly. He was nearly on top of them before he realised what was happening. He stood stock-still as another rocket flash lit the sky overhead and betrayed the bodies before him. One appeared to be crouched over another as it lay prostate on the sand. There was a moment before the darkness restored itself in which a face turned up towards him.

Sam clutched his knife, ready to remove the obstacle if necessary, but all intentions were halted when he heard her speak. "Who's there? He's dying. Will ye not help him?"

Sam had been away from home for a very long time. In his late teens he'd been forced to take a train to Devon with its own special stop. Thereafter he'd only been able to return to Ireland for holidays. Now, on a beach in the Middle East, in the middle of the night, in the middle of a war, he was being asked for help by an Irishwoman. Her voice stripped him of all his sensibilities. He was supposed to lead the operation – to ignore all else and get the job done. Against all reason he took his red LED from his belt and lit her face.

In the midst of deepest misery that smile caught him, full of hope, of faith. He hesitated longer than he should have on a beautiful face and then panned the torch down. Her arms, to the elbows, were enveloped in blood. The child at her knees was labouring for air, the fingers on both her hands were interwoven as she desperately tried to stem the catastrophic bleed, and Sam's decision was made. He unrolled the med pack in his kit and without a word went to work, packing and strapping one wound and knowing what he would have to do with another. Out of bandages and gauze, he applied a tourniquet to the boy's other, upper leg knowing that with it the kid would lose the limb, but without it he would lose his life.

Sam refused to speak to the woman. She fired what sounded like questions at him in a guttural tongue, all of which he failed to understand. She then attempted what sounded like a subtly different language. He knew what she was doing: testing this stranger – Hebrew or Arabic. His arrival on the sand was undoubtedly suspicious. He knew she'd think it more likely that he was Israeli given that he'd come from the sea, yet he sensed more confusion than hostility.

He finished the job, content that he'd done all that could be expected of him in the circumstances. She rattled off more questions as he reached down for a final check on the boy's pulse. Frustrated, she reverted to English, her shoulders falling in resignation at his persistent silence. He understood her annoyance: that he couldn't be there for good reason yet he'd done what she'd asked of him. He packed up to go and she threw her arms around his neck and hugged him hard.

"Thank you," she whispered, and he found that he wanted to relent.

"No hassle," he replied, and felt the shock shudder through her. Even with just two words his accent was indisputable. She pulled back and although the light had burned part of his night vision he could sense her staring at him. Just then Min crawled up from behind and swearing like no other man under Sam's command would get away with, made clear in raw Glaswegian his feelings on contact with the natives.

They extracted, Sam's stocky sergeant panting incredulous questions at him as they ran. He knew, though, somehow, that he'd see that woman again. He couldn't have imagined how, such was the simultaneous humanity and depravity of what their next meeting would bring.

———

THE FIRING CONTINUED ALL NIGHT, both incoming and desperate, pointless return fire from Gaza into the night sky as fighters hunted for a gunship they had no hope of seeing, let alone hitting.

The Israeli Defence Force reacted with its usual restraint by blowing up anything and everything with the firm intention of filling the few unoccupied patches of land in Gaza with makeshift coffins.

Sam and his men yomped across beaches and through shitty, shell-holed streets all night, avoiding everyone, which took time. They'd been shown satellite images of the port and been briefed on its layout, so they knew it was woefully inadequate for such a heavily populated city, but even they were taken aback. They dug in for a day's rest at the edge of the breakwater as the sun snuck over the Mediterranean.

It gradually revealed a harbour no bigger than some of the fishing ports he'd worked in his youth. Despite the increasing daylight they could hear the Israeli attacks continuing inland and it began to register that this was less of an operation to complete, as one to withdraw from with as little exposure as possible.

There was no sign of the ship. Day passed into night as they waited for its arrival, one man on sentry, three asleep. They had, by diktat, no firearms. Sending soldiers into friendly territory without authorisation was one thing and could be denied, but not if they were carrying. Sam's patrol was well equipped, nonetheless, for hand-to-hand combat.

By the early hours they were defecating in small bags and their bodies were encrusted with salt. As their ration packs were worked through, they contemplated the looming need to eat discarded fish from the small boats a few hundred yards away. No man could afford to get sick, though, and of greater concern was their water supply. If the ship didn't show up soon, Sam knew they'd have to break cover and fill their deflatable bottles.

———

THE SHIP NEVER DID ARRIVE.

"It's a blockade," Min eventually whispered what Sam had suspected.

"Yeah," he conceded. "I reckon Hamas pinged a few rockets over the fence. Good timing."

"It's our own fault, pal. Whoever thought this was a good idea should be stood up and shot twice. This is what they always do if Hamas don't behave. They shut down aid. Block the seas. I mean, did our lot not think about that?"

"Sure that's your first mistake."

"What?"

"Thinking that our lot think things through."

"Aye," Min said. "What next?"

"Well, the ship's not going to be allowed in. So we need to make contact, and plan our extraction."

Given that deniability was essential, they'd only been issued with smartphones which in themselves were still relatively rare. They'd been packed in watertight commercially available cases. There were applications on the devices that encrypted or scrambled conversations, but they knew that Israel was on the ball with all comms and that any signal out of Gaza stood a more than even chance of interception. Such concerns were secondary, however, as they had to get a signal first. Min had brought a small pebble which gathered together any cellular bandwidth and turned it into a comm channel, but even with that they could find nothing. No amount of hopeful arm extending and staring into the face of the phones brought any breakthrough. It was clear that their makeshift bunker on the breakwater was in a black spot.

Sam opted to go alone in search of what, at best, would be 2G. He cast off his kit, discarded all but the blade sheathed against his inner left leg and headed for the city. His Arabic was limited to "please", "thank you" and "excuse me" – his three essentials for any deployment. But he hoped he wouldn't need them, that he would secure comms long before he left the harbour. Unfortunately, like everything on that op, it went belly-up.

The glow from the smartphone screen lit his face every time he stroked it to life and so he was forced to walk roughly five hundred metres between each attempt. The constant checking led him straight into Gaza City, and as he plunged deeper into its density he became increasingly conscious that his bearings were gradually muddling. Sam was always confident that he'd be able to sniff out the sea eventually, given how he'd been reared, but what he hadn't planned for were the patrols.

The first one he encountered was a collection of three, each man carrying a heavy weapon. Rocket-propelled grenades were silhouetted over their shoulders like tulips before bloom. Hamas fighters, demonstrating to the population that they were prepared to take on the Apaches, Cobras and whatever other helicopters the Israeli Air Force had at its disposal.

The initial gaggle was far from alert. They smoked and talked, oblivious to his presence as they passed less than two feet from him. Stupidly he assumed there would be spacing between any patrols stalking the streets and he huddled in a doorway, watching their backs weave around a corner before igniting the screen on the smartphone. It turned out to be the best and worst action of the night. He immediately heard a shout as a second patrol picked up the glow and started barking orders at him. He concentrated on trying to lower his heart rate, knowing that it was no time to kick the shit out of himself for getting caught so quickly and easily, and hunted for options. Remaining silent, he told himself that as far as the men were concerned, he was guilty of little more than breaking some sort of curfew. He debated pretending to be a western journalist or aid worker, but knew that it would only prolong the agony and that ultimately, he didn't have time to talk his way out of the situation. Fight, or flight he reasoned, and worked out his next steps as he waited for the men to get to him. Looking around one last time, he decided to do all he could to avoid drawing fire in such a built-up area then stood still, deciding which of them needed disabling first.

They arrived in one lump as if congealed together in a spittoon, which made his work much easier. Sam placed his phone in the pouch above his coccyx and eased one foot behind for stability. The patrolmen noticed his stance and raised their arms immediately – an AK and a homemade Carl Gustav pistol.

Coaxed by the poor light they came closer to get a better look. Untrained assailants often stand either beyond accurate firing distance or too close to prevent an unarmed attack. Both mistakes narrow their advantage considerably. Sam knew the Gustav weapon to be dreadfully inexact and that a Kalashnikov was hard to handle. Of the three men, the only one who eyed him with sufficient wariness or had the wit to stand outside his striking arc appeared to have been issued a mortar tube.

What Sam didn't want was collateral damage: dead children in the houses on either side of him or noise attracting anyone else to the scene. That meant the three men needed to be taken down hard and that they would more than likely suffer permanent damage, or worse.

The youngest was the most excitable; Sam imagined he had most to prove. He gesticulated his Kalashnikov at Sam and, predictably, edged forward in the process. There was no shoulder butt on his model, so Sam dipped to the side and grabbed the barrel and mag to take the youth's teeth out with the stock. He heard them break as he ducked and rose with his fist to hammer the holder of the Gustav with a disarming blow to the sweetmeats. As the second man folded, the gun presented nicely and Sam twisted it from his grip, turning it on the mortar man, who was suddenly outnumbered by two guns to one.

"Min fadlik la!" he pleaded, and gave up immediately, crouching to his knees with his hands in the air. Sam walked behind him and kicked him in the back to make sure he was face down and unnerved at the prospect of what would happen next.

He set the guns down and incapacitated the younger man with a blow so heavy it could have killed him. The second fighter was lying in a knot, drawing his knees to cover his groin as he moaned in pain. Sam rolled him face down with a kick and placed his knee across the man's shoulder blade, and pulling his chin backwards.

"Rajul mayit," the man hissed in anger, but the stretch on his throat choked him nearly as much as Sam's ramming of the small gun's magazine down his gullet. He ripped a scarf from the man's neck and lashed it around his head while the mortar man panted and prayed. As soon as the knot was tied Sam struck out sideways to his right, hammering the jaw of the mortar man before he too could make any further noise. The lower frame of his face shattered and his head shook away and then back. He too wore a Keffiyeh so Sam tore strips off it and wedged them into the man's hanging jaw. Finding cable ties on the belt of the second man, Sam strung two together and clicked them tight around the mortar man's face before securing his hands and feet similarly. A small radio was tucked into the man's thigh pocket. He removed it and rotated the dial on top to 'off'. The radio was of no use to Sam, it would carry any transmission only as far as the line of sight. He dropped it and dragged each of the men into a side street and silently swearing at himself, was forced to leave it at that. He began a steady-paced run north, needing to place distance between him and the scene. It would likely only be a matter of minutes before the men were discovered.

He'd only covered about twenty metres when he saw yet another patrol and realised that their station or briefing room must be close by. This time, he could see few options. The new street left him more exposed; there was no obvious side road in which to shelter and his heaving chest betrayed his breath on the cool air. He stepped back into inadequate gloom, and watched.

The new patrol was different. He watched them as they rolled down the street, fingers parallel with their gun barrels, entirely distinct from their predecessors. They were properly spaced too and Sam knew his luck had expired. He'd left at least one of their colleagues conscious and had visions of him flapping like a seal, head and tail raised as his pals went past. There was virtually no chance of evading capture and less prospect of fighting his way out.

He tried to dismiss the feeling of hopelessness. He'd been trained to believe that there was always a way, yet in those moments demanding a decision, he couldn't find it. Capture by the Palestinians would be a nightmare. Hamas would assume he was there to identify their rocket positions, making him Sayeret Matkal – the Israeli equivalent of the UK's Special Reconnaissance Unit. They might assume him to be Shayetet 13, Israel's answer to his own SBS. Either way, he would be considered a prize hostage or even an opportune candidate for slaughter and revenge given the brutality of the air assault on Gaza. There was no way his own unit could claim him without upsetting Israel and the Palestinians, and the United States might not be too happy with the UK either. Sam was on his own.

The Hamas fighters spun on the balls of their feet, marking out sight lines and using what little light there was to clear the area. They were so much better than the previous unit that Sam wondered whether they had tried to make contact with the incapacitated men and had taken the lack of response as an indicator of an incursion.

All is not lost he kept telling himself, driving his heart rate down, as the first man approached. But instead of finding an alternative, he found himself regulating his own body, readying for any sliver of an opportunity to present itself. *All is not lost.*

The first man got closer as Sam pushed aside the urge to step forward and offer a gentle surrender. He was keen to avoid unnecessary shooting but knew the risks that could come with the hysteria of an arrest. The chance of an instant execution was high. He'd seen tempers in the Arab world explode in a matter of seconds and witnessed crowds goad gunmen into extrajudicial murder.

The lead man was ten steps ahead of three others, so close now that Sam caught the sweet, strawberry scent of hookah smoke off him as he turned his back, still unaware of Sam's presence in the shadow. With no attractive option, Sam stood still and waited to see how things would pan out, keeping an eye on the weapon and calculating how likely it was that he could successfully disarm the man and slot his pals with singles without killing anyone in the surrounding homes. He pressed back hard against the wall.

Inevitably, the first man spun back towards him, and he braced to move forward but was suddenly masked from the patrol when a door to his left flung open. Instinct told him to pause, and he heard a woman barking at the men in what sounded to his untrained ear to be faltering Arabic. Sam had no idea why the Hamas fighters were listening instead of firing but their boots and voices soon battered off a stream of echoes around the walls of the tight little street and he remained sandwiched between the door and the wall behind.

He waited silently in the hope that the woman would simply close the door again. Instead, when the men were out of sight, she spoke. "I think you'd better come in."

Chapter 4

They'd occasionally reminisced about that encounter, over too much drink. Back then Sam hadn't tended to overanalyse things, but how they'd met that second time forever felt beyond incredible. Shannon had thought that perhaps God had sent him, but he was of the view that God would have sent her someone altogether more wholesome.

"He sent me someone useful, then," she'd joked, unintentionally souring the mood as they remembered the use to which she had put him.

Maybe there had been a plan. Of the hundreds of little streets in Gaza, and the two million people crammed in there, he'd managed to meet the same woman twice in the space of a few days.

———

THE DOOR CLOSED. She put one hand on his chest and walked him backwards through the tiny flat, a finger to her lips in a command of silence. His mind should have been on the job, yet he found her confidence captivating. When she lifted the pressure he stopped. Leaving her left hand where it was, she reached behind him to open a rear door, winding her upper body past him to look outside. He noticed her T-shirt sway, betraying that she'd dressed quickly, and he caught the smell of sleep from her as she leaned across.

Satisfied that the back entrance was clear, she moved around him and bid him outside where they dodged garbage and the stench of rotting meat through what was little more than an open sewer. They walked for about two hundred metres through a tight back alley, past other houses and their detritus, packed into everything from plastic bags to pillow cases. The backs of the homes stood an arm's span from a tall, rear wall, creating a thin strip through which Sam could hear the scurry of rodents as they made their way through. He assumed that bin collections had become a thing of the past in Gaza. Suddenly, the woman turned and opened another door and waved him inside a new house. Sam made his way as quietly as possible across the stone floor of the new, open space, and was grateful to hear her soft Irish accent again. "You're grand, there's nobody in here."

"Who are you?" he asked.

"Who the fuck are you, more like?" she hissed.

He laughed aloud – she'd posed a fair question, but she immediately shushed him.

"I'm Shannon." She met his silence with an extended hand, her shake strong.

In normal circumstances Sam wouldn't say anything to anyone, least of all about who he was or what he was doing, but these circumstances weren't normal. She had saved his skin and he had saved a kid dying in her arms. She was obviously some sort of aid worker; he was obviously some sort of trouble. And she was from home and he was from home, and she was exceptionally, breathtakingly beautiful.

He'd have to lie through his teeth or say nothing.

"You're Irish," she said.

He stayed silent, staring at her, finding himself wanting to talk.

She stared back, moving just a fraction closer, searching his eyes.

"I heard it. On the beach. You're northern. But Irish."

He held her eye, stacking the blocks. The Semtex explosive they'd been sent to retrieve had come from Ireland, concealed on an aid ship. Everything thus far suggested the woman was ...

"You with an NGO?"

"Well, I'm not a Palestinian, am I?"

Sam resisted the urge to smile. Much as he doubted it, the woman could be the link between the IRA and Hamas.

"So who are you?"

Their eyes locked and she bored into him. He'd caught a glimpse of a stairwell to the front of the building which he thought must lead to an un-shuttered window, as the dawn glow gave him enough light to be aware of the emptiness of the room, save for a rolled rug against one wall. He turned, slowly but instinctively, using that light to get a better view of her. She moved too, her face tilted up to his, her hair dishevelled, her eyes deep, dark and somehow warm, despite her rather abrasive benevolence. She'd all but skipped through the alley in flimsy sandals, and he'd been aware of her athletic build in her simple, worn-out jeans and plain t-shirt. He could now see her smooth, sallow skin in the light, the curve of her cheekbone. He noticed her lips, full yet parted just slightly in the middle. There was no dictating his heart rate now, higher than it had been when facing the fighters in the alley.

"What do you want?" her voice had fallen to a whisper, as if she'd thought it rather than said it.

He tried to focus, to think. He'd seen her trying to save that child, desperate to help the kid when others would have been running. Now she looked at him with a searching frustration that gently morphed into encouragement, her eye brows falling from a frown to soften her face, the beginning of a kind smile on her lips. She was not afraid of him, he could feel her strength of character, her courage. This was an Irish woman who'd chosen to toil in one of the world's worst human environments. She didn't need to be here, she didn't need to help him, yet she had placed herself at risk to do just that. He found himself wanting to speak, but his throat and jaw were tightening. He felt ill-equipped for the intensity of her almost silent scrutiny.

"Well, whatever you're here for you're in deep shit," she eventually broke the current.

He tried to regain some composure and latched onto the distraction of his phone, looking for a signal.

"You need to rethink the route of your night-time stroll. This is not the area to be wandering about at night. Knew you straight away in the light of your fancy phone," she said. "Lit up like the Liffey."

He let out a chuckle, grateful for her humour despite the dreadful mess that had been created.

"Did the kid make it?" he managed.

"He did."

There was no thanks given; there was none required. Even then he knew they wouldn't need to talk much. Something had been forged between them on that beach, in the blood.

"I need to get a signal," he told her.

"No chance. Mobile network is the first thing that goes down when there's a row. Israel controls the phone masts."

He looked up from his screen, grateful for the excuse to lock eyes with her again. Only an Irish person could characterise a rocket exchange as a row. She looked right back, a knowing smile on her lips. He knew she knew what he was thinking, but there was no time.

"I really need to make a call," he was almost grateful for the distraction.

She sighed, tilted her head to her shoulder and looked at him again for a moment.

"I know where there's a satphone," she said.

"Serious?"

"But I might need another favour."

Sam waited for the request, but she bit her lip then, as if debating with herself.

"Where are your men?" she asked.

"Not far. We need comms. Really soon, like."

Shannon had nerve. He knew she was making him wait – she saw his silence and raised it, looking at him coyly, trying to give the air of neediness, but he sensed this woman needed for little.

"I could really do with that satphone."

"I know."

"Well, can I borrow it?"

"Can you help me?"

"I'm not intending to hang around for long."

"Don't need you to," she said shrugging, but he hoped he saw disappointment in her gesture.

"You get me the phone and I'll help if I can."

He was willing her to be trembling inside as he was – the feeling that makes a leg stride falter. He was also confused. They were just meeting yet they already had a past. He had a job to get on with and she was a distraction he was happy about. He shook his mind free of his wayward thoughts. She helped concentrate his mind.

"How do I know you'll help?"

"I'm in a hurry, you have me at a disadvantage."

Her shoulders sagged. She turned her head to the wall and gave up her lie. "It's here."

She led him up a concrete staircase. It snaked around and revealed another floor, but continued upwards towards a door. Beside the door lay a heavy Peli case that she refused to let him carry as she opened the door out onto a flat roof. She laid it quietly on the dusty surface and eased the plastic latches to reveal an old M4 Nera device.

"We use it for interviews with radio stations."

"Radio stations?"

"Across the world. To get the message out. Tell people what's really happening here, on the ground. Helps us raise funds to set up schools."

Sam eyed the device and sensed threat – not from the woman but maybe from what he was about to do. Making a voice call felt risky, but then his mind ticked through some latent fail-safes. Keep it easy, he told himself. Sound civilian. There will be eavesdroppers.

"Hold this button down while you dial," he heard her say as he tried to think through what he would say. "Then hands off and wait."

She handed him headphones and a microphone. He looked at her, willing her to leave him to make the call, but she stood, watching him.

"It would be better…" he began.

"I'm not leaving you," she crossed her arms. "These rooves are all joined together. You think I'm gonna let you tear off into the night with my kit?"

He knew she wasn't worried that he was going to pinch her phone, the case alone would be too cumbersome to run off with. But he found himself reluctant to challenge her, to be rude, to insist she go.

"It would be better for you," he tilted his head from side to side.

"I can decide what's good for me," she replied, and nodded to the unit.

He hadn't the time to debate, so turned and held down a button with one finger, screwing his eyes shut, recalling the digits before pressing them out on the keypad. He opened his eyes quickly, feeling overexposed, and ran his gaze continually over the surrounding silent houses as the dialling tone kicked in.

"Hello, could you put me through to Apartment Six-Three-A, please?"

There was a momentary falter as the desk clerk realised what type of call this was.

"One moment, please," came the reply and the faint tapping on a keyboard. "Ehm, it's late, sir, can I say who's calling?"

"It's Paul, Simon's brother," Sam said, and watched the woman's head cock in curiosity. He tapped off the disciples on his left hand, making sure he'd got the correct one for the correct day.

"Can you give me five minutes, sir? The concierge has no directions to wake residents. I'd like to make sure your brother is up first if that's ok."

"Fine." Sam was pretending to be irritated. "I'll call back."

"Thank you, sir, apologies."

Sam hit the red button and looked at the woman.

Shannon.

She met his gaze and smiled. He felt his irritation at her presence pass. For five minutes they sat like that, a long time, although to him it didn't feel like that; an age without a name, as they kept eye contact. She had nothing to call him by but she appeared not to care.

Then he was dialling again, and the clerk had done his job.

"Hi, Paul, how are you doing?"

The voice was mature and the fact that its owner had prepped and assumed the story so quickly told Sam that this man was senior enough. He spoke just as a brother might – delighted to hear from him, but a tuned-in eavesdropper would identify a flaw: Sam's accent was Irish and his brother's was English. Sam was still looking at Shannon as he fabricated small talk, blethered about being well and working hard and still her eyes met his.

A number was read to him. "That's where Mum is staying. Give her a call soon. She's really keen to hear from you. Don't leave it too long this time."

Sam broke from Shannon and tapped the digits into his phone, knowing that among them were coordinates. There was more inconsequential patter and the call ended. He entered a scramble of random numbers on the satphone keypad and he realised, with some discomfort and annoyance, that he was doubting Shannon. His intention was to prevent her from hitting redial.

"Ok," he said. "Soon as I can, I'll come back and sort out whatever it is you need in return."

She smiled. "How do I know?"

He paused, keen to get going, keen to stay. "You know," he said, then left her on the roof.

He paused on the ground floor, drawing out his phone. He didn't need signal to consult the map saved and hidden in a jogging app.

On the street Sam walked with intent, marking off the road names as and when they were displayed. Having a destination gave him confidence and the fledgling daylight made his presence on the street less conspicuous. He met no patrols as he followed the coordinates a mile inland to a confusingly nondescript street. He was wondering what the significance of the location was when his hand lit up and he lifted the phone. The image of a cake slice had appeared on the screen: a wireless connection. The crescents increased as he approached a half-built house, three storeys high and without windows or doors. He walked in through the concrete and twisted steel bar and his cake slice was complete.

Crouching against a wall in a room at the centre of the house he worked the phone, wishing Min was with him for his tech know-how. Sam remembered to open an app within an app, then waited. When it offered him a bar in which to type, he composed his message, encrypted it and got it away. He waited, tapping the phone against his knuckles, standing, moving around a little, then crouching again to keep his muscles alive. The back of his mind wrested with some hidden irritation or guilt, something he'd done or hadn't done. Then the response, unscrambled by the app and far from expected: *Extraction negative. Target vessel re-routed to port of Ashdod. Proceed and complete.*

Sam's confusion was hammered out on the phone as he tapped and enlarged the map. What the hell? What are they saying? The orders looked like lunacy and a suspicion rose to the surface that they were being set up for failure.

The map was showing him the Gaza cage. Ashdod was north of that, firmly in Israeli-controlled territory. He knew there was no chance of breaking through the IDF's land border security. There was no sensible way out of Gaza, save for Palestinian tunnels, and considering any such alliance with Hamas was off-the-scale stupid. The only way was by sea but they had no boats. He measured on the tiny map offered by the screen: twenty-eight nautical miles in an onshore breeze. Ashdod was not a swim away.

He hadn't doubted that he would keep his promise to return to the woman, but now he was left with no choice. He used the walk back to make a plan and calm his mind, weaving through the small streets, trusting his instincts. He felt increasingly at ease with his purpose, somehow convinced by the woman's unexpected intervention that everything was working out as it ought to. To carry out his orders he would have to get help. It seemed to fit, and he found himself wanting to go back. He'd made a promise, after all. He couldn't have imagined what she would ask of him.

Chapter 5

That night rattled through Sam's mind for much of the flight home from Afghanistan. Short of Isla's arrival, meeting Shannon had been the best thing to ever happen to him. He found himself wondering how things might have been if he'd never met her at all. He'd still be in the dust and the dirt, fighting hard with neither thought nor fear. He'd certainly not be feeling this breath-robbing pain. The guilt would not be there. But, then, neither would Isla.

He pulled focus to the coffins lashed to the base of the C-17's cargo bay and thanked God that he hadn't known the poor unfortunates inside. It was almost laughable that some idiot at Kandahar Airfield thought it acceptable to place a recently bereaved bootneck beside caskets.

He imagined it was part of the grieving process; seeing death in everything, thoughts tumbling through a life short-lived. It felt important to remember their beginning together, now that they had their end. The details he could never share with anyone, and certainly not the person who might one day most want to know. Would Isla ask? And what would he say? Sam slipped into a waking dream, increasingly oblivious to all around him, finding a kind of comfort in revisiting the beats of how they'd bonded, over a terrible compact.

He surfaced as the plane landed and was ushered off the plane on the blind side to prevent the relatives of the dead seeing a bedraggled Royal Marine emerge on foot while their loved ones had to be carried, draped in the symbols of an unreciprocated loyalty. The dead guardsmen had been woefully unprepared for Taliban tactics. Sam had often seen them moving through the dusk, skylined and making noise, completely oblivious to the signs of mines and ambush.

From RAF Lyneham he was taken to the nearby military town of Wootton Bassett to buy civilian clothes. English officers could travel freely in their kit but he had to fly from Bristol to Belfast where attitudes towards the UK military varied hugely.

It wasn't until he reached the civilian airport that a real plan began to form. It had always been thus, his mind and heart would darken for long periods as he wallowed in the horrors but on every occasion something pointed him in the right direction. Thereafter he'd work hard to get to that point in his imagination where everything would be as good as it could possibly be. He treated it as a form of internal therapy in which he'd listen to himself moan before eventually shaking it off.

Dressed in badly fitting clothes, Sam found himself struggling with the thought of his imminent reunion with his daughter. His throat grew thick and he could feel his eyes begin to flounder in a rising tide. He knew that without a distraction he might lose a fight he'd become accustomed to winning – normally he could beat emotion, as if suppressing incoming enemy fire.

Mercifully he found a gnarled newspaper discarded on a vacant seat. He whipped it up before him and opened it at a random page. Breathing deeply and scanning hard to distract himself his eyes fell upon an advert for an auction to be held just outside Belfast.

No reserve! the ad screamed, listing a large aluminium sailing boat as the key lot. He had no idea what it was worth or what it might sell for, but he knew instantly that he would buy it. It felt as though his dead wife, in her gentle way, had somehow drawn him towards it. From that point on he had a goal. The next steps fell into place on the short hop home.

———

SAM JOINED the line behind ordinary commuters as they queued to disembark from the plane. He'd emerged from his meanderings as the tyres hit the tarmac and looked around properly for the first time. It was always a heavy grounding being dropped suddenly, far from any reference point, among civilians who were indifferent and oblivious to all that was happening in their name. They had not the slightest idea or care about where the weathered-looking man among them was coming from – it was for him to adjust, not them. His language, his behaviour – even his look, would all need constantly sense checked from this point on, he was among real people now. He straightened his back and gripped the headrests on either side of the aisle as the attendant opened the doors, bracing for a meeting that made him more nervous than any contact in the desert.

The airport was small, the walk to the terminal short. He bypassed the bag carousel and kept moving.

Sam never craved human touch in times of distress. Death, when it often visited, was on deployment; he and his men almost expected to die, and there was no comfort in the field. That's not to say there was no reaction – there was always a reaction, usually more death. Yet to be smothered in hugs as he was when he stepped off that flight was a relatively new sensation that was simultaneously consoling and terrible.

First came Isla, breaking from her grandparents, walking slowly towards him raising her little arms for a lift. To see her tears and bury his face in her neck and smell her hair – the smell of her mam, was to finally acknowledge that Shannon was dead. He nearly lost it as she shook against him, all her pain bundling out in almost silent sobs. She gulped for air but made little noise, her tiny arms gripping him so tight. He forced his own tears back, heaving slowly and forcefully into his chest, and gradually felt her relief course through him like a shot of strong whiskey, easing her arms, content that he was really there, home, holding her. He clung to her nearly as much as she did him, a little limpet mine threatening his detonation. He turned them both, unable to raise his face to Shannon's parents or his own; both pairs crying while they waited patiently.

Eventually, with Isla still on his shoulder, Sam walked towards his in-laws and swung an arm around them too. It occurred to him that he'd never done more than shake Shannon's father's hand before. A bear of a man, he hugged back and shuddered out his grief. Her mother, often given to emotion, was probably the steadiest of all.

Then came Sam's own parents. "So sorry, son," his dad said. They paused in a huddle for a few silent moments.

His mother wept and rubbed Isla's back. "Need to let you know there's reporters outside."

At that Sam was able to rally. They needed a means to get out of the airport and that was something he could usefully distract himself with.

He knew George Best Belfast City Airport well. After they'd married he and Shannon had built a house in Northern Ireland – nesting, perhaps. Preparing for Isla. And ever since he'd flown home on leave.

He knew there'd be no easy exit past the press, so he told the others to leave and tell the reporters he'd missed the flight and would catch the next one. He watched them move off, Isla holding his mum's hand and looking back at him. He waved and nodded to reassure her, then moved over to the car hire desks and watched through the sliding doors as the journalists were informed before gathering up their kits and wandering off. The interruption provided a moment of relief before he strolled outside and made for the flyover to re-join his family. Sam had made a life's work of not having his photograph taken. He'd exploited social media but never been used by it and was confident he wouldn't be recognised. The walk brought a chance to get a breath. But the brief moment he was alone also brought home the damage done to his daughter. If his heart hurt this bad, hers was utterly broken, and he promised himself that nothing would ever cause that to happen again.

For the next week they found themselves soaked in sympathy. Ordinarily Sam would have shunned such intrusion. His intensely private nature meant he recoiled at a stranger's touch. He was awkward, reserved and removed. Shannon was the opposite. She made friends easily. She'd been huggy, touchy, happy. And so it was that his parents' house – their temporary home given the mess forensics had made of their own house, became like an arrivals terminal as people he vaguely knew streamed through the door and crowded the rooms, grappling him and kissing Isla. The sheen on their cheeks reflected a loss that had evidently affected them deeply.

They were of a kind – overseas aid or charity workers, for the most part; those who picked up the pieces amid the destruction left by people like him. Contrary to his expectations, he found himself drawing huge comfort from their presence. They told him stories of his wife, of a life well lived, of her importance on the planet. He took in with gratitude tales of the little acts of kindness she'd performed to make life valuable again in places where war had depleted its currency.

The whole time Isla never left his side, which was just as he wanted it.

After a few days he knew it was time.

Sam dosed Isla with Calpol to make sure she'd sleep while he did what he needed to do. Despite the short distance, he'd been avoiding going back to what had been their home. He'd banished the thought of going through the front door, replacing that previous warmth and joy with horror. He'd wondered about leaving it – those memories intact – the call from the kitchen, the dozens of magnets on the fridge, the scamper of little feet, the sweep and hug and noticing the changes she's made since his last leave.

But it had to be done. It took nine minutes to get there, he knew because Isla used to make him time it. He put the key in the door, left the light off and pushed in to the silence. He moved through the hall, touching the ridge of the frame as he'd always done, touch wood I got home, then stood in the living room to absorb what had happened there. For an hour he looked slowly back and forth, piecing together what little he knew of events, standing mostly still, tracing the progress of the investigators in the fine dust from their settled chemicals. Then he walked the half mile to a very different type of house, a place entirely without warmth, the root of the evil that had taken his wife from their daughter. The house of horrors was well known in the area, the landlord, a local factory owner, had finally done what should have been done years earlier and emptied it of the scum that had caused Shannon to act as she had. Sam would have his time with that greedy bastard too.

———

SAM BLACKED OUT THE FUNERAL, other than noting that while music can be a comfort it can also draw the most insulated mind into the shuddering bleakness of bereavement. He'd chosen her favourite tunes, and almost regretted it. Shannon had loved singing and she'd eventually broken him down, turning slide guitar from a migraine-inducing screech to a tolerable whine. It was an indication of her happiness. Any time he heard Waylon or Johnny crooning from the kitchen, he knew she'd be swaying around with Isla, laughing hard and beaming that beautiful smile.

Two days later he was back on a plane, his daughter at his side. She had no idea where they were going and he had no idea what she would think of his plan. But when they arrived at an obscure auctioneer yard in Maidstone, Kent, she got it immediately. There, standing clear above the fence, was a 57-foot Norwegian-built cutter. The auction would be in Belfast, but the boat had been impounded in England.

"What do you think of that, wee woman?" he asked.

"Nice," she replied.

"You'd get your own cabin, your own bunk."

"Is that where we're going to live, Daddy?" she asked, her voice betraying excitement for the first time since he'd been home. In that moment she sounded like a five-year-old again.

"It is, darlin'," he replied, and climbed the fence as if it were a gnarly cargo net. He rolled over the barbed top and caught the panic on her face. "Don't worry, snugs, I'm not going to leave you outside," he said, changing his mind about going to the gate and forcing it open. Instead he rolled down the far side and ripped the bottom edge of a weak spot to let her through.

The hull would have been sound had it not been for the pointless behaviour of customs officers who had evidently been given tungsten-tipped drill bits for Christmas. Holes had been bored every three feet and the bulkheads torn out. She was still a beautiful craft though – spacious enough to live aboard, small enough for him to handle on his own. Isla's delight at finding a forward cabin sealed it.

"Daddy, it's so cool."

Because of the drug bust that had led to the boat's detention, there was TV interest at the auction, so he bid online. Fully aware that circumstances meant their house sale would take an age, Sam was forced to borrow against the monies due from Shannon's life insurance, which didn't feel as bad as he'd imagined. Over two weeks wielding a welder, he got her seaworthy and sailed her home. Isla was with him every step of the way, making her new cabin cosy.

Each night thereafter they sailed to a different bay. He was determined to assure Isla that nobody would come for him, as they had for her mam. Nobody could find them, he told her, not if they kept moving.

She was given to panic in her dreams and she often

visited at night, tucking her toes against his back. He watched her those mornings as she woke, the horror dawning and then peacefulness creeping back once she had reached out and confirmed he was really there. It gave him comfort too to know she was not alone. He wondered whether he needed her company just as much as she needed his.

The healing had begun, but it would take forever and there were pressing problems. He needed to work out how he would support her financially, and how he could douse the hatred inside him for the man who had taken her mother.

Chapter 6

I t had seemed like madness to Sam and the handful of men with whom he went through selection when they'd been briefed on the exploits of their forebears.

"So we'll be swimmer canoeists," Min had said that night. They'd been staring with exhaustion into pint glasses full of tap water, such were the demands on their aching bodies.

"If we make it through," Sam had grunted.

"If I can haul your arse up that bloody hill and you can haul mine, we stand an even chance." They'd spent the day doing just that, carrying one another on their shoulders in the driving rain up and down a mountain in preparation for a task they knew they'd be set.

"Doesn't really do them justice, does it?"

"What?"

"Swimmer canoeists."

"They boys were pure mental. And what about the kit!"

Sam had smiled at what they'd been told. Members of the original Special Boat Squadron, as it had been known, were issued with none of the fancy equipment that they, even as lowly marines, now had.

"It was the submarine stuff that got me," Sam confessed. "They had balls big as mangoes."

"Aye," Min chuckled.

They'd been regaled with tales of how their predecessors had raided and bombed all over Europe during the war, having been dropped into the sea from a submarine that would surface for as little as five minutes before leaving them to their own devices.

"Not a wetsuit between them."

The lesson had included a description of how the men had plastered grease over a woolly jersey in an effort to retain heat in the sea.

"And those canoes were crap, like. If we make it through, you reckon we'll ever have to do the like of what they got up to?"

"I dunno, Min," Sam had said. "I think every generation has their tests. Our gear is better but we're more dependent on it, I reckon. And our enemies are better equipped than theirs were. Maybe it all evens out."

"Aye." Min had drained his pint of water. "Cot time, pal. Who knows when they'll haul us out of the bloody things."

———

WHILE THE STORIES had seemed madness during selection, they didn't so much now.

Sam stared at the kayaks Shannon had obtained for them and immediately recalled that session, the classroom, the old film they'd been shown. There had been PowerPoint slides of the boats the original SBS men had been deployed in, flimsy and slow. He smiled.

"What's funny?" Shannon asked, as they stood at the water's edge.

"Nothing." His eyes flitted up to her then back to the boats on the ground.

The team he was leading was made up of highly trained kayakers who could shoot rapids and paddle for two days without sleep. But that was in navy-issue boats. He dated what lay before him to the seventies – dangerous canvas-coated tubs with rounded hulls, no spraydecks to keep the water out and little legroom. Min would fit lengthwise – but he was as broad as he was long. At fifteen stone Sam was about average and would manage, but the other two men were big units. How they were going to navigate around the might of the Israeli Navy in the yokes on offer was beyond him. Despite his reservations he thought back to what their predecessors had achieved and imagined the wartime SBS men would have envied the craft on offer.

The whole thing was full of irony and he couldn't help but smile again as he thought of their call sign, simple and brief: Charlie.

"Are they no good?" Shannon had watched his frown change into a grin as he'd been shown what she'd managed to obtain for him. Her hand went to her hip, her brow furrowed, confused at his reaction.

"'Charlie don't surf'," he muttered, looking up from the kayaks to the rolling waves crashing up the beach.

"Are they not good enough for ye? Because there's no end of boats available here in Gaza. Just say the word, I'll get you a gin palace if you'd prefer?"

He turned to her. "The movie," he said. "*Apocalypse Now.* Charlie is indeed about to surf," he said. All the way to the most militarised waters in the Mediterranean, he thought. "Thank you. These will do well."

The sea state was shocking, well beyond what the navy would describe as "marginal". Had they been training, he'd have pulled the plug. Plenty of SBS men had died on or under the sea and to Sam it looked that they stood a pretty fair chance of adding to that toll. His only consolation was that so long as they were careful, there was virtually no way the matchbox-like vessels would appear on any Israeli radar.

He looked up, her gaze fell to the little kayaks.

"Will ye be ok?" she said, more gently than he'd heard her speak before.

"They know what they're doing," Sam said.

"Whatever it is, I hope it's worth it," she replied.

"I'd better go get them."

She looked up then and he saw that her eyes glistened. "Mind yourself," she said, "please."

She turned and walked away, he watched her for longer than he had time for.

There was a certain satisfaction when the burn began in his shoulders as muscle memory kicked in and he shovelled the running sea beneath him to climb over the breakers. After ten minutes they had each gone beyond the rip and they paused to muster and bail out with sawn-off Coke cans they'd gathered from the stinking heaps of rubbish scattered around the harbour. The kayaks were tippy and rolled all over the place, and their round hulls made them hard to steer but each man got in sync with such peculiarities after a while.

The six-hour paddle gave him time to process what Shannon had done for his team. And what she had asked of him. He wrestled with an alien hope that her willingness to help him was not simply down to what she'd requested in return. It had been so long since he'd felt a connection to anyone, and never like that. He thought of her eyes, her smile, her scent. She stayed in his sights as he reached and hauled the paddle. She dulled the pain in his trapezius, deltoids and triceps. She dragged him and his men through the eastern Med.

He'd have preferred a tandem configuration: four kayaks in a straight line was the safest way to avoid losing one another. But it was also the surest way to be detected – from the air or satellite an observer could mistake them for a larger vessel, so he'd opted for pairs and knew Min would mind the diver, just as he and his buddy were doing. It was inevitable there would be capsizes, but Eskimo rolls in these ramshackle boats would only result in a sinking. They'd need to slip out of the hulls and use one another to invert and empty the boats of water before clambering back in.

His main concern, though, was to work out how to complete the task that Shannon had set him. He'd briefed the others on what they would do when they arrived at the port, but he hadn't told them he would be vanishing again.

Shannon appeared tough, headstrong and committed – a bad combination. He'd tried to negotiate when asking for her help, but he'd had nothing to offer. He'd insisted she involve nobody else, but she'd ignored him. He'd stood in her flat, on the marble floor with its fine dusting of sand, and eventually accepted everything she demanded. It seemed like lunacy after the fact, but she'd been so compelling and so determined that hers was the right course of action that she'd left him with little choice. All he was asking for were some small boats – what she was demanding was totally out of whack.

"He's a predatory paedophile," she'd said, failing to

understand his reluctance. "He rapes kids. Surely you can see the sense?"

He'd stared at her, frustrated at being sidetracked like this. "I have to get my team into Israel and out of the Middle East as quickly as possible. This is not what I'm here for," he explained, but he knew it was a mistake as soon as he'd said it.

"Well, what *are* you here for?" she'd countered.

He closed his eyes, paused and dismissed the question. "We need the boats."

"And I need a favour, and you give the impression that you're the type of person who can help with this favour, and, frankly, if you don't, then you and your little band of brothers from the beach are on your own-ee-oh."

He would always remember that phrase. It was often said to him when he was wee and it wedged itself in a little space in his mind.

"Well, where is this man?" Sam resigned himself to at least pretend to consider what she was asking.

"He's in Jerusalem, usually."

"Jerusalem's a long bloody way from Ashdod."

"It's two moons by camel," she said, which nearly made him laugh. "But for someone who is proposing to ignore a naval blockade, international protocol and the might of the Israeli Defence Forces, I should think that would be a piece ... of piss."

Sam was silenced by the dictionary she seemed to have at her disposal. Her access to vocabulary unbalanced him ever after. Words devoted themselves to her – her capacity to pluck the pertinent phrase from the air and insert it into any argument, as if stacking letters in pigeonholes in a post room. She could gut any adversary. He gave up.

"So, I find him, in the middle of a major city, and ..."

"You'll find him no problem because he's at the UN building."

She had an answer to everything.

"And then what?"

"And then you do what you do," she said matter-of-factly.

"I kill him?"

They stared at each other. It seemed pretty clear that she wanted Sam to kill him.

"So a senior figure in some UN peacekeeping outfit turns up dead and the Israelis just ignore it?"

"Not the point," she said. "Point is, every time he comes to Gaza he won't be able to abuse children under the pretence that he's here to help them."

"And you have evidence that this guy is doing this?"

"Well, if you want to hang around, I can bring you half a dozen little boys who have been left bleeding by this bastard. If you want to hang around, I'll bring you their distraught parents. If you want to hang around, you can listen to how their lives have been ruptured like their ..." She stopped, and turned away for a brief moment.

"Ok," he relented. "But why doesn't someone here just take him out – Hamas or Fatah or someone?"

"Cause he's dishing out money and he's feeding families. He's supplying hospitals and he's the dog's balls to the right people. You think this place is any less vulnerable to corruption than any other hellhole on earth?"

Sam said nothing. It was a well-trodden path, that of the paedophile. He was broadly aware of all that had occurred in his own country, how those attracted to children had insinuated themselves into positions of moral superiority to feed their addiction. He'd never understand how anyone could justify satiating their own desires at the distress of children. They often claimed to believe that what they were doing wasn't wrong, but the lengths they went to to cover it up always suggested otherwise.

"So do you want the boats or not?" she'd pressed.

"Yes."

"A friend will bring them to the harbour tonight."

"I asked you not to involve anybody else."

"Well, I'm not carrying the bloody boats, and you lot can't very well walk around Gaza in your cargo pants and face paint, can you?"

"You trust this bloke?"

"I don't trust anyone really, but, yes, he's not about to bust your bollocks."

Sam wondered whether her Irishness was part of the attraction. Almost everything she said reminded him of home – a point of reference right from the outset. She made him smile, like they had a secret language.

And so it was set.

He was soaked. And chafed. And rashed. Every bloody job he did as an officer in the SBS resulted in his extremities being punished: feet, fingers, arse, sack. The unhappy quartet that often froze, rubbed or blistered under extreme conditions. They'd changed back into their wet kit, placing their civvies in their dry bags and stuffing them into the transoms, but the bailing and sponging of water kept their crotches sodden with salt water, like they were ladling pain onto their penises. The rubbing of the caked salt had resulted in abrasions as he pulled stroke after stroke, distracted as he was by running through the various scenarios with Shannon. What if *she* was trying to stroke him? Could this be a woman scorned who wanted an ex-lover removed? He honestly didn't think so, but he had no evidence of the man's offences. He'd no idea how he would even manage to get to Jerusalem, never having been there before. He'd never even been to Israel or Palestine, for that matter.

Sam had always tried to remain open minded about people he met, until persuaded otherwise. Nobody, he knew, was without flaws, least of all him. He erred towards trust, which was a weakness, and was aware that the woman had caught his breath, sucker-punched him, and that he was vulnerable as a result. It remained a lingering worry that she could be the contact due to receive the old IRA explosives. She could be a militant sympathiser – she could be a bloody Hamas operative for all he knew. He traced her: her ability to speak Arabic, a white Irishwoman in a war-torn state, giving aid, in possession of a satellite phone. Had he not already fallen too far, he would likely have placed her at a remove from them one way or another. Little wonder his team was incredulous at his decision to accept her help and carry on with this ridiculous operation.

Yet there was no doubt that his thoughts of her made the paddle easier. Using a similar strategy to the horrendous yomps of his training days in Wales and Devon, he allowed his mind to carry him away as his body thundered pain signals towards his brain. His back and arms might be screaming, an inferno might be burning in his shoulders, but his mind countered it.

It was on the crest of such distractions that they arrived at Ashdod, a stinking industrial port on Israel's south-west coast. The sea was choked with detritus and they picked up plastic bag after plastic bag on their paddles. They lapped quietly around the edge of an enormous breakwater of a huge harbour with multiple berths and an astonishing military presence. It was going to be a challenge to even locate the correct ship without being caught, never mind getting aboard and removing the explosives.

During other operations Sam would normally have had a crash vest full of flares and comms kit. Inside the kayak would be his rifle of choice, an L119 carbine, the stubby little C8. He'd also have a handgun, a Sig usually.

Not this time. All they had were their wetsuits, boots and fins. They stood next to no chance.

Chapter 7

The absence of radios was the main hurdle. Sam and two of his men stayed beyond the breakwater, spaced apart, and they sent the strongest and smallest paddler in to hunt for the mercy ship. There was always a reluctance to send such a close friend into any sort of danger, but Sam and Min had served together for a long time and Sam knew that if his reticence ever showed, Min would request redeployment. Sam also knew that of all the men in the service, Min would get the job done with minimal fuss or risk of compromise.

The wait outside the enormous harbour wall was uncomfortable. Maintaining sight of one another was virtually impossible on the swell, forcing Sam to paddle hard north and south to ensure Sparky and the diver were ok. The soaking had left them frozen despite the decent sea temperature. He willed Min to find the mercy ship and hurry back to get them.

After an hour of exhausting work just holding position, Sam spied movement in the reflection of a street lamp thrown out across the sea. The flick of a paddle, then it was gone. Min was almost beside him before Sam caught sight of him again; a sign of good practice.

"You're no goanie believe this," Min called to him. "I went all the way in, cleared the military docks and then the merchant quays, and guess what?"

"I'm not really in the mood for guessing, Min," Sam shouted back.

"It's near the mouth of the bloody harbour. It's lashed up tae an old wall in the middle of the place. I went straight past it on the way in. I thought she was an ancient wreck abandoned, but on the way out I took another look cos I couldnae find her inside, and sure as hell there she was."

"How close is it?" Sam plunged his paddle deep to swivel his kayak.

"Half a mile, tops."

"The Israelis can't be that interested in her, then."

"Naw." Min's reply was whipped away by the breeze.

"You get him," Sam held his paddle and pointed north towards an invisible man, "and we'll follow you in."

Sam saw Min's blades plunge and pull, then disappear. He rounded up the man to the south and they moved in towards the harbour. Twenty minutes later, with adrenaline pumping heat into them, they began to see the outline of the old quay. It was really little more than a random wall in the middle of the sea – a navigation hazard, Sam imagined, probably built on a natural rock formation many decades before. Far removed from the merchant quays and poorly lit in comparison to the naval docks, its positioning was a small blessing. The military quays were sufficiently illuminated to be seen from space and the effect plunged the surrounding water into almost complete darkness. They paddled in without detection, and using hand signals and small whistles

Sam and Min directed boarding via the ship's seaward quarter. The diver was left to corral the kayaks at sea level on the blind side as they had no painters to secure them.

In part, they followed the briefing: Sam with an open palm directing Sparky to the starboard side to keep watch for incoming vessels through the anchor eye. He should have been the man to handle the explosives, but Min had more experience, especially of close combat in confined quarters and ships were tight spaces below deck.

Methodically they combed through and cleared every inch of the stinking boat that was packed to the teeth with tinned food, toiletries and blankets. Both men knew that Semtex could be kept in just about anything because as plastic explosives went it was pretty stable. To make matters worse, the stuff they were looking for was old. That meant the markers – the colouring and odour added to it, would likely be depleted or absent. Both men had infiltrated IRA arms dumps in the past and they expected the Semtex to be in oblong strips, possibly wrapped in black and have the texture of stiff dough.

But the adrenaline charge from climbing aboard undetected quickly wore off.

"We'll need to sharpen up," Sam said. "We've had a tough run. Tiredness will make us sloppy."

"Aye," Min replied. "OK."

It struck Sam that the IRA might have concealed the stuff in some tinned food and so he began to scan the labels for a tell, but that rapidly proved to be a hopeless pursuit – there were thousands of cans on board.

Sam stood still as Min moved through the bulkhead doors ahead of him. There was a generator running somewhere – he could hear the gentle hum of power coursing through the steel hull. Did that mean there were people on board? He knew it was necessary to keep systems alive, batteries charged, so it didn't follow that the Israelis who'd impounded the ship would automatically have kept a team on board, but he had to assume that they weren't alone.

Min came back and in a low voice said what Sam had been thinking.

"Needle in a bloody haystack, pal."

"Think like they did when they stored the stuff," Sam said. "What would you do? Where would you put it?"

"Well, they're no goanie put it in the engine room, are they? If that went up, it would take the ship down."

"It's heat resistant, though, remember. But I agree, I don't think they'll have wanted it near the engine, and I can't see them wanting it anywhere near sleeping quarters."

"I wouldnae want tae bunk beside it but the people who stowed it might not have known what it was, aye?" Sam nodded in resignation. The people transporting the gear could well have been kept in the dark. "Which just means it could be anywhere." Min looked around at the bank of tins. "You don't think?"

"We're not going to open a thousand cans."

"I could swally a tin o' beans alright."

"I'd say we're looking for somewhere cold and far away from the clattering and banging of the waves, but I can't see it being on the bridge either."

"If it was me, I'd pack it low, keep centre of gravity down, least movement in the sea."

"Ok, let's move towards the bilges."

They made their way deep into the hull, moving as quietly as possible down steel stairways. Still there was no sign of life, no indication that anyone was on board. Both men knew, however, that there could be a team asleep in any of the cabins and if that was the case, there would be someone on watch.

When they got as low as they could go they gazed around under torchlight, confirming that the task of finding a small amount of anything was potentially gargantuan. The substance could be concealed just about anywhere.

"Think, Min. When we've found this stuff before, how was it stored?"

Min paused, his back to his boss. Before special forces, the two men had been attached to a special reconnaissance unit in Northern Ireland. One of the more bizarre roles they'd played was to take IRA weapons from hides and leave them to the armoury to be interfered with, only to return them exactly the way they'd found them. It had been a good buzz at the time.

"Pipes," Min eventually said, turning quickly. "I mind it being in sealed pipes."

"Really?" Sam had no such recollection.

"Aye, like, greased pipes with screw-on heads. Watertight."

"Ok," Sam said, sweeping around with his torch. But once they started to look, they found pipes everywhere. Most were painted the same colour as the hull itself, with varying degrees of rust sneaking through like pimples. "We'll need to trace them – see where they're likely to go. There'll be intakes for cooling the engine and probably the generators, out for the waste, heating and who the hell knows what else. Some might be carrying electrical cable."

"We canny really go round tapping them, aye?"

Sam shook his head. Unusual noise was sure to raise a response. "We may as well start here and work up. If we have no joy, we can come back here and go down."

Min moved ahead of Sam, running his hand along a

three-inch pipe then stopping. "That's warm, could be the exchange taking heat away from the engine or something." He switched to another and moved off.

Sam selected a lower pipe and crouched as he clambered forward. They traced the tubes through watertight bulkheads, finding them again on the other side of steel walls, moving higher and higher into the superstructure. It was time-consuming and Sam was acutely aware that the stuff could just as easily be packed inside a can of spaghetti hoops in the galley.

"Wheesht." Min halted on the third deck up.

"What?" Sam whispered, alert to any noise ahead.

"We've a new one here."

"A new what?"

"A new pipe. This does'nae make any sense."

Sam walked through a bulkhead door to join Min who was pointing his LED into the corner of a new space, then peering round to the other side of the door to double-check.

"See what I mean?"

"There's an extra pipe?"

"Aye. It looks like it's a continuation from the room before but, you're naw – it's no' really. It just starts up in this compartment and runs to the end of it, and if I check round the corner ..." Min stepped ten feet and leaned around the metal door. His head popped back and a wry smile crept across his face, "it does'nae go through into there."

"So this is a dummy pipe?"

"One way tae find out."

Min crouched at an end while Sam got to his knees and gripped the other end of the rogue pipe. They pulled hard and it came away with a bang. Both men fell back, suddenly careful with the tube and also listening for any attention they might have attracted. They gently rolled forward, cradling the pipe as if it were a small child, and placed it on a metal shelf.

"What's at your end?"

"Internal cap," Min muttered, drawing his blade and going to work.

Sam resisted the urge to tell his friend to go easy. He saw Min sheath the knife and swap it for his torch, which he then shone into the pipe.

"Well?"

"It's packed – I can just about smell it."

"Sure?"

"Completely."

"How tightly stowed is it?"

"No movement."

"If this is full, that's a hell of a haul."

"Aye."

"That's a lot more than we were led to believe."

"Makes you understand why they were keen to take the risk of sending us. Do we need to look for more?"

"The int only said one batch, but we can keep an eye on the way out. Let's leave it in this tube – might be the best way to get it off."

"For sure. It's snug as a bug in there. Drawing it out would mean juggling the stuff."

Min resealed the cap and the men each took an end, gripping tightly as they moved up through the ship to deck level, counting pipes as they went.

"Anything?"

"Naw, all normal."

"Me too. This must be all of it."

They found a rope in a port-side locker and called Sparky back.

"It's in the tube, check it over. All yours," Min told him.

Sparky looked the tube over, removed the caps and prodded the substance with his fingers.

"We can move it like this," he looked up at his seniors. "Without a detonator, it's pretty stable."

Sam wound two rolling hitches to it before sending Min down to collect the lowering tube. When he felt the weight slacken, he dropped the rope to allow Min to drag the tube behind his kayak and out of the harbour.

They mustered a mile outside the breakwater. Sam fired up the phone, sent a message and while they waited he broke the news to the others. The sea was calming but the mood turned rough.

"I need to go ashore again. I have unfinished business."

"What? What business?" Min growled.

"I need you to get the explosives to the ship. I'll be in touch as soon as I can."

"You never told me about any orders." For the second time in a couple of days Min's voice was raised in a manner that only a friend could get away with while speaking to a commanding officer.

"I'm not able to get into it, Min."

"Well, I'm not able to let you go ashore alone. What are we to say to the extraction crew?"

Sam motioned Min further from the two men, conscious that he had the tube tethered around his waist and that drawing him aside came with pain for his sergeant.

"You need to tell them that something came up. It's non-negotiable, Min. I'm sorry, I can't get into it but I need to get ashore before sunrise."

In the middle of the debate the phone buzzed against Sam's chest: they had orders. Sam looked at the screen and handed it to Min. "Coordinates are in there. Your course is two-nine-zero. Sixteen nautical miles offshore is the RV. A Zodiac will pick you up," he told them.

"Are they aware of this?"

"Who?"

"The brass?"

"No, and there will be hell to pay, but I need you to trust me."

"What am I tae tell them?"

"Min, I had to do a deal to get the kayaks. I have to do my side."

"What deal? Tae hell with any deal! You know the score – we do the job, we get tae fuck. Never mind any bloody deal."

He could feel rather than see Min's hardened stare.

"I have to see this through, Min. I promised."

"Bollocks tae yer promise. We're done here. Let's go!"

"Not this time, Min."

"This isnae on, pal."

"It's essential, Min. Please don't make me pull rank, not with you."

"You fucking look after yerself," he barked, then twisted the kayak and hauled hard on the blades, pulling the other men and a tube of high-grade explosives in his wake.

Sam turned, seeking a sheltered spot to land and sort himself out.

He'd have a lot of explaining to do when he got back, but the operation had been successful and he prayed for the wind to be at his back for the debrief.

Chapter 8

There were guns everywhere. Sam was at ease around automatic weapons, but not when strung over the shoulders of sulky teenagers. Jerusalem was proving to be an eye-opener.

The market on Jaffa Road was a cacophony of colour. Fruit tumbled from the pitched stalls left and right, produce of the land of milk and honey. He caught the noise of arguments everywhere he went. Some might call them debates, but they were heated and heavy. Haggling seemed to be the local currency because not once did he see shekels exchanged.

Streams of children trotted along in single file with rangy youths before and aft, each carrying a rifle. At either end of the closed street were scowling soldiers, young and conscripted, bored by their sedate posting. He watched them wave their detector wands over the torsos of shoppers in half-arsed fashion. It was useful to observe for a while , he decided, to note that almost every building had a guard of some sort and that weapons were not just tolerated, they were expected. What these people were scared of, he realised, were not pistols – they were suicide vests.

Money would have been a problem but that Shannon had handed him a bundle as he'd left Gaza. He'd discarded his wet kit in Ashdod, bought some cheap but new clothes and boarded the only transport going north, a sherut to Tel Aviv. The shared minibus–taxi affair had been an experience too. Companionship was discouraged; suited Sam just fine.

Tel Aviv to Jerusalem involved a similar arrangement and by that sherut ride he'd settled a little into the country's ways, adopting and adapting so as not to stand out. There were people of all shades, he often struggled to tell the difference between the Jews and the Arabs. He didn't have to speak because nobody spoke to him – in fact, no one paid him any attention at all until the driver insisted on an extra ten dollars to take him into the Arab section in the east of the city. He claimed Jews were afraid to go there, which, as Sam later discovered, was bollocks. He didn't have any US dollars anyway, so he got out and walked. Although the hops had been short, the waits had been long and it had taken him a full day to get to there.

The American Colony Hotel was his only point of reference – he'd remembered a few stories from SBS colleagues who had performed close protection there for a former prime minister and had spoken fondly of its underground cavern. It was a place to begin, but he changed his mind instantly after inquiring about the cost of a room. He had no credit cards, no identification and he would need more cash in the very near future. Not far around the corner he found the cheaper Christmas Hotel. There he ate, studied tourist maps of the city and eventually got the first proper rest he'd had in a week. Still, the pause before sleep brought anxiety, and he had plenty to worry about. What he couldn't afford was to get caught. A life in an Israeli jail was not attractive. Nor was the fallout the presence a man with his background would bring for his unit. This job had to be done carefully. He would need to take his time and do it right.

———

THE CALL to prayer woke him, a six-hour sleep having chipped the edge off his unease. Sam stared out of the hotel window at the exodus of men streaming towards the Old City and the mosque. He'd seen it all before, but not in the city where it had all begun. There was something intriguing about the herd of humans driving forward in front of him. He sat by his window for a while, enjoying the curiosity of a new place and its Friday routine. Shutters came down as dust swirled up and he decided to follow the sandals through the sandpit to Herod's Gate. He knew he should get on with what needed to be done, but hated wasting opportunities. This was a new place, with ancient importance, and he wanted to see it.

The smells of the old walled city were at different times dreadful, intense and exotic. The stench of donkey dung at the perimeter was quickly replaced by sweetness, the must of age and, eventually, by burning incense sticks. Muslims filtered towards the raised domes as shuckling Orthodox Jews prayed below them at the Western Wall, filling the cracks in enormous stones with folded paper. It was quite a distraction from the task at hand and it kindled in him some semblance of understanding. His mind was drawn back to Iraq and Afghanistan. For the first time he felt he was observing the genesis of the conflict that had deposited him and his pals into those wars and so many others into their graves.

Sam found a bench above the Western Wall Plaza and sat long into the evening as Friday prayers became Shabbat; the occupation of the city rotating from one faith to another. Security tightened and the police were swapped out for well-armoured replacements. Tension was building, so Sam decided to avoid being asked for identification he didn't possess and reluctantly sidled off into the night. Lingering in his mind was the fact that he was in trouble. He should not be there, he had not followed orders. He knew that the woman had altered something, that suddenly his job had shifted from being the most pressing thing in his mind. It had been years since he'd had an alternative focus, and he found himself caring less about the shit storm he would face when he returned.

He knew that his status back home would shift to AWOL, but there was no way British security apparatus could appeal to the Israelis to track a man who wasn't supposed to be there. He had no electronics and had left no footprint, and for the first time in a very long time he felt an element of freedom and relished the ability to explore undetected and without orders, save those set by Shannon. He left the city walls and wandered through places familiar from the Bible stories of his childhood, remembering blood on doors, plagues and locusts. May as well be hung for a sheep as a lamb, he thought. From Mount Olive he stared back down at the city. The light licked off the Golden Dome, shadows cast long from church spires, synagogues and minarets – all reaching for God, each battling for space and primacy. To his left the dead were crammed, buried in the Promised Land at great personal expense. He thought of the cost of their repatriation and then of the price paid by the families of his fellow bootnecks. Then he thought of the kids in Gaza who'd had their futures destroyed by a rapist before their existence had even properly begun. He decided that there was nothing more important than life, but that for the deserving to live free, others might not live at all.

Chapter 9

He found it liberating to be without the responsibility of leading men. Ordinarily his time on a job would have been consumed with briefings and preparation, but he had no kit to check and no intelligence packs to consult. All he possessed was a name and an ill-defined outcome to achieve.

Prejudice, preconception and all manner of undesirable emotions made themselves known to him during that week. He hadn't expected Palestinian men to hold hands and he found himself double-checking his sensibilities. He'd always considered himself pretty liberal, despite having spent his service surrounded, in political terms, by those to starboard of the right wing. Sam felt that people ought to be left alone unless they caused others harm or hassle. As rules went, he'd always been guided by that simple and straightforward premise. He found himself sense-checking to ensure that he hadn't inadvertently subsumed any personal hang-ups in terms of race, religion or romantic inclination. It made him wonder whether he was preparing for something, daring to imagine a different life away from the navy. He wandered through the city questioning himself, now that he finally had time to think about such things. Had the military and all of its grunt and fuck clouded his principles? The constant changes in the cultural command of the city and its religious icons made him interrogate his own faith – his comfortable conclusion that any person who lived a decent and generous life would find their way to God regardless of what denomination they were reared in. Jerusalem, though, challenged his ideas of himself, and not in a good way. Having grown up in Northern Ireland, the notion that people could be hostile towards others without even knowing them wasn't new to Sam, but Israel and Palestine were on a whole different level. The feelings of injustice were plastered on the walls that towered into the sky to keep peoples apart. The divisions helped him reason out his own hitherto thoughtless dalliance with the region. His grip on what Afghanistan and Iraq had really been about grew on him subtly, yet he knew he'd never understand it properly.

Sam felt drawn to the dustier, dirtier eastern quarter of the city. It had a warmer lack of order, greater animation in speech, mannerism and madness. He found it soothing, friendly and familiar – a million miles from barracks life, until he sat to eat a falafel pitta on a bench by the old city's ancient walls and a man pissed against the stones less than a foot from his head.

The more affluent part of Jerusalem was an austere affair. He saw lots of handshakes but few smiles. Sam sensed that everybody felt under siege. The inhabitants seemed set in a hard stance, as if convinced they were on the cusp of losing all they had worked for. That, at least, was not alien to him.

Sam tailed his man for two days: from the UN building

to his home, from his home to a café, from the café to work. He was honest with himself; it wasn't just the fear of getting caught that made him cautious. While he didn't really doubt what Shannon had told him about the man, they had said so little to one another. He wanted to be able to get out the other side, to be able to tell her that he'd done what he promised, but he needed some assurance that the man was no good. In time, he got it.

The man meandered irritatingly around a few bars, sipping cocktail drinks from delicate little glasses. It made him a tough tail. Sam would never normally follow someone alone; he'd be part of a team that rotated and swapped control of the mark. Everyone would be kept up to date on each minute detail through commentary on a closed net, like a stream of consciousness. In Jerusalem, though, he had no radio and nobody else to spread the risk and sow doubt into the mind of a suspicious mark. What he was doing went against all his training, he should be on a ship heading home, not contemplating murder on behalf of a woman he'd just met. Perhaps, he realised, the target wasn't the only one driven by his desires.

Eventually the man went to a small independent cinema. Sam dandered off to wait a few hundred metres away but not before he checked what was showing. A poster on the billboard told him it was a film for the UK's Channel Four about the death of a cameraman who'd been filming in Gaza. At least the target's cover was consistent.

Through the glass facade he could see a reception with drinks, glad-handing and air kisses, so Sam waited outside until it ended. Eventually, hugs complete the man left the building on his own and made a mobile phone call. He walked slowly for a few minutes, checking his watch repeatedly, then climbed slowly up a steep footpath to higher ground, towards a heath.

As dusk fell it became easier to track him. The man's steps slowed further when he entered an ornately paved public area. Sam checked his location using translations for tourists on street signs: Lion's Fountain, a plaque told him, Hebron Road. Bushes and trees surrounded what Sam assumed would be a water feature. Through gaps in the foliage the view of the city's lights was impressive. He didn't realise what the place was until it was too late.

Within seconds he'd lost the man amid high hedges. Sam began to hunt, a little too desperately given that he had other options; he knew where the mark lived and worked and could pick him up again the next day. But his sudden disappearance worried Sam that his mark may have caught sight of the tail, so he speeded up and would have compromised himself had it not been for two men – one with a broad hat and suit and a man in a leather jacket. The man with the hat was loitering for no apparent reason and the leather-jacket man was looking towards Sam. Even in the half-light he could make out leather man's excitement, although it wasn't pronounced enough to cast much of a shadow.

Sam closed his eyes for a moment and reminded himself of yet another failing: he had little sense of some elements of civilian life. The Marines had given him skills few others possessed, but immersion in military life had left enormous gaps in his civilian understanding. Leather-jacket man beckoned him towards the bushes: Sam was being cruised.

He ignored the amorous suitor and began a hunt through the hedges in pursuit of his mark. Moments later he heard suppressed grunts in the gloom and saw the face of a boy rising and the mark clutching his trousers and securing them at the waist. They'd made enough noise to conceal Sam's arrival, and as the kid was being paid he obtained all the proof he required. The boy was no older than twelve. The mark left the heath onto the main street and walked quickly in the direction of his home. Sam thought it prudent to get there first.

———

HE THOUGHT ABOUT IT NON-STOP — how he would approach her when he saw her again. What would he say? What would he do? Later, Sam realised he'd thought about it more than he'd thought about anything else — he must have because for the duration of their separation he ignored any sensible notion that entered his head. He rehearsed it, refined it, adopted different scenarios, built conversations designed to provoke the right opportunity.

The first problem had been finding her again. He forced himself to consider how so easily she could have deceived him. She had perfect deniability: if he got caught killing the paedophile, no story he could plausibly tell could possibly make her complicit. He wasn't supposed to be in Jerusalem — he had to deny having been in Gaza. As far as anyone anywhere was concerned, she and he had never met. But it didn't feel like that, and he remained as sure as he could be that she'd been on the same page.

In the end, the name of her NGO was all he needed. On Abu Taleb, not far from the dusty court gates, he found a shabby little café that sold internet time for a few shekels. Finding her humanitarian outfit, he wrote down the land-line number for its office in Gaza and called it from a payphone through a stinking handset. The greeting was in Arabic, a male voice.

"Is Shannon there, please?"

The line rattled like a drum as the receiver was dropped. He heard sandals slap away from the phone.

"Hello?" she said eventually. The gentle rise of her voice in query sent a shudder through him, and his meticulously rehearsed words warped as he reverted, introverted, to type.

"It's done," he said.

She didn't miss a beat, no matter how disturbing the message must have been. There was no pause, no panic.

"Are you ok?" Which took him aback. She sounded so gentle.

"Yes."

"Is there anything I can do to help?"

As the years rolled past, her endless concern for others would never cease to amaze him, but in that moment he loved her.

"You could, eh …" he threw risk at the wall and said it, "would you like to meet up before I have to go?"

"Yes," she said immediately.

"Thank fuck for that," he blurted out and she giggled, a cheeky, involuntary little laugh.

Then there was silence. And it was a beautiful silence. He closed his eyes. He could hear her breathing and it was calm, and he was calm, and their silence was in sync. There was no awkwardness, just a relief, and an incredible peace born of incredible violence.

———

"TELL ME ABOUT IT," she said.

"No."

She paused. "Yes, I want to know."

He looked at her resting, cradled in the crook of his arm, her incredible eyes upturned to him. "Why?"

He hadn't expected to be asked to recount the detail.

"Because it's on me," she said.

She wasn't revelling in the man's demise, he realised. She was taking responsibility for it.

"It was rough." Sam had no intention of telling her everything. He was accustomed to boxing up the bad stuff and stacking it away. He had no desire to go over it again himself, never mind making her go through it too.

"I insist, Sam."

She used his name a lot, which he found oddly disarming. Nobody ever used his name, except maybe Min, and that was only when they were alone. As a bootneck or in the service, he was always just "Irish" or "Ireland", which suited him fine. Latterly, he'd become "sir", which sat rather less comfortably.

Shannon said his name once more, then lay still for a long time. He knew she knew she wouldn't have to press any further. The story would come, as he knew that every story would come. He later pinpointed that moment as the time she began to ease his conscience, becoming his confidant, his cure.

"I found him easily enough and I tailed him a little and got to know his ways. I saw what you saw, his desire for boys."

She shifted uneasily, so he paused. Then she ran her hand over his bare chest and squeezed gently: go on.

"I did it at his flat. The night I saw him with the kid." He didn't elaborate on what had happened on the heath, but he knew he'd have to give her some information to prevent a deep dive. "His place had a low veranda, like a balcony, except smaller. I swung up onto his patio thing and cracked the door."

He paused to look at her, hoping that would be explanation enough, but all he could see was the parting of her hair, the short mane now straggled by exertion. Her hand did the job her eyes could not. Her fingers gently crabbed his skin as she demanded more detail.

"He fought hard. He was lying down when I entered his room, no covers, no clothes, and he was awake. Makes it hard. To get a grip. It's sometimes tougher to deal with someone prostrate than upright, and he was slippery as a mackerel."

Sam stopped again and was about to roll away under the pretence of getting a glass of water, but she held him and tightened her arm in a tiny flex.

"Go on."

"There's nothing to be gained here," he said.

"Keep going," she whispered.

Sam sighed. "Well, I reached for him and he lashed out, moved back, used his feet. His legs were surprisingly strong and it took a while to grapple, you know. I mean – seriously, what's the benefit of this?"

"It's not fair that it's in your head alone," she said, which confused him as much as it sounded completely solid as an explanation.

He thought about what more to say. He hadn't wanted the man's blood on him – he didn't trust the man's blood but he didn't want to say that to her. He increased pace and injected flippancy into the telling in the hope of getting through it, as if writing a sentence and speeding up before running out of page.

"I got hold of his foot and used his weight to turn it,

snapped his ankle and then had to get to his head to stop the screaming. Then it was over, he was dead, and I was covered from head to toe in his DNA."

There was silence and he held his breath for whatever verdict he was due. He half expected her to rise and leave.

She spoke then, shifting gear. "Can you be traced?"

Sam wondered what sort of woman he was lying with. Her main concern appeared to be for him.

"Probably. He made a serious racket and I needed to get out of that flat quickly, so I washed him with a cloth best I could. I doubt it was enough."

She lay tense against him. "Can the Israelis trace your DNA – to link it to you?"

"Is my DNA on record, you mean?"

"Yeah, can they, like, subpoena it or something from the Brits?"

"Well, I'm sure it's on record in the navy somewhere. They've got my blood group and possibly samples and stuff. I've spent a bit of time in the infirmary."

"No shit," she said, poking an unsightly scar across his abdomen.

"But I doubt the British would share that kind of information and, sure, how would the Israelis know I'd been there?"

"They know," she said. "They know who's been in and out of their country. If they didn't arrest you, then they were playing with you. Watching you or tracking you."

She spoke with conviction. Israel was a small country with a big army and a serious dedication to its own protection. He had no reason to doubt her sincerity, but it made him question his ability to act covertly, and her ambivalence to the likelihood of his capture.

"You must have thought I'd be lifted, then."

She said nothing for a moment. "I'm sorry," she said, looking up at him. "I shouldn't have, and now I wouldn't have. But I had a weird confidence it would be ok. And I didn't know you then."

"You don't know me now," he said, regretting it instantly.

"I know you, Sam Ireland," she said, snuggling back in.

They were quiet and he let it slide into a contentment he'd never felt before. He'd opened up further than he'd ever done and it didn't feel at all uncomfortable, although she must have felt he'd gone far enough and she closed it down.

"He's gone now and kids are safer. That's all that matters."

She never knew about the terrible bludgeoning it took to kill the man. Sam never spoke of the horrific skull-crushing blows he'd had to deliver. The way the man had suffered and lashed around in agony. Yes, the world was a tiny bit safer for some kids, but only a few.

Chapter 10

If getting into Israel had been hard, Sam found getting out of it nearly impossible. His inclination was, as ever, to go coastal. He'd only been in Jerusalem a week but he quickly got twitchy at the stale dryness and his inability to see the sea.

Shannon borrowed a car to travel up to meet him. It was safer that way, she'd said. There was no way he'd get into Gaza without papers. Pick a place, tell me where you are.

He'd consulted a map, chosen a coastal fortress town and got himself there using yet another sherut. Once there he felt more at ease and called her again.

When it was time to part she drove him south to Tel Aviv and gave him enough shekels to spend a few nights in the most disgusting hostel he'd ever seen – a needle-infested pit with blood on the sheetless bed. He slept on the beach. As dawn broke he went in search of a boat in the hope that a skipper might agree to take him to sea. But doubt crept in – Shannon had worried him with questions about his DNA and what capture would mean. The creeping daylight brought a harsh realisation that his planned escape was daft. He reasoned that a brutal-looking bloke trying to hitch a lift from fishermen or offering to crew a sailing boat would raise considerable suspicion. The navy would throw him to the wolves if he got picked up by the IDF or Israeli police. He opted, instead, for caution, and decided to steal a yacht and head in whatever direction the charts on board took him.

And therein lay the first of his extraction problems: Tel Aviv's main marina was incredibly small. He swam into it to get beyond the security fence with minimal fuss, but rapidly worked out the challenge that theft of a boat posed. Of the half dozen yachts he broke into, none had charts that mapped an area beyond the immediate vicinity and the reason was clear: Israel was surrounded by hostile countries, so there was no point in sailors buying charts for day cruises when there was nowhere safe for them to travel to. Embarking upon anything other than a pretty lengthy voyage meant skippers would inevitably find themselves in Arab, or Muslim, terrain.

He found one chart, far less detailed than he would have liked, that had both Cyprus and the Israeli coast, so he settled on Larnaca as his destination, about one hundred and eighty nautical miles away. But, again, disquiet set in. Larnaca was much too far for a slow beamy yacht to get away to without detection. If someone noticed the boat missing, the authorities would be on him within hours, and so he gave up on his second bright idea of the day and tinkered his thinking in another direction.

In the corner of a car park stood a bundle of sailing dinghies and a few racing boats with more substantial lifting keels, and through the crazed window of a nearby shed

Sam saw sets of sails. He gazed at the boats, initially without real thought, before a gradual warmth crept in. The boats were plainly suffering from underuse – the ropes and sheets were gently greening, but the rigs appeared in good shape. One boat was particularly appealing; he didn't recognise the make but it had a compass, an open transom and a retractable bowsprit. It was about twenty feet long and substantially built. He estimated it was capable of between six and sixteen knots, which, with a favourable breeze, could get him to Cyprus in less than twenty-four hours. More importantly, he thought, nobody would expect a yoke like that to sail to Cyprus. No customs officer at the other end would imagine for a moment that a racing dinghy could come from another country, and so would likely ignore it. If he left at night, it could get him well offshore before anyone knew it was gone.

He used what money he had to buy breakfast and stock up on water, energy bars and sunscreen. He buried his provisions in the sand beneath him on the beach and settled in for a day's dozing ahead of the trip.

———

"YOU ARE ONE LUCKY BASTARD," his superior snarled at him as he spat out the findings. "Discontinued in the interests of public justice."

Utter disgust.

Sam had known he was facing likely dismissal. On top of that a hefty fine was probable, plus up to a year in prison.

So, he had to agree, he was one lucky bastard.

His lawyer had appraised him of the likely outcomes: lieutenants who appeared before military courts don't normally escape lightly, he was warned, unless charged with some sort of assault; assault was almost encouraged. Those up on fraud charges were ushered away into oblivion and never heard of again in the hope that the press didn't get wind of what went on with missing MoD kit. But for absence and negligence to his team, which was all they could prove he had done, Sam knew he could have been in very, very deep water.

He was due to be listed simply by rank and as belonging to the Royal Navy on publication of the verdict, and was as amazed as anyone when the charges were kicked out. Only then was it evident just how sensitive the operation that his Charlie team was involved in, had been. His boss's bosses had taken the view that no detail whatsoever should be given out, even in the comparatively closed environment of a court martial.

That didn't mean he could remain in the Special Boat Service, though. His belligerent refusal to go into any detail about what he had been doing had infuriated his major. Despite not managing to get him convicted, his commanding officer ensured that the brass busted him back to the Marine Corps. Sam regarded the major's behaviour as petulant. A tough enough guy who had apparently been a particularly good rugby player in his youth, his attitude was straight out of Tory central office. Perhaps because of his upbringing or education, his compassion was strictly limited to those within his own tax code. Regardless of Sam's officer status, the major had continued to treat him as a grunt and deemed Sam's men expendable and distasteful in equal measure. They were his fodder and Sam was his well-trained collie who had stepped too far out of line. In spite of the operation's success, the major's inability to wear insubordination hurtled his temper into orbit.

Sam read the judgement and part of him wanted to

take the hit on the chin. He knew he'd made rash and questionable decisions, but he'd met an incredible person and all previous focus had since become blurred. Provided he wasn't going to prison, a promising new passage lay ahead of him. Yet the work that had gone into becoming a special forces officer had been gargantuan. The physical and mental sacrifice had taken more than a chunk of him, and although he hadn't fully appreciated the extent of that toll at the time of selection, he'd loved being a member of the elite fighting force. They got no thanks for what they did, successful operations were never acknowledged, but through that achievement he knew he was at the very top of his game. He knew that few could ever be asked to do the things he did, and he knew he'd miss that terribly. At the age of thirty-five he was a Royal Marine once more.

It took two months for him to reason it all out and find his pace again, helped largely by a very welcome distraction. Shannon and he married in the garden of his folks' house, by the sea, on a sunny day. Her family came north and mixed easily with his own. There were some rough enough ratings present from his rise through the ranks, as well as his pals from home. There were no politics, just gallons of rum, and they danced and sang all night as guitars and banjos were handed around. Everyone took their turn to perform – a proper Irish affair. It later made him choke to think of that day, at the top of the tide. Given how he earned a quid, he never imagined that his wife's travels would end before his.

Chapter 11

The wedding seemed like a distant memory, as he stood amid the prints of strangers - a yeti-like trail in the fine fingerprint powder that dusted what had once been a happy home. He tried to console himself that what he was about to do was no different than what Shannon had asked of him those years before in Gaza.

In the garage he lifted a box of gloves he used for working with epoxy resin and put one pair on, removing another for later. He had a full-face dust mask hanging on the tool board and a dozen cellophane dust suits that Shannon had bought to protect his clothes from paint and filler. In the bathroom he found the boxes of toiletries they had pinched from hotels around the world and he took out the shower caps.

Then he thought through his next movements, just as he had for any serious undertaking a hundred times before. At 0230 he made his move and walked the four miles to where the factory owner lived. Sam knew the man had migrant workers bunked up in his own house – that way rent could be charged and most of the paltry pay they received ended up right back in the owner's pocket.

In a lane hidden from the road he checked the ground for piercing objects and placed the shower caps on his feet and head. He looked like a Tellytubby in the dust suit but the mask must have made him look terrifying. Then he was free to put on the second pair of gloves over the first, which he hoped would avoid any cross-contamination. He was conscious that his DNA could have landed just about anywhere on the outward skin of the first pair.

It took him two minutes to get inside. He had no idea where the owner slept, so he eased cautiously around the spacious house. At 0400 he realised that his plan had a flaw: a mobile phone buzzed, then grew louder until it became an alarm. There was movement, a shuffle and muffled conversation in Russian.

Shift work.

The factory operation was enormous. The owner made his fortune from tourist trinkets that were sold in shops the length and breadth of the island. In green and gold and with folk ballads on a loop, these shops rammed fake Ireland down the throats of visitors, who in turn lapped up the little plaques and poems and brought them home to their relatives as gifts. The irony was that they were made by Eastern Europeans in what was, in fact, part of the United Kingdom. And those poor bastards evidently worked around the clock.

Beside a bathroom was a door that, he was grateful to discover, concealed an airing cupboard. He turned as he slipped inside. There were few sheets or towels stacked on the timber shelves. Crushed between a hoover and a copper tank, he bided his time and listened as a small army readied itself for a day of painting stuff green. By 0430, all were gone.

Sam inched the door open and crept quickly through the large house trying door after door. He found rooms crammed with beds, sheets strewn across them tallying with the pace the occupants had vacated their sleeping quarters. With only two doors unopened he began to wonder whether the owner had left with his workforce, but he turned the handle of the final bedroom and received his first shock of the morning.

His eyes followed the hump of a body in the bed from toe to top where – eyes wide open, the factory owner lay, staring at him.

Sam had grown up in the area and as a child had known the man to see. He had barely changed.

"You're looking well, Sam," the owner said, without moving.

Sam almost laughed. The sarcastic bastard had probably been expecting a visit.

"Tell me where he is."

"Who knows?" the owner said. "I employ them all through an agent."

"Then where's the agent?"

"He'll tell you nothing, Sam. He probably doesn't even know the boy. My agent doesn't care for chick nor child. He beats them and batters them and keeps them in line. I don't bother asking anything about them."

The carelessness in the man's tone drew Sam's temper. He tried to calm himself, to think methodically, to act and leave no trace.

The man had known Sam would come, but obviously hadn't thought about what that would mean.

"Where's the agent?" Sam asked again, trying to bring his heart rate down.

The owner snorted. "Dublin, far as I know."

"You'll need to do better than that."

"You'd have no joy with him – he's enormous. He'd eat you for breakfast."

"You'll tell me where he is."

"Can't," was all the owner said, and Sam wondered whether he was resigned to his fate or whether he'd misunderstood his predicament.

Sam had always known how promiscuous the man was, and thus what was important to him. Stepping forward with a following uppercut, Sam caved his nose into his face then tore back the festering duvet, grabbed the triumvirate of his genitalia and gave it a full twist. The man gargled and screamed. Sam eased the grip as he laboured to gain composure and shift to persuasive mode.

"Alright, Sam," he panted, his face awash with blood and his nose ruptured. "Alright, alright, I've got a number for him. I'll give you his number!"

Sam didn't want him going anywhere for a phone or a pen and paper, so he gave his tackle another half turn and with that came all he needed. The man gestured to a mobile phone by the bed and gasped out the pin code. Then it was straightforward: contacts, name, number and address. Sam knew he wouldn't remember the phone number and resisted the urge to text it to himself, but the address burned into his mind.

He looked down at the factory owner and tried again to persuade himself to be the better man – to walk away and leave him there in his stinking sheets. But he'd thought it through, over and over. This was a man of an age, he'd never change. Sam knew that if he walked away, the owner would get straight on the phone. The gangmaster who knew the whereabouts of Shannon's killer would be tipped off and his efforts would be in vain.

Sam wavered for just that moment, but the decision had been made days before. The police would have thirty suspects ahead of him, all who hot bunked in the owner's own bloody house. He leaned forward and drew the factory owner's tenure of abuse to a permanent close.

———

DESTROYING the coveralls and gloves was straightforward. Shannon, a half-hearted environmentalist, had often complained that all day, every day a fire burned at the edge of the sprawling factory, and the memory of her mild moaning gave Sam the idea of how to prevent the plods from tracking him down: he'd literally blow smoke all over the place. The factory had acres of sheds, dozens of lorries, tonnes of rubbish. There were also hundreds of workers, so Sam's face was just one among many in the half light. He approached the bonfire from upwind, deposited his small bundle and waited until it joined the factory waste as ash. The walk home was consumed with the address he'd obtained being repeated over and over in his head, while working out how to get to Dublin without being picked up on any cameras or by the tollbooths on the way.

Isla was still asleep when he got back. He washed well and climbed into the bed parallel to hers, content that he had the roots of a plan to get to the gangmaster. Then he lay back and waited for the guilt to coast over him like a sea fog, imagining what Shannon would have made of it all. She'd developed an uncanny knack of drawing out the dark stuff and making him deal with it. Although her ultimate aim had been to civilianise him, she'd known that to berate him would be to lose him; to defeat her subtle but steady progress. While gently driving him away from more extreme behaviour she had never failed to persuade him that there was dignity or sense in his decisions, however wrong his subsequent actions may have been. "Right instinct, wrong answer," she'd often said, as she gradually helped him find a way to resist similar impulses in the future. He craved that now. He ached for her guidance as he closed his eyes.

Chapter 12

In what now seemed like another life, Sam had learned that every snippet of information led somewhere provided it was properly interrogated. It may be filed away and forgotten until required, but those tiny skills, tips or connections had the potential to trigger a breakthrough that could make the difference between life and death. The latter was his priority.

He'd spent a day persuading himself that what he was about to do was for his daughter, and for his wife. He needed to know that what had been done to them couldn't be done to anyone else. Sam clung to the truth in that, but to scratch the surface would have been to admit that he also wanted to strangle the hurt inside him and vengeance seemed like a logical first move. The way things worked out, that proved correct; all manner of problems were solved by his actions that week. And all manner of problems were created.

A significant part of the SBS post-selection training had focused on surveillance, and some of what he'd been taught, and put into practice on future deployments, brought deviousness to a whole new level. The courses had reinforced just how difficult it is to avoid detection. For the first time, he wondered whether the skills instilled in him could have a use beyond the military. Regardless, he couldn't get caught, not now that Isla's future was dependent upon his presence. Nothing would place him in Dublin.

Years spent sanding, painting, rigging and delivering boats all around the Irish coast had taught him that boat ownership in Ireland is generally a pretty thankless pastime. The weather could be good for about two months of the year, and seldom the same two. He knew there were sheds up and down the country in which vessels hibernated for up to nine months at a time. He settled on one nearby yard where he knew two dozen suitably fast examples would be standing.

He borrowed his dad's car because it ran on petrol and filled it to the throat at the nearest forecourt. CCTV footage of him fuelling a car could not arise suspicion, whereas similar images of him stockpiling unleaded in barrels would certainly become evidence in any future court case. Then he gathered together every jerrycan and container he could find and drove the lot into the garage at the home he'd shared with Shannon. There he siphoned at least half the tank out of the car and into the containers. Later that night he deposited them at the high-tide mark in a quiet cove a few miles away.

———

SAM TUCKED ISLA IN, left her in the care of her grandparents who had long since stopped questioning his movements, and went back to the garage. There he kitted up, grabbed his old bike and cycled the three miles to the boatyard. It didn't take long to get into the shed and to identify a six-metre rigid inflatable with a nice Yamaha 175 horsepower outboard engine on the back. He rolled the RIB down the slipway, launched her and hauled the trailer back to the shed, leaving the boats as he had found them, minus one. Gloved, with a balaclava on and in a full drysuit, he tossed the bike aboard, sculled offshore, lowered the outboard and made gentle progress to pick up the fuel.

Fully stocked, he broke for open water and was soon planing at thirty knots down the east coast towards Dublin Bay. Customs posed a concern but even if he was pulled up and boarded, he had nothing on the boat that would warrant investigation. All he required for this job was a nautical chart, determination, the pocket map of Dublin he'd taken from his folks' house, and his bare hands.

Pretty little Bullock Harbour, close to Dalkey on Dublin's gold coast, was on his mind. Years before, he'd done a few maintenance jobs in it and reckoned that was anonymous enough for his needs. He went over and over the timing in his head. It was dark now and it needed to be dark when he arrived. By the chart, he reckoned it was 135 miles away. At thirty knots that would take him just under four hours and he anticipated landing at the perfectly sleepy 0400 Greenwich Mean Time.

There was a stiff south-easterly blowing when he crossed Dublin Bay that allowed him to tie the RIB outside the harbour wall, largely out of sight and in slightly deeper water. He hoped that might allow him to leave in a hurry, or at a time of his choosing. If he got it wrong, however, the boat would be beached and he'd be at the mercy of the flood tide.

He stripped off his drysuit, under which he wore paint-spattered jeans and a scabby old fleece, and stuffed it in the seat locker, his intention to pass as a construction worker. He rolled a buff up over his chin and flipped on a scruffy cap. The bike was slung over his shoulder and he scaled the slippery surface of the wrong side of the harbour wall as quickly as he was able.

It took him an hour of enjoyable cycling to get to the north inner city. His view of Dublin Port and the East Link were undisturbed. He crossed the Liffey and made his way a few streets in towards Mountjoy, where he had to consult the fold-out map for directions.

The address the factory owner had given him was an apartment near Summerhill, and when he looked at the street layout he was glad he'd opted for the pushbike. It was anonymous and it allowed him to get in and out of the area without having to cross a carriageway or get snarled in the one-way traffic system.

Time was tight, so he didn't spend as much as he should have conducting a proper recce. What he ought to have done was stop some distance away and work his way in gradually, listening and watching. But as sure as the sun rose and set, the tide would turn, and he wanted to get the information he needed and find the boat floating so that he could get back to Isla. Had he done the job properly, things would undoubtedly have turned out differently.

The apartment complex was almost U-shaped in appearance. He cycled in past an ornamental roundabout and quickly identified the correct staircase. Sam climbed the stairs as if they were his own to remove any possibility of being mistaken for a thief. Head down and with the exertion of the cycle and the stairs pumping in his ears he didn't hear what he otherwise might have if he'd applied proper caution. It wasn't until he reached the top of the two flights that he caught a muffled commotion. Drawing his eye along a landing he realised it was coming from the apartment he intended to visit. His shoulders fell a little. So much for surprising the gangmaster in his sleep.

As he walked towards the door he heard a scream and a slap followed by dull thuds and sobbing. He caught a woman's voice, a growl, another slap and decided that he'd listened long enough. Convinced a woman was being attacked, Sam put his shoulder to the door — and bounced back off it immediately. Sam's frame was far short of that of a bodybuilder, but he was just out of theatre and as fit as a trout. At six feet tall, fifteen stone and carrying no excess, he'd never put his weight to a domestic door frame and seen it stand up. The apartment had evidently been prepared for unwelcome visitors, which told him all sorts of things about what he might find on the other side, if he managed to find a way in.

He needn't have worried — his attempted intrusion wasn't in vain. The door opened before him and there, in glorious underpants and a wife-beater vest, stood a mountain of a man. For the second time in the space of a minute Sam questioned his luck while hastily registering the man's features and knowing a battle was inevitable. Doubtless this was the man he had come to see. The bloke's shoulders bulged from recent exertion as he leaned forward into the door frame, one hand on each edge. The fingers on one were ornamented with gold and slathered in blood. This was eighteen stone of pure ignorance, Sam concluded. The man was plainly unperturbed, confident and badly mistaken.

Sam debated whether to wade straight in, but his hastiness had not served him well so far. He decided to take stock, to try to draw the hulk out of his comfort zone.

"I've called the Guards," he said, imagining that the man would assume he was a neighbour.

"Good, good," he replied, which was not really what Sam had been hoping for. "Then they can take yer one away for harassment."

Sam noted how well the man had assimilated Dublin parlance. His Eastern European tone was mixed with more than a little of the vernacular. Sam ducked a fraction and turned his head to peer under a colossal arm and, as hoped, the man followed his gaze to find a woman in black crawling towards a sofa before reaching out to grip its arm. Obviously the man deemed Sam no threat because he turned further inside the apartment to shout at the woman to stop bleeding on his furniture. As he yelled, his right hand dropped off the steel door frame.

Sam stepped left and used his entire body weight and both arms to take the man's swinging hand and give its wrist a full turn anticlockwise, breaking it immediately and dislocating the man's elbow in the process. It was a simple enough move but one that rarely presented itself as an opportunity. It was also excruciatingly painful. Sam was aware first-hand that some wounds are so severe that they cut off the messages being sent to the brain, often leaving a combatant able to continue fighting. The trick was to do just enough damage to ensure that the pain endured. Sam needed the gangmaster to remain conscious but disabled. He wanted the scope to inflict more pain in order to get the answers he'd come for.

A heavy blow to the side of the throat forced the man back inside the apartment and down to the floor, giving Sam enough space to close the door. He glanced at the woman, who was gradually recovering. Sam had intervened in a domestic before and knew it was precarious. He understood why it happened but nonetheless found it interesting that in such situations a person being saved from a savage beating can turn violently against a good Samaritan, so he tried to keep an eye on the woman to see what way she might go. While the thug laboured for breath at his feet there was a certain comfort in what she gasped. "Thank you," was all she managed, and his assumptions were challenged again. He realised that he had expected her to be a domestic slave or sex worker, but she was plainly Irish – and something else about her seemed out of place. He was turning his attention back to the man but was distracted by what he'd seen. She was well enough dressed – understated and practical. Someone under duress would be forced to dress provocatively or have no choice but to wear clothing provided for them from a discount store like Lidl or Aldi. Her facial wounds were limited to a cut across the temple that was bleeding hard and a rapidly blossoming black eye. Judging by the way she attempted to cradle herself he knew the bastard on the floor had also gone to work on her torso. Perhaps he was a boxer or a martial artist. They tended to wear down the trunk, varying and concealing their punishment.

Sam stared down at the panting mass. Confident that the gangster was sufficiently incapacitated for the moment, he stepped on his face and walked over him to help the woman up. She was sore and gently sobbing but he needed information.

"Anyone else in this flat?"

"I don't think so," she said. "I only got here a bit before you."

"Why?"

"Looking for a woman that was supposed to be in trouble."

"You police?"

"No."

"Any weapons?"

"I'd be amazed if there weren't," she wheezed.

"Does he live alone?"

"I don't know," she said.

"So who are you?" he asked, slightly annoyed that she knew so little.

"I'll tell you in a minute. Can we not just get out of here?"

She made a fair point. He realised that she thought he was just a neighbour – a saviour, so it was her turn to be exasperated.

"Yes, sorry, go on ahead, I need some time with him."

Her damaged face turned quizzical.

Sam moved away from her to clear the rest of the flat, all four rooms of it, and returned to the woman. "Can you walk?"

"Not really. Can you help me?"

Sam looked at the gangmaster, then back at her, then thought of the time.

"I'll help you into the jacks for a minute, then I'll get you out."

"No," she said.

"I need you to wait in the bathroom."

"I will in me bollocks," she said, and nodded to the bloke on the floor. "Do whatever you have to do."

Sam stared at her.

"That's not ideal," he said.

He didn't want anyone else to hear what he needed to know. That would lead to identification, which would lead to the factory owner, which would lead to Portlaoise Prison, which would leave Isla alone. Again.

"Ideal?" Her tone ticked up on the incredulous register and she looked at him, re-evaluating his presence, his purpose.

"Get in the fucking bogs or I will leave you here with him."

Sam's tone was deliberately harsh but she was fit for it and shrugged, painfully. He got the impression there was a long history between the pair and she wanted to watch.

He scooped her up and she groaned in pain as he left her sitting on the toilet lid and shut the door. He'd no idea how much she heard as he went to work on the man. To Sam it took forever, and he was deeply worried that the noise would rouse a real neighbour and bring the police. The man was both physically and mentally tough, but he had no ideological commitment to a cause. Taliban fighters might be inept and weak, Sam thought as he varied the techniques, but their hearts are strong. Their information is tough to tap because they believe what they're doing is right. This big bastard, he reckoned, had no such emotional attachment to his work, but once he realised Sam's demands were deeply personal, he understood that he wouldn't be left alive unless he choked out the details. Sam got there in the end.

Then he had a decision to make: disable or decommission. Sam couldn't kill the man unless he killed the witness too, and he had no intention of hurting the woman. So he went for two simple enough fixes. The first was disgusting but took sex out of the equation for the man forever. And the second ensured he would never again raise his fists in anger. Sam then retrieved the woman from the bathroom, pulled the buff up his face once more and tried to debrief her, which proved tricky because she juked around his head to try to get a view of the sobbing mound on the floor.

"We're leaving now and we need to do so quietly."

"What did you do to him?"

"He'll live," Sam said, and watched her shoulders sag a little. "We need to go. How did you get here?"

"I drove."

"Can you drive now?"

"What do you think?" she said.

Sam didn't think it was a good idea – she could barely stand. "If I leave you outside, will you call the cops?"

"For what reason would I call the Guards?"

Sam stared at her for a moment, trying to work her out.

"What would I say to them? That I came to get a girl from a pimp and he beat the shit out of me, and then some fella from the north came and cut his bollocks off?" She was incredulous.

"I didn't cut his bollocks off," he said, but their heads turned in synchronicity and he noticed how the man's torn shorts were creeping in blood as a tea towel might mopping a drink spill. It was definitely time to go. "Look, I'll drive you to a hospital. I hope you've a car with a big boot."

IT WAS A HAIRDRESSER'S CAR. Sam lowered her into the passenger seat and got his bike, released the front wheel and was forced to leave the back one sticking out the rear. "Where's the hospital?"

She gave him directions, but when they passed the Mater Emergency Department he began to wonder where she was taking him. Ordinarily he would have invested some thinking time in keeping track of their direction, speed and where the sun would rise, but he had the little map as backup. What he didn't have was much darkness left, so he was keen to get the unexpected mess sorted, the woman the help she needed and start moving back towards the boat.

"I could use someone like you," she said quietly. "You obviously know what that bastard was up to."

"All I know is he brings in foreign workers and skims them."

"Illegals too, mostly women," she said. "He brings them over, promises cleaning or office work and within hours of being picked up at Dublin Airport they've been raped at least twice."

Sam stayed silent but felt fairly satisfied that the man had been neutered.

"They're in houses just like these." She winced as she tried to raise her arm to gesture at the Georgian terraces sweeping past. "And the gregarious men of Ireland enjoy them every day, whether they're drugged or half-dead. They don't give a rat's ass."

None of this surprised Sam. He'd seen it all before in Helmand, in Poole, in Palestine. Flashes of his wife appeared before him. He swiped them away as if an advert had popped up on his phone, but her image kept bouncing back. He knew then that he wouldn't make the tide.

They coasted through the north inner city, along yet another beautiful street. He detested towns, could not abide the claustrophobia and proximity to people that city life insisted upon, but Dublin was different. There is space in Dublin, he thought. The streets were broad, the houses simple but statuesque, and the architecture untouched by bombing missions or terrorism. He'd always felt at ease in the Pale, a city with mischief around every corner.

This woman, though, was rapidly destroying that image

for him. She was talking about the shitheads who spent their wages on exploited women. She insisted the johns must know that the victims had been trafficked. She talked about drugs and crime gangs and how useless the Gardaí was. Then suddenly she ordered him to turn right, as if he had made a stupid mistake. There followed a hard left and a long laneway, a set of plush gates and eventually an austere old convent. An old sign for a school hung from a low, rotten stump.

Sam looked up and pitied the children who had been educated – or incarcerated – in what must to them have been a frightening place. He parked on noisy weed-infested gravel and helped the woman out of the low vehicle. He half carried her up a stone staircase and it was plain to him that she had no intention of going to hospital. Along a corridor they reached a small, barren office. She leaned away from him to flick on a fan heater and muttered that the nuns would not be happy if they knew she had it. Organised religion and misery in Ireland, Sam thought, once went hand in glove. By the time he got her sat down, he knew the tide had turned and that the boat would be bottomed out. His parents would look after Isla, yet again, but he was stranded now until the flood.

Over three hours they talked, or rather he listened, as he dressed her wounds. In the Royal Marines a body is a body – a machine of sorts, and where there is damage someone has to get in there and try to fix it. Sam had forgotten the niceties of civilian life and when he checked her over she shuddered and seemed to panic slightly. He examined her ribcage and her spine and he stopped when he realised, a little too late, that she was alarmed. He stood back, hands upturned, eye down, asking without asking whether he was to proceed. She screwed her eyes shut, sighed deeply as if gathering latent strength, and nodded. The silent exchange made him conscious that her crusade against abuse might have been borne of personal experience.

He wrapped it up, deciding that if anything was broken, it couldn't be too serious given that she was still talking and, he felt, almost pitching to him. He became less aware of what she was saying than of the spark in her eyes, and through it he followed the shake and nod of every heartfelt gesticulation. Her gentle commitment made him think of his dead wife and he knew that whatever this woman was working up to, he would help her achieve.

And so from that unexpected exchange, the kindling of a new occupation was ignited in Sam's mind. From there, a clandestine little company was born; a means of income, a pathway from perdition. But he knew he had to get to Lithuania first and make another withdrawal before he could start depositing in any absolution account.

Chapter 13

Sam found himself at an enormous disadvantage. He couldn't speak Lithuanian – but at least Lithuanians used the Latin alphabet. Nor had he any Russian other than the capability to order two beers and to inquire of strangers whether *they* spoke English. He'd spent time in the Russian Caucasus, up to no good, so it wasn't sensible for someone like him to be found in that part of the world with no explanation.

A young woman came to his aid on the plane to Vilnius. She was a bubbly, friendly girl with a pretty, plump face, who tried to strike up a conversation from the moment of buckle up.

"Hello, how are you?" she began.

His instinct was to recoil, to revert to rudeness. He didn't want anyone to remember him. "Grand," was his effort to dismiss her, but she wasn't giving up.

"I am going home for first time in two years," she chattered happily. "I am very pleased to be doing this."

He noted how she rounded all her words perfectly, as if trying out elocution lessons on him.

"Good for you," was all he offered, but she was determined. On and on she went, about her catering job in Dublin and about how much she loved Ireland. And then came the questions, inevitably, about why he was visiting her country. That was when he realised the opportunity and began an elaborate fabrication on the hoof. He'd done it before, creating an alias from thin air. Ideally he would live it inside his head for a while so it would hold up when questioned, but there was no time. It came rather easily to him, which he often thought was both a blessing and confirmation that he was not as decent a person as he wanted to be. Anyone who can lie like that has a dark element inside them, he reckoned.

Sam saw the *Irish Daily Star* in the pouch in front of her and pointed. "I work for them." Her head followed his gaze to the seat in front.

"These people?" She gestured to the backs of the heads of the people in front.

"No. The newspaper – the *Star*."

"Oooh," she replied, interested. "What do you do for the *Star*?"

"I'm an investigator." He found himself suddenly brimming with bullshit. "I find people for journalists. Then the reporters go and interview them."

"And who are you looking for?" she inquired, leaning in and lowering her voice as much as the racket from the jet engines would allow.

Sam mirrored her. "A murderer." Let that sink in, he thought, hoping for awe. Hope misplaced.

"Well, you're coming to the correct country," she

replied. "So many murderers I know," she sat back up and waved her hand dismissively.

Which wasn't really what Sam had anticipated.

She went quiet and they sat for a long time, arms tucked in like chicken wings, as they puttered around with the unpacking and consumption of tiny sausages and obliterated eggs from the on-board meal. And then he struck.

"I have pretty good expenses," he told her. "I could use your help."

"Not that type of woman," she hissed at him, eyes flashing anger.

"No, no, that's not what I meant. Really – that's not what I meant."

He let her stew for a while and sure enough she came back in better humour. "So what *do* you mean?"

"A translator, to help me find the murderer."

"Oh." She sounded surprised. "Yes, I can do that."

And then the babble began again, an endless witter of relentless zest for life. The young woman seemed to Sam able to find fun in the most mundane things. She would have been an uplifting influence if he hadn't had so much on his mind. He zoned her out and pretended to sleep, but she didn't stop until touchdown.

The following day they met in the old town. He handed her a note, his best guess at spelling the name of Shannon's killer. Granted, it was hard to know how accurate he'd got it, given that it had been gargled to him by a man in extreme pain because of the weight being applied to a pressure point. With a knowing, superior air the girl took his pencil, corrected his spelling and began walking. He had no choice but to follow.

They entered a beautiful building on the edge of the old town – marble steps, open foyer and severe-looking security guards. A woman at a central workstation appeared no less forbidding and greeted them with a stare rather than a smile. She said nothing, but the vacuum was filled by Sam's bright companion who managed to woo the woman out of her post-Soviet slumber. At one point he actually saw her blink. Something was written on a piece of paper and then they were at a computer terminal in another room; after which they were on the street again, walking alongside a trolleybus. Vilnius struck him as a city of two halves – the first a riddle of old cobbled streets and beautiful renaissance hotels and homes, the second a downtown area pleading for seediness and sex and bling and big black BMWs.

"What was that place?" he asked.

"Is newspaper. I tell them you are from newspaper in Ireland. They are willing to help."

"So where are we going now?"

She ignored him until eventually they arrived at an imposing detached, dilapidated construction. Their feet crunched in the snow but the girl stared up at the hundreds of broken windows above. All around them were cracked streets and pavements falling into the gutters. An occasional fast-food outlet looked onto the wasteland from which grew this Soviet era bloc of a building. The young woman looked at him.

"He's in there."

"Really? What is it?"

"Is a prison."

"Bollocks," he muttered in disappointment.

She looked confused. "You don't want a murderer in jail?"

"No—yes—of course. But I wanted, you know, to get someone to interview him – to expose him."

"Then you're lucky," she said.

And then they were on the march again. He knew she was showing off her knowledge of the place and enjoying the power of it all, but he was growing tired of her lack of communication. He couldn't deny, however, that she appeared to be saving him time and effort, and all the marching around had helped him get his bearings a little. "Right, where are we going now and why am I lucky?"

"You are very, very lucky," she said. "He is to be going court today."

"How do you know that?" "Newspaper," she said, with a quizzical tone that suggested he ought to try harder to keep up.

"OK?"

"I have uncle working at court."

To be fair, that did strike Sam as very, very lucky. And a little unlucky, because court didn't sound like an ideal place to snuff someone if you wanted to get away with it. And his priority had to be getting away with it. He didn't fancy spending thirty years away from Isla, and certainly not in the building at their tail.

The young woman was a whirlwind of energy. Sam could barely keep up with her as she wound him through the streets of Vilnius. They passed contemporary minimalist shops selling watches worth thousands, and markets for the poor that looked like little more than food banks. The place reminded him of Moscow, where people were either destitute or filthy, horribly, braggingly rich. They eventually stopped on what looked like the main street and she turned to face an imposing building with unnecessarily high doors hung between gargantuan pillars.

"Wait here," she commanded, her bossiness again betraying a desire to impress; he was on her turf and she was evidently competent. As he stood there, he mused over how much effort this woman had saved him. Sam was confident that he could find just about anyone, just about anywhere, but doing so took time. With language barriers and when his often well-concealed Irish charm fell dead – as he suspected it would in this society, it could be a struggle. This woman was a lucky charm – a bustling little dynamo of endless resourcefulness and contacts and he did, indeed, feel very, very lucky.

When she emerged, she was excited. She lowered her voice to a stage whisper. "He can get you in!"

Sam shook his head in wonder. Less than twenty-four hours after they'd landed, she had him a face to face. Of course he had absolutely no idea what to do with this opportunity, so he needed to think fast. "When's he due up?"

"What?"

"When will he be here?"

She looked at her watch for effect. "Three hours."

This was, frankly, not the best news.

"Thank you so much," he began. "Shall we meet here in a few hours, then?" Her face fell into unabashed disappointment. He scrabbled to atone. "I can pay you now if you'd like?"

"Why Irishmen are always trying to pay me money," she replied, making a statement rather than asking a question.

"But we agreed I'd pay you from my expenses? You've been a huge help."

"So now you not need me?" she tilted her head forward, her brow creased, suddenly angry.

"Yes," he struggled. "Yes, I need you. Why is he in prison?" he tried.

"He is fighting with police," she shrugged, as if everyone fought with police.

"And when did he come back to Lithuania?"

"This I don't know."

"OK. Thank you. Will we meet later?"

"Then you pay me later," she said, and he realised she was enjoying the importance of her new role and was keen for it not to end. And, of course, not taking the money kept her in the game for more fun later. He tried to suppress the irritation – he didn't want to bring any trouble her way, or towards her uncle, but he needed that one-to-one with Shannon's murderer. There was no way he'd get another chance.

The solution presented itself as he haggled with the girl over her refusal to accept immediate payment. An arse-about-face negotiation. He took a gamble and asked her for guidance.

"Do you know diabetes?"

"Of course," she said, moderately offended. "You need insulin?"

"Yes." What he really needed was what came with it.

"Ok," she sighed, and they were off again, through the pretty part of town this time. They came to a chemist, where she put out her hand for cash and then stomped off. He heard her barking orders at a fat woman in a white coat. They had an argument; the younger woman prevailed and came back with a vial.

"Thank you," he said, "but I need the needle too – the syringe."

"Why you not bring with you?"

Sam thought that was a good question.

"Left it at the hotel."

"You must stay far away," was all she said as she turned to once more set-to with the pharmacist. She emerged victorious and it was time to part ways.

"Thank you. I need to go and …" He shook the bag a little.

"Yes," she said, not moving.

"I really need a few hours. I'll meet you at the court at two o'clock, ok?"

She looked at the bag in his hand, appeared to accept that he had something to do and agreed. "As you are wishing," she said, turning and strolling away.

Sam shook the discomfort of the exchange away and turned towards where the trolleybus had passed them earlier.

He'd spotted a metalworks on the far side of the road as they'd walked towards the jail. When he got there, he was disappointed. Beyond the trolleybus cables was a train track. The metalworks were so close, yet so far away, and there was no obvious means of getting over the line. At length he gave up looking, skipped over the barrier, ran across the sleepers and hurled himself at the fence on the far side, telling himself not to care about the many people watching him do it. There was no time for messing around. A ten-minute fast walk took him to the gates of the factory and the rapid click and buzz of welders told him he was in the right place.

Sam worked his way quietly around the furthest side of the imposing shed and found the delivery bay. There he found what he was looking for standing three barrels tall, in bright blue, with the universal skull symbol on them. The letters HF were marked in bold: hydrofluoric acid. Because of the foreign text, he had no idea if it was pure, but he had no time and was out of options. He broke the seal and gingerly filled half a centimetre of the syringe, carefully replacing the needle cover. It was a distant memory but he recalled the warnings he'd been given when he'd trained at a rigging factory as a teenager. Used to clean stainless steel, he and the others on the course were told in no uncertain terms that a drop of HF acid on your skin could cause severe damage, take it internally and the next stop was multiple organ failure.

Sam worked his way back to Vilnius centre, constantly checking his time. The next step was one that could help hugely.

He hunted for a gorilla pit and with only one hour left, slight desperation was creeping in. At a very fast walk he covered about a mile and finally caught sight of a "York" sign above a door. Like the acid warning label, some brands were universal. He bounded upstairs and as he opened a door into a heavy-weights gym, every shaven, thick head in the room rotated robotically towards him.

The next bit was tricky. He did his usual.

"*Vyh guh-vah-REE-tyeh pah ahn-GLEES-kee?*" he tried from memory. Do you speak English? he thought he'd said. Except he was speaking Russian, which was far from ideal. He knew that many Lithuanians still hated Russia.

The body builders just looked at him, some slugging from what he assumed were supplement shakes. Eventually one powder monkey stepped forward and shrugged. *A little*, he seemed to suggest.

Sam began to gesture in an uncomfortable sign language, eventually withdrawing the syringe and miming an injection into the buttock. The man watched and his eyes betrayed no recognition, yet he nodded once and then summoned someone over with a barely discernible flick of his head.

A second man with shoulders the size of watermelons motioned Sam towards a changing room. Nervous that he was on shaky ground, he followed; barely confident that his build was sufficient to suggest he threw a few barbells about.

Watermelon man rooted in his bag and produced a small, familiar-looking glass bottle, the type that some of Sam's pals had. Post-training, he'd seen them shoot that shit into their arse muscles, he'd seen the nose bleeds as they squatted and pressed and gradually made themselves too big to move quickly.

Sam pulled out his cash and scraped off a few sheets, which seemed to surprise and please the man.

"*Spaseeba*," he tried, thinking he'd said thank you. The watermelons just shrugged. Sam turned and left, with an irksome feeling that despite the time pressures, things were going rather too well.

He paused in a side street to carefully add the steroids to the acid, then made for the court. He had no idea how long the plastic of the syringe would last with that stuff in it, and it already felt warm to the touch. The thought that it could seep into his pocket made him hold his jacket away from his body slightly and increase his pace.

On the steps standing sentry was his trusty translator. She ushered him inside without any greeting and led him to a man in uniform, who greeted him with nothing more than a short glance. The man turned without a word and began walking, which told Sam that the young woman hadn't licked her manner off the ground. She, contrary to her form to date, remained behind.

The man opened an enormous dark timber door and walked Sam down a series of echoey marble corridors, Sam filing the route away in case he needed to get out at speed. They passed nobody, and the windows into adjoining rooms were above head height. Sam didn't like to think about what had gone on behind the closed doors they passed during the

Cold War. The man slowed and stopped, opening a door to a room before walking away without so much as a nod of the head or a word spoken. This is going too smoothly he thought, only mildly concerned about how he would get out again if things went badly, but more worried about the syringe, which was hot but appeared to be holding up. He scanned the room for cameras and paced a little. Like the rest of the building he'd seen so far, the only windows were above head height and covered in some sort of film – the type Belfast pubs had used during the Troubles to stop gunmen picking out their targets. He could make out the dark blur of legs walking past and reckoned that the room was half below street level.

After half an hour the door opened and two fully attired policemen came in. They had the whole outfit: batons, knee pads, elbow pads, padded baseball hats, stab jackets, handguns. Panic tried to rise in him as he realised this was not a fight he could win. Wary that the girl had declined to come with him, he immediately thought he'd been screwed and was about to get lifted. He thought of the window above and how he might smash it and use the furniture to get up there and out onto the street. He told himself to hold his nerve to see what would unfold as the guards lined the wall and stood at a regimented ease before him; Sam bracing for the arrest. Then their heads turned towards the door and more guards appeared, hauling in a man about Sam's size, and he knew he was looking at Shannon's killer.

Sam's heart hammered hard, his jaw tightened. The man was fair, scarred and snarling, tugging and shaking his shoulders against the arms that gripped him. He looked like he craved conflict and stared at Sam, goading him, confident he could fight, despite his arms being secured behind his back. Sam wondered who the man thought he was. The display of aggression gave Sam a moment to consider his next move. He needed to be alone with the man, and so opted for authority and nodded to the police officers to leave, which, to his complete amazement, they did. He had no idea what the officers had been told about him – he imagined they thought him some sort of overseas police officer of rank. Their compliance with his gesture only served to make him worry about whether the planets were aligning in his favour, or it was all about to come to a dreadful conclusion.

Suddenly it was just Shannon's killer, and Shannon's husband; a widower, with a weapon. The door closed with a heavy click and the man's attitude changed. His eyes narrowed and he regarded Sam again, curious, trying to work out who he was.

"You were in Northern Ireland."

The man's head flicked an inch and froze. Sam could see he was being understood.

"You came to my house. You murdered my wife," Sam said, as evenly as he was able.

The man's pupils widened involuntarily; his mind unable to keep up with the confusion of seeing Sam there. Maybe it was Sam's accent, maybe he had seen him around the village when he'd been home on leave. Regardless, he knew he was in the shit.

Sam had all the conformation he required and chose not to spend time with a dead man. Stepping forward he hammered the syringe into his thigh, palming the plunger in the same movement. The man fell back, slouched, against the wall, shock taking the air from his lungs. Terror filled his eyes as he looked to his leg.

Sam watched, hopeful it would take hours, if not days, for him to die.

Traces of steroids wouldn't attract any attention in a prison. He was confident that a place like that would be awash with anabolics. Sam didn't care how they explained the acid – he suspected they would ignore it, assuming they bothered with an autopsy at all.

He placed the needle carefully in its sheath, returned the syringe to his pocket and reached for the door. He nodded to the officers outside, maintaining the air of seniority, and walked briskly back, retracing the turns in reverse.

Three hours later, having spent all his cash on a translator, her uncle, steroids and a teddy for Isla, he was back at the airport, twitching for his flight to London to be called.

It was only after he got through security at Heathrow - all but home and hosed, that he began to think about what he'd done, and what Shannon would have said. Any satisfaction was short lived, as he wondered whether he was gradually unpicking her good work, given the risks he'd taken. He was guilty of murder, for sure. But that wasn't what caused the ache creeping through him. He'd not been home, where he was truly needed. He'd pursued vengeance, satisfaction and purpose. He was guilty of grief.

Chapter 14

He'd received a tap on his shoulder one morning as they prepared to patrol from a forward operating post – the dustiest, dirtiest, most dangerous compound they'd occupied all tour. The sandbag walls of the makeshift fort were the only protection they had; well, aside from some pretty heavy general-purpose machine guns, a truckload of artillery and a mortar team.

He was filling in his hole, the one he'd slept in for two weeks, dug by his own giant paw, when he was informed that a keen lieutenant had arrived and was being flown to the outpost to relieve him. With hindsight he wondered whether someone somewhere had realised how much time he'd spent on the ground and how many of his men had been sent home without legs. Everyone knew they'd had a hell of a tour, and although Sam's men had taken out a dozen Taliban positions, the landmines had literally crippled them.

His troop was blisteringly brutal, probably among the best few sections of Royal Marines he'd ever served with.

The young ones were brave and smart; the corporals and sergeants across the board were experienced and committed. During larger ops they'd managed to trim the Taliban right back without losing a single bootneck, but it was the bloody IEDs that had taken the toll. He'd applied tourniquet after tourniquet – on one occasion three to the same man, in an horrific loss of livelihoods. He lost count of the number of times he'd knelt by one of his men as they growled to suppress the shock of seeing their limbs in sinew beside them.

There were occasions when it was simply too dangerous to let the medics get close to the wounded. One man down is bad; two explosions ought to be preventable. It went against general orders but in his mind it was sensible: better to lose the boss than the medic. So, insisting that the doc retrace his steps with the rest of the section, he tended the maimed. His reasoning was that they could make it back without him, but without the expertise of the morphine man they might not make it back at all. It was a way of alleviating the guilt associated with leading men to their deaths. The responsibility was his.

He'd found that no matter how brave they were, the men in his unit were scared at times. People often confuse the two, he told them. Bravery is not fearlessness. Bravery is the suppression of fear to accomplish what you think needs to be done. His men had loads of bravery, but they trusted him to make the right decisions. As they should – he was in his thirties and in bootneck terms he'd been around the block. Except that no detector can trace every mine; no section can sweep ahead of every footstep, particularly at night. Those crippled were on his conscience while his own hands and feet, remarkably, remained with him.

As forty loomed closer than thirty, his back began to

stiffen. The bergen never felt any lighter and his kit seemed permanently saturated in the blood of others. Countless times he'd hauled the bodies of brave little marines to casevacs in the full knowledge that if the catastrophic bleed didn't take them, the PTSD might. He knew too that the hidden plague would come to him, but he didn't have time to contract anything back then. He believed, contrary to what many said, that post-traumatic stress was treated pretty seriously in the corps. Sam always looked upon it as a kind of virus that would inevitably spread throughout his troop. His thinking was that he couldn't catch it until that dreadful tour was finished, but he never doubted it would come.

It wasn't until he got home that the cracks began to appear and let the darkness in. It started with terror, which he found hard to take. It came at night, triggered in sleep, and was dreadful. He'd heard people talk of flashbacks, others of reliving the hell. For him, closing his eyes was like going to the movies. Everything was so vivid, so real, and yet so embarrassingly ordinary once the sun rose. Darkness for a period became his enemy, perhaps because for the most part death had visited at night, like when an allied army unit got their range wrong and blew the shit out of his position, then denied it. Or when they were too fresh to the field to understand how the Taliban was working in any given area.

Until then panic had been unusual to him, but that changed in an instant. He'd wake up suddenly, eyes wide open, ready to burst out, and realise that sleep had taken him to hell again. And the anxiety didn't end there. It endured for hours as he lay awake and listened and jerked; he was frightened. Even under extreme fire, even with bits of bootneck hanging from rocks or plastered over walls, he'd seldom been afraid. But there was no adrenaline to protect him at night, in bed, beside his wife. There was no rifle or GPMG to counter his fear and shoot up the enemy. There was just silence, and darkness, and cowardice. It crept through him like the dawn over sea, enveloping and exposing him and, according to Shannon, making him human again.

Sam had never been dependent upon anyone. Until Shannon. All through the school years he'd taken his own path – often the most difficult, occasionally losing friends in the process. He could have been popular if he'd toed the line and done what the other boys were doing, but his outlook was different. Usually very different. He couldn't stand by and watch some of the things that went on and laugh nervously as the others did or shrug it off and keep his mouth shut or his paws in his pockets. But what appeared to many to be a strength, he knew to be a flaw. It had served him badly. He'd fallen into trouble and been ushered into the military, where the last of his youth was spent out and the framing of his adulthood was set.

Thereafter came Shannon – the only person to have seen inside his mind and understood. Yet he was regressing without her. Slipping back while trying to tell himself that his actions were justified, warranted; trying to block out the fact that he was doing what he was doing because he wanted to.

His mind drifted back to a shameful incident in Belfast that still gusted guilt over him during darker, maudlin moments. She'd consoled him afterwards, and for the first time he wondered whether she'd thought it had been, perhaps in part, her fault.

It had been on that unexpected period of leave. Against all odds he'd been allowed home for Christmas and it was the first time he'd had the chance to spend it with Isla and only the second he'd spent with Shannon.

He and Isla were happy, hand in hand on a climbing escalator in Belfast's Victoria Square shopping centre. They planned to buy her mother a Christmas present. Isla was full of chat while Sam constantly scanned. He couldn't help it. On leave he did relax a little, lower his alert level as much as he could, but there was nothing he could do to stop himself taking in his surroundings, probably seeking out threat and making sure he had the capacity to react. Ahead of him was a man who was facing the wrong way, looking beneath Sam, at his little girl. His mouth was open, his tongue wide and flat, his head nodding slightly. There was no doubt in Sam's mind – this was a slobbering, salivating pervert who had forgotten himself and was ogling his child. Sam went off, like a grenade tossed into a bunker.

His feet reached the end of the moving stairs and he reached for the man, plucking him from the ground and throttling him with his back against a glass wall.

"Fuck are you looking at?" was all Sam could manage to growl, his teeth ground shut in anger, the man's body giving way to shock and fear. Then there was screaming and slapping and Isla crying and the man in a mess on the ground. Somebody called for security and two women arrived up in his face calling him for every name they could muster. He lifted Isla up, drew her in and turned to walk away. It was only then he realised what he had done.

"He's got a learning disability, you bloody animal!" he heard a woman shout.

He turned back and looked at the scene, at the people gathered around. All Sam could see were the man's feet. One other woman could have been his mother. She was distraught and wailing beside him. Sam closed his eyes and his heart sank. A swollen ball of nausea travelled up his chest. He had the overwhelming urge to return and plead an apology but he could see the woman would wear none of it.

"What's *wrong* with you?" she screamed, stunned, from her position crouched by the man.

And then Sam prioritised: he chose Isla over his conscience. He turned and left, holding her tight, saying over and over again that everything would be all right, ignoring her questions about why he had hit the man. He didn't even remember hitting him – he couldn't say for sure that he had. If she was right, Sam knew the man could be in real difficulty. He took her away.

There were still tears and terror and snot when they got home. Isla ran straight to her mother and told her everything in one great stream of distress. Shannon looked at him in horror, and then gradually relented as it dawned on her that remorse, rather than anger, was his main affliction. She calmed Isla down as only she could back then, and later coaxed it all out of him. He told her he'd thought the man was looking at Isla, she told him that's not how people like that behave. She made him acknowledge that he might be looking for trouble where no trouble lurked, that he was constantly primed to explode and that he had to be aware of that and work hard at acting like a human. She spoke to him for hours, making him face up to the fact that strengths and reactions in war were weaknesses in real life.

She reasoned it out objectively. Had she tried to shower him with shit and niceties, he would have taken no comfort. But she drew him to a conclusion of sorts, without letting him off the hook.

"You fucked up today," she said, cutting but necessary.

"I know, I'm so sorry, Shan. It's just there, it's in me."

"That's why it won't be the last time. You'll do it again. But you need to address it each time, to feel the hurt. Then maybe it will happen less often."

"Don't hold back, Shan, will you, darlin'?"

"No point, Sam. You need to realise that other people aren't like you. You've been surrounded by commandos for years, hon, so it's not your fault that you're tuned to the fucking moon. But if you're going to get out, you have to learn to live like us. Not everyone is the enemy. There isn't risk round every corner. And you need to realise that other people are no match for you. They chucked in red meat and wanted you to come out cross. Now you have to retrain for ordinary life."

He stared at her. He knew she was right, but he didn't know how to get there.

"What you did was out of love and protection."

He snorted.

"It was, Sam. Your instincts are good – to protect Isla, to look after her, but your instincts are to fight *immediately* and instead you need to fight clever. Consider that fighting isn't the first and only option. You have to get used to being around different types of people – gentle people, confused people, folk who aren't familiar with fast decisions and quick reactions. That man must have been so scared when he saw you coming at him today."

"Aagh, I can't even remember going at him," he rasped, as the shame overwhelmed him. And then more and more came tumbling out. He told her of the sleepless nights, of the horrors in the dark, of the weakness he felt. Shannon siphoned out the pain and when the flow began it was hard to stop. In the end, he even told her of the nightmares he'd had of harming her and Isla. She assured him that he didn't scare her, that she felt safe with him and that she was positive he would never hurt them. The relief, eventually, was enormous.

Sam knew that that was the beginning of his final extraction from the Royal Marines, a phased dislocation designed to make him a normal man again. And then the person who shackled him to sanity was murdered, and he needed to find a way to do it alone.

Chapter 15

"Just fooking leave me alone."

Sam stared at the girl. She couldn't have been more than seventeen years old. She was sitting up and swaying on top of soiled sheets but in her head could well have been floating on clean, cotton clouds. He couldn't begin to imagine what had been pumped into her. She could barely sit and her arms flailed around as she grappled for purchase in the putrid air of the tiny room.

The charity woman had sent him to the address – a block of flats in Tallaght, south-west Dublin. He hadn't needed to force entry, which was just as well because he hadn't brought any heavy kit or weapons. The door had been wide open and the smell of perfume and rubber tumbled down the stairwell.

The charity woman's briefing had been scant: an address and an assertion that there were at least four girls in the flat. He could locate only two – a worry, but also a waste of money because he'd hired a people carrier at the airport. If the intel had been accurate, he would have rented a smaller vehicle that would have been easier to park and put a smaller dent in his dwindling finances.

The girl lunged away from him to the side of her bed and popped back up, shuddering like a diving board post-diver, her head wobbling furiously. He stooped to pick her up and recoiled immediately when he caught sight of the needle in her hand.

"Whoa, whoa, whoa," he spluttered, "I'm here to help you, I'm not gonna hurt you, I'm not a punter. I'm here to take you home."

"Fook-a off yourself," she drawled. The poor kid was bombed beyond sense.

And Sam was short on time. "Who runs this place?"

She just stared at him.

"I do," a voice came from behind.

He turned to face a well-preserved fifty-something — glamorous, perhaps, hair in an ornate weave on top of her painstakingly crafted facade. Sam scanned her for as long as he could, noticing her coat and handbag. She must have just returned to the flat. He tried to get more of a fix, but he was wary of the kid with the pointy, probably infection-ridden weapon to his right.

The older woman began to talk, confident and dismissive. "So you're here to help them, are you?"

"What are you — like a madam or something?"

"I am an employer," she said, "And I also have people to answer to, and they will be back very soon."

Sam reassessed his plan not to hurt anyone. Her selfishness made him cross — her willingness to treat these kids as tools. He'd been told the boss was Romanian, but he'd obviously hired locally to give his grim exploits a native branding. The mutton was taking a phone from her bag, so it was decision time. She tapped in her code and ten held it to her ear.

Taking a step to his left he curled her phone arm behind her back.

"Don't you touch me—don't you dare touch—get your hands off me!" The woman kicked, spat, swore and screamed as Sam wheeled her and pressed her against the wall. He took the phone and fumbled with it, stopping the call. Then a flash of an opportunity presented itself, remembering how they'd seized phones off Taliban spotters and used them for intelligence. He leaned in harder against the woman, his free arm finding the settings, passcode menu and quickly changed it to four zeros and she swung her scrawny elbows at him. He stuffed it in his pocket and tore a leather strap, not unlike a belt, from a radiator. He found it alarmingly moist. He shoved her to his right and bound her hands to the railing of the bed, the kid edging lazily out of the way, eyes wide open at the display. As he pinned her down to make the lashing secure, her bouffant slumped and he rather imagined that this wasn't the first occasion someone had lashed the old pigeon to a headboard.

The woman's cursing was reaching alarming levels. He rifled quickly through her handbag, and found a purse with at least a dozen neatly arranged credit cards. There was also a gnarled curl of fifty euro notes, the proceeds of sex, he assumed, and so due to the girls he'd been sent to retrieve. It all went in his pockets.

He turned to the kid, now cowering in the corner, the needle held in front of her like a dagger. She was pretty far gone and needed help. Shannon would have hugged her, Sam thought, used reason and psychology and empathy. He, instead, slapped the syringe out of her hand, found a bag under the bed and bucked every piece of non-kinky clothing into it. Then he hoisted her over his shoulder and carried her down the stairwell to the car. He rolled her into the back seat while she shouted and gave out and made him wish he'd brought someone with him. He locked her in and turned to go back to the flat but she started bouncing about so much that the alarm went off. Sam paused for a second and looked to the sky, feeling sure someone would call the Guards. He still had the other girl to get out of the flat, and despite the noise he thought of the story of the chicken, the bag of corn, the fox and the boat, so to quell the alarm he decided to take the first one back up with him.

At the top of the stairs he found the second girl, slightly older and moderately more sober, packed and ready to go.

"Great, come on," he said, turning. The one over his shoulder was getting heavyish. She was still kicking when she put her hands against the wall to curtail his rotation. "Can you tell her to take it easy?"

To his amazement the second girl formed a fist and hit the kid with such force that the wriggling stopped. Sam didn't have the time to reason it out. He just grunted and swung fully round, faced down the stairs and made for the car. The aggressive one followed.

He put them both in the back and hurried to the front, looking up at the windows around him, climbed in and started driving. That the violent one was behind him made him cross. The whole extraction had been full of mistakes and he resolved to ensure that the next one was properly planned and risk assessed. Civilian life had made him sloppy, too easily distracted.

When he got to Dublin Airport he realised that breaking the girls out of the brothel was the least of his problems. He parked outside the shiny new departure terminal and was immediately accosted by a Nazi parking attendant.

"Drop off only," the man started as soon as he got out of the vehicle. Sam ignored him and made for the rear door. He tugged the handle but it wouldn't open, then the parking Nazi was at his back. "I said, drop off only!"

"I am dropping off," Sam muttered, staring at the girl in the back, who stared defiantly back. He was confused.

"You'll need to move on now."

Sam turned to face the attendant. "You said drop off – I am dropping off."

"Then drop off and clear out." The man stood with his arms folded.

Sam tried the handle again and shook the door. The girl turned away from him.

"Open the bloody door," he growled at the window, but the woman stared straight ahead. What the hell is this about? he thought.

"That's it, I'm calling the Guards," the attendant said, reaching for the radio on his shoulder.

Sam walked around the car and got into the driver's seat. He hunted for the central locking button and thumped it hard. As soon as the doors clicked, he heard the girl lock her own door again. He did it again, she responded the same way. He turned to her.

"What are you doing? I'm trying to get you away from here."

"I'm not going back," she said.

"What?"

"I'm not going back to my home country." She stared out the window at the attendant who was now knocking on the window.

Sam wished he had a phone to call the charity woman

but he'd deliberately not brought one so that he couldn't be tracked in the event of something going wrong. He wondered what else could possibly *go* wrong.

"Look, I need to drop you here. There's someone inside going to help you."

"How do I know you do not just send me to another country for same?"

"Same?"

"More sex. Different country, more of same."

Sam turned forwards and looked in the rear-view mirror, ignoring the hammering on the window, and tried to place her look and accent. "Where are you from?"

"Albania," she said.

"Look, the woman inside works for a charity, understand?"

"I know charity."

"Tell her you don't want to go back to Albania. She'll do her best for you."

The woman slumped and crossed her arms in a kind of sulk and her childish reaction made him realise that she was younger than he'd first thought. Her work had evidently aged her.

He unlocked the doors again, got out and marched around to the pavement only to be greeted by a guard.

"This man is holding up the thoroughfare, guard," the attendant announced.

"What's the problem?" The guard turned to Sam who opened the door just to have it pulled shut again, which Sam knew didn't look great. The guard leaned in to take a look at the rear seats and tutted. "And how old are these women?" his voice almost began to sing.

"I'm just delivering them for a flight." Sam pulled the door again.

"One of them doesn't look at all well." The guard looked at Sam, weighing up the situation.

"Give me a minute," Sam said, hunting in his pocket for the slip of paper with the charity woman's phone number on it. He was about to get the guard to call it when he remembered the madam's phone. He strode back to the driver's side, the guard shouting.

"Hang on, there! I need to know what's going on here."

Sam reached into his pocket and sat into the car again to make the call.

"Hello?"

He turned away from the women. "It's Sam. I'm outside. I've got a problem."

"Outside where?" Charity sounded like she was driving, which was not at all good. She was supposed to be on the concourse waiting for the women to be delivered.

"Terminal Two?" Sam said.

"Already?"

"This is the time we arranged?"

"I'm still fifteen minutes away," she said, which almost annoyed him more than anything that had gone before.

Sam hung up, realising that this might be something he would have to learn in any new business. Charity workers were brilliant people, but he knew from the way Shannon had got on that they were not altogether organised, and compared to the navy they could be sketchy when it came to the execution of simple operations. Their passion crowded their practicality and they argued over how things ought to be done even in the midst of actually doing them. He found such silliness exhausting.

He went back to the guard. "There's a woman coming, she'll explain everything."

The attendant stepped forward. "Well, you'll have to move on – you're blocking the way."

The guard turned on the parking Nazi. "They'll stay here until I am satisfied with what's going on."

"But he's blocking the ..."

Sam and the cop turned to look at the light traffic depositing passengers. There was plenty of space all along the drop-off point. The attendant refolded his arms in annoyance. Sam tried the door one last time but the woman pulled it shut. He leaned against the car and waited.

It took the full fifteen minutes for Charity to arrive. She pulled up in front of the people carrier and took the guard aside. Sam could just about hear her remonstrating him. She, at least, had identification and plane tickets for the girls. After establishing that the guard wanted to know who Sam was – and Sam didn't want anyone to know that, he tried to open the door again so he could clear off but the woman pulled it shut, as expected. Charity moved towards Sam with an apologetic smile that turned to concern when she realised that one of the girls was semi-conscious. She wanted to know why and Sam wanted to know how any of that mattered in the circumstances.

"Look, there are two issues here – getting them out of the vehicle and getting them on the flight."

Charity tried the door, nodding encouragingly through the window, and coaxed the fully conscious woman out of the car. She stood, unsure, and allowed Charity to rub her shoulder. Sam heard the cop at his back.

"Sir, I'm going to need to see some identification," the guard began, as a massive white Mercedes screeched up behind and a shaven-headed thug emerged. The man simply walked forward, grabbed the more conscious girl by the upper arm and led her away. Sam looked skyward and wondered again how he had ended up in such a situation. He looked to the guard to intervene but the guard looked terrified.

Sam tried to cajole the officer into doing something. "This is now a kidnap situation. Are you going to allow two vulnerable women to be taken against their will?"

"I ... I'll radio for assistance."

"Seriously?" Charity said. Having pulled the wobbly woman out of the car she was now shielding her against the open door by standing in front of the kid.

"So I'm to sort this bloody mess out while you panic, you prick!" Sam shouted at the guard. His anger rose at being forced, in full view of countless security cameras, to deal with the skinhead. He had to remind himself to be smart and not let his temper take over, especially when his actions were very likely being recorded.

Beyond the guard Sam saw a clear Perspex box fixed to the wall with prohibited items and a sign appealing for dangerous articles to be deposited prior to departure. He looked at the cans of deodorant, razor blades and cigarette lighters and settled upon a tool, obviously discarded by a travelling builder or joiner. As the thug moved to return to the people carrier Sam walked over, lent a boot strike to the Perspex box and retrieved a Stanley knife. He drew the blade while the thug faced a much too gentle accosting from the guard and bent down to slash two of the Mercedes' tyres.

It was clear that the thug had balls. To try and take two women, on his own, in front of a man, a cop, a woman and a jobsworth traffic attendant suggested confidence or reck-lessness. Unsurprisingly, he got cross watching his car lean in towards the kerb, and Sam turned to face him. The whole fight became quite convoluted and took a short age, but Sam managed to come out on top – with a chewed ear, a possible broken nose and dozens of people watching him extricate himself from his opponent. The charity woman stared at him as he rose from the incapacitated lump on the footpath and he had to shout at her to jolt her into action.

"Get the women and get them inside!"

Charity dragged the doped girl to the Merc, retrieved the other woman who had fallen into complete, compliant silence, and made for the concourse. All the while the guard flapped his arms, unsure what to do beyond call for his colleagues.

Sam pushed past the jobsworth, climbed into the hire car, slammed his door shut and caught the reflection of the Irish police arriving in force as he drove away. The chasing posse pulled in to get an explanation from their man on the scene, which allowed him the chance to turn the corner and swerve immediately into an Enterprise car-hire slot. He was out of the car before the wailing vehicles screamed past in pursuit of a car that was already behind them. The people carrier was nearly returned before it had been rented – the same staff, slightly baffled, were on shift.

He'd hired the vehicle corporate so that the only ID required was his licence – a fake he'd held since his previous employment and long since forgotten by his old bosses. It was only just still in date. He asked the staff to delete his stolen credit card details and handed over some of the madam's cash instead, counting out the notes he'd intended to give to the trafficked girls. There looked to be a few thousand in the roll.

He dropped an extra fifty euro on the counter. "You might want to clean the back seat. Nothing serious," he told them, then walked into the thoroughfare and jumped on the bus to Belfast.

Chapter 16

"First comes dignity, captain!"

"First comes discipline," screamed the epauleted Russian.

Not for the first time Sam questioned the wisdom of his choice of new career, thinking of Shannon and what she would have made of what he was doing. His eyes tightened and his lips thinned at the reflection. *So I died, you left the military and jumped straight into a shit fight? Well done, Sam, that's just what Isla needs.* He could hear her as clearly as if she were on the ship with him.

"Take me to the crew, captain!"

Sam looked on in amazement at the little Dubliner as he squared up to the ship's skipper. At five foot seven he was dinky in comparison, yet appeared to know no fear. Sam wondered whether his own presence had been needed at all.

"No," replied the officer, shaking his head, dumbfounded. "You are not welcome on this ship. You must leave."

Even after years in the Marines, special forces and of

hauling himself around harbours and oceans, Sam shared a little of the captain's surprise that they had made it onto his bridge. His ship was still at sea, after all. A hostile boarding of a commercial vessel in Irish waters was not what he would have reasonably expected.

Sam had been reluctant to answer when Charity called with another job. The Dublin Airport debacle had left him feeling exposed, yet nobody had come looking for him and, mercifully, the wrestling match hadn't made the news or social media. Still, his face was now on record somewhere and those CCTV images made him want to stay out of Dublin for a while. Then the charity woman had mentioned ships and, suddenly, he found himself interested.

All Charity had told him was that a man who dealt with exploited seafarers would meet him at the gates to Dublin Port. Sam took the bus and found the bloke sitting in his car talking on a Bluetooth speakerphone. He knocked on the window and was beckoned into the passenger seat where he enjoyed five minutes of the man's colourful conversation as he tried to persuade some foreign bloke to take on his penalty points for speeding on a motorbike. It was a fun listen.

"If I get any more, I'll lose my licence," he explained to the person on the other end. "Yer man won't care. He's leaving in a few weeks anyway. They'll not chase him to Poland for three points." Sam could hear chatter on the other end, then the man replied. "Sound, brother, talk to ye." The little man closed the call. "Fran," he said, and leaned over to shake Sam's hand.

"Sam."

"So you've been with the Brits, have you?"

Normally this would put him on notice – so many people in Ireland are inherently hostile to the UK's armed forces, but it was obvious to Sam that Fran was taking the piss.

"Yes," was all Sam said, and they settled in like they'd known each other forever as Fran explained the job.

"Ship full of Filipinos under a flag of convenience heading for the port as we speak. The ship's run by a Russian shipping agency. Issues on board with the poor treatment of the ratings, the blue-collar grafters."

Sam appreciated the brevity of the briefing but had questions. "How do you know about this?"

"SMS, my friend, text message – the wonders of technology." Fran held up his phone and shook it with a roguish grin before tapping and reading from the screen.

"Dear, Mr Fran," he began, and turned to Sam with a smile, "from MV *Gallant* at anchor in Fort Lauderdale. We due Dublin six week. Please help. No good on ship. No pay many day. 2 month. No permitted leave ship. Many crew. 15 Filipino. Not return home in year. Please help us."

"Seriously?"

"Modern slavery, brother, hidden before our very eyes," Fran said dramatically. "Every port has a Mission to Seafarers and every mission has a little booklet. And my number, brother, is in that booklet."

Sam knew of the mission, a religious organisation designed to cater to the spiritual needs of those in peril on the seas. He'd seen the booklets too, but he'd never read one. "Why your number?" he asked.

"I'm the rep for the ITF – the International Transport Workers' Federation."

"A trade union?"

"Exactly, brother, but you wouldn't know anything about that, would you? You're not allowed to organise, being at the beck and call of her Majesty, wha?" He chuckled.

They drove into the port and Fran waved merrily at scowling stevedores. Sam got a sense of why the little man might need him. "You don't seem too popular around here," he said.

"They love me, really," said Fran, his cheery disposition masking a serious determination. "They just get pissed off when I arrest a ship and their shift runs over."

"You can arrest a ship?"

"I can, brother! Under maritime law, and that's what you and me are going to get up to today."

To Sam that sounded like more fun than trailing hookers out of disease-ridden flats. These were the type of seamen he could deal with. They parked up and Fran led Sam across to a tall building covered in glass.

As they entered an office a man in a tie dropped his head into his hands in despair. "Ah, Fran, man, not again. I told the wife I'd be home to watch the young one." Sam saw a waterproof coat on a hanger and could make out "harbour master" embroidered on the chest.

"Well, comrade, with cooperation and goodwill towards your fellow human beings, we'll be out of your way in a jiffy."

"What is it, Fran?" asked the harbour master.

"A big shiny red ship is sitting on the edge of Dublin Bay. Belize flag, Russian captain, fifteen Filipinos on board. No pay for two months. No agreement and no right to leave. I want them unionised and paid or allowed ashore for repatriation."

"Ah, look," the harbour master shook his head. "Why today? I'm about to go on me holidays. Could you not have come tomorrow?"

"I'll do you a deal," said Fran. "I'll not arrest the ship at the quay if you can get me out there to sort it. Then, if I can get an agreement and the men paid, I'll allow it in. Your men can unload it and send it on its merry way."

"And if there's no agreement?"

"Then I'll arrest it at sea and you'll have the dock clear for the next ship that comes along. But what I'm suggesting leaves you with a chance to get home before dinner."

"S'pose if I say no, the harbour will be crawling with press again?"

Sam stiffened – that hadn't been part of his reckoning.

Fran smiled like a Bond villain. "I don't want that any more than you do, comrade."

The harbour master stared at Fran for a few moments before speaking on a radio and telling the pilot boat crew to free up a seat.

"Two," said Fran.

"Who's your pal?" asked the harbour master, tipping his head.

"This is a brother in arms," said Fran, winking at Sam.

The harbour master grunted and lifted a box of Bensons off his table. He snatched up a mobile phone and moved to a small balcony, closing the door behind him.

Fran turned to Sam. "Ever been in a pilot boat?"

"No," Sam surprised himself.

"I hate the things," Fran said. "Make me sick to the stomach."

"I've seen plenty," Sam said.

"I bet you have, brother."

"So, what's next, who's the master calling?"

"The wife, I'd say." Fran beamed. "I'll try not to make a bollocks of him."

"Are we really going to take this ship?"

"If they don't buckle. See, my friend, shipping is big business. Captains get paid more if they're qualified to enter ports without a pilot, but no captain knows every port. If a ship gets it arse ways and runs aground, that snarls up traffic for hours – days even. And it's the speed of the turn-around that's vital to these big companies and to the commercial port. If a dock gets locked up or ships can't come in, that fella," he pointed to the figure pluming smoke into the air, "gets it in the neck."

"What about the dockers – how do you get them to play ball? Surely if the captain lets them, they'll unload?"

"If the ships get ashore, then I play the union card."

"Which is what?"

"The dockers are unionised. They're part of an umbrella trade union group. I call their organiser, he calls the head stevedore, they take off their hard hats and sit on their posteriors."

Sam shook his head gently at the deviousness of the plan. This was a job he might enjoy.

———

THE PILOT BOAT hammered through the waves rather than over them.

"Glad you're happy." Fran glared mockingly at Sam.

As they neared the ship a tiny rope ladder was flung over the side and for the first time he saw concern in the little Dubliner's eyes. Sam was in his element but Fran stood on the foredeck as the pilot boat leapt and plunged, its bow seeking to drive against the ship to keep it as close to stationary as possible. Fran held his hands out for balance, his man bag battering up and down under his flailing arm, as if he were riding a skateboard for the first time.

As a wave crest neared Sam swept out and grabbed the ladder with one arm and Fran's underarm with the other, hefting the little man onto the first rung. After that Fran had no choice but to keep going, bag flapping in the wind and he was up and away like a mortar out of a tube. Sam followed fast and Fran treated him to a heel on the forehead near the top, as the pilot boat withdrew and headed back to port.

On board, Fran was elated, pumping and ready to rumble. A bulky Russian met them at the top, complete with clipboard.

"Pilot, yes?"

"Yes, pilot," Fran lied, and Sam watched as he scribbled "Mickey Mouse" as a signature on the proffered page. "Take me to the bridge!"

The Russian complied and up steep steps they went, winding through the ship until they came to a modern, well-provisioned command room.

Fran marched across the bridge and hit the ground at a hurtle. "Captain, you're a cunt." Which took Sam aback, never mind the man to whom it was directed.

"Who are you?" fired the wide-eyed skipper, his face turning purple.

"International Transport Workers' Federation!" Fran announced with gusto.

The captain realised he'd been rumbled. "No, no, no! Get off this ship! Get off – you have no right here!" he screamed.

From Fran's reaction Sam saw that boarding cargo vessels was nothing new to him – Fran had pulled this stunt before.

"I have every right, as you well know, captain," Fran began in his florid, eloquent way, then reeled off some ancient law of the sea. Sam was thoroughly entertained and there was just enough edge to the proceedings to resurrect a recently absent buzz up his neck, brought about by the potential of engagement. Fran was animated, passionate, committed and enormously funny, and the antics of the little rascal's performance made him realise how much he missed that rush.

"Sixty days at sea, no pay, captain! You have crew on board who haven't been allowed ashore for one year, captain – one year!"

"No!" roared the Russian. "We pay them."

"A dollar a day, captain. Would you work for a dollar a day?"

"This is what they sign up for!"

"Well, where are the contracts, captain?" Fran shouted back, tilted forward, his hands in the air. "Show them to me!" he roared, plainly convinced that no contracts would be forthcoming.

The ding-dong went on for about fifteen minutes during which time the first officer came up and, although Sam had virtually no Russian, his gesticulations to the captain motioned a lifting movement, and a sideways hoist and deposit. Sam thought it was pretty clear that the officer was suggesting that he and Fran be thrown overboard. This, Sam felt, was probably part of the ill-defined role for which he'd been hired, so he stepped between the arguing men and the first officer and stared the new arrival down. Like a dog scolded, the first officer retreated.

The captain radioed ashore and requested help, which the harbour master duly refused, along with permission to dock until matters were resolved. The captain's second call was to his shipping agency employer and, after much discussion, it was agreed to take the unwelcome guests to see the crew. In the bowels of the ship they came across ten small frightened Filipinos in orange jumpsuits, sitting round a table in a grubby little mess room. The captain stood, arms folded in an attempt to fill the doorway until Fran rounded on him.

"Fuck off, captain," he said, "or you will not get to unload this ship all week."

Interestingly for Sam, the unloading of the cargo appeared to be the most pressing matter, and so the captain withdrew with a snarl. Fran got to work and Sam stood sentry.

"Who speaks English?" Fran smiled with surprise when all the men raised their hands. "Excellent," said Fran. "I am here to help you. ITF. Now, who texted me?"

A little man fidgeted with his phone, eyes on the table, then timidly raised his hand. The others turned to him in astonishment.

"I did not know you would come," said the man, softly.

"Well, here I am, brother, and if you all stick together, we can get this sorted out. More pay and off the boat, home to your families. But you need to stay together. Do you understand?"

Sam found their body language fascinating. The men were afraid, some more than others. What wasn't at all clear, however, was whether they were of one mind.

Fran picked out one man who was glowering at the sailor who had made the contact. "What's your problem?" he pointed at him. "Are you scared of the captain? Don't you want paid a fair wage?"

This man, whom Fran had exposed, was bigger than the others. Sam realised why he'd been singled out. Fran was a master of negotiation: pick the big one in a fight – the rest will buckle.

"Aaaah, is problem for me," he spluttered. "I need monies for sending home."

Fran set about bringing the man into the group, folding him into a fellowship. "How much do you send home, my man?" his tone became softer.

"Maybe … maybe, eh, thirty dollars every month."

"My friend," said Fran, "you should be earning thirty dollars every day. Lookit – you should be earning sixty dollars a day, but we are people of the world and we know you were signed up in Manila where exploitation is a national sport."

"They have our sea books," said the man, shaking his head in despair.

"If you work as one and refuse to do your jobs and say you won't unlock the holds and help unload this ship, I can get you thirty dollars a day. You can join the union, I can get your sea books and you can all get off this ship."

The men looked sceptical. Sam knew enough about commercial shipping to work out that the papers in their sea books were their licence to operate; without them, they were unemployed. But he also wondered about the books' worth if they breached their contracts and their hiring agent back in the Philippines found out.

Fran lowered his tone again, persuasive, coaxing the men to trust him. Then he left them to discuss the options among themselves.

Outside the door the captain and first officer were attempting to eavesdrop, but the hum of the ship made that virtually impossible. They demanded to know which of the crew had called Fran, who in turn swore at them with utter contempt and hinted that Sam was some sort of trained assassin who would slaughter them in their sleep if they so much as scolded the crew. Sam thought it great craic.

Eventually Fran returned to the mess and withdrew a laptop and papers from which he signed all the men up to union membership. He made call after call, booked flights, a minibus and allowed the men to prepare to dock the ship. The pilot boat returned with the real pilot on board and the vessel was guided between the piers and tied up to the quay. The captain signed the agreements and Sam watched with incredulity as he withdrew hundreds of thousands of dollars from the ship's safe and began to count out the cash.

With each man paid and their sea books released, Fran marched them off the ship to be whisked to the airport. The whole thing had taken less than five hours. Fran and Sam went drinking and arose the next day to hear that the ship's name had been changed, a new crew had been flown in and the agreements torn up.

"Ah, well, fuck it anyway," said Fran. He looked more distressed than his patter suggested, a deep frown, lips drawn thin. Sam reckoned he was worried for the men and their future, perhaps the thought of more seafarers being treated badly on the ship in future. Sam saw in him a mischievous little man with his heart in the right place. "I'll get that ship next time it comes to Ireland and we'll do it all over again."

So through Charity's referral, Sam had a new client, and began to see a way through financially for the first time in ages.

Chapter 17

Six months passed and Isla adjusted. Her sleeping improved and, gradually, when enraptured by the discoveries of life, as any five-year-old ought to be, her smiles returned, sparingly. Three nights out of four she slept in her own cabin. That pleased Sam – of course, but it also left a kind of void.

He spent scant time addressing his own head issues. He filled his days with jobs: sanding, varnishing, servicing the engine, setting the rig. The boat was in beautiful shape, but his mind was a mess.

As Isla edged towards contentment, his thoughts became occupied by a hostile force that was distorted by noise. He remembered exactly when it began: as he was standing on the crosstrees of the mast, twenty feet up and working on something that was working just fine. Perhaps it was the view from up there that did it – it was similar to an observation post on high ground over the plains of Afghanistan. He received a radio transmission in his head and nearly fell backwards onto the deck below.

"Casevac." The squelch and the break up were unmistakable, the volume painful. He swiped at his head to remove an earpiece that wasn't there. It felt like a cupped hand had hit him hard on the side of the skull and shattered his eardrum. He hugged the mast, slid to the lower spreaders and sat still for a very long time. He began to wonder whether he'd imagined it as it had struck from nowhere – he'd had no thought in his head at that moment about Helmand or the corps or anything else. Only Isla's calls shook him from what he reluctantly accepted was fear.

The noises returned periodically in unwelcome bursts, but Sam could detect no trigger, no reason. After each and without any idea of how to counter them, he sought distraction through physical exertion. He'd swim off the boat, or take Isla to new islands and leave her at the highest point where they could still see each other. Then he belted hard and fast around the shore to the point of puking. She was confused by his retching and he told her it was just part of training for muscles, as was the hundred push-ups he forced himself into while she tried to count for him. She stumbled after thirty but they got there eventually.

Sam imagined his mind softening as his body hardened. He wanted his alertness to subside when he was alone with Isla. He wanted the pain endured in the Afghan mountains to clear from his peripheral vision. At times it felt that if he looked anywhere other than straight ahead, the horror would be waiting for him on the edges. He kept seeing dust and charring on the faces of those with whom he'd served, the torn lips, the exposed teeth. Men trying to talk through their disfigured mouths, unaware of their permanent facial contortion or imminent death. The most frustrating nightmare was the one in which he was helpless to do any good; his inability to stem the flow of rich warm blood into the arid earth of a land where no man had any business to be. He knew most of the dream stemmed from what had been the longest day of his life.

Sam saw it happen but he didn't hear it simultaneously. The dust went up like water out of a blowhole, straight and true and although it happened only fifty feet away, the sound somehow took minutes to break into his head. They'd been patrolling between two hills, in a line, on their way to deal with two Taliban touts who'd been reporting on their movements for days. Back at the OP his men were scanning the mobile phone signals for intel. If they could confirm that the two men they'd been watching were sending information to the enemy, they could remove them. Otherwise, they had to let the pair carry on.

Sam knew that tracking the men was dangerous – that they could deliberately draw his team into fire, but it had been his call to carry on regardless. Too many of his men had been shot and his patience with their rules of engagement was exhausted. He wanted some peace. He got anything but.

"Get the doc! Get the doc!"

The shouting belonged to him but it didn't feel like he was talking. He moved forward, scraping the earth with a prod in an attempt to avoid further mines and crouched by his injured lead man. He turned and directed the others to drop and stop, but sent two towards higher ground to secure cover for what would be an extraction of the casualty. From then on it became a horror show. He knelt in silence, unable to comprehend what was happening. Plume after plume erupted, but the noise just wasn't there and he couldn't understand why. He watched in utter silence as devices exploded and threw bits of four more marines into the air.

"Nobody move! Nobody move! Doc, no movement. Triage from where you stand, tell me what's needed."

Sam didn't know whether they were in a minefield, if someone was detonating devices remotely or whether they were on a timer. He hunted around as the deafness subsided. The medic hurled Sam his bag and he administered what he could, but they were out of morphine within minutes. He found it remarkably easy to screen out the screaming as he concentrated on the medic's instructions and moved between his men, unwilling to leave them without attention, despite the risk of further explosions. He packed their wounds and tightened the tourniquets as they writhed in agony. Then they sat in the sun and waited. It took all day as they burned and blistered in the dirt. On the ridgeline around their position they could see friendlies arrive to keep them covered from secondary attack. He remembered wishing it – craving the approach of a Taliban wave. How he didn't die that day remained a mystery to him. Part of him thought they should all perish in that valley.

When the casualty evacuation helicopters eventually arrived, they ignored every warning. Their crews appeared with stretchers and stood in the middle of that valley and triggered nothing. One by one his men were taken into the sky, all beyond mending. Two died on the way back to Bastion, two never walked again, one would never utter another word. He got a medal that later helped save him from dishonourable discharge, but he felt he should have got dead.

LIVING on the boat brought a certain peace and solitude that seemed to suit them both. The constant stream of work lifted a weight off him. He only had two clients but they kept him as busy as he needed to be and removed the persistent worry he'd had over his ability to provide for Isla. It was still only six months since they'd lost Shannon and he'd come to believe that they should not force their healing, but just take their time. His parents or Shannon's were always keen to take Isla when he went away for a few days' work, and she was happy to go with them. There were other distractions too. Sam was unfamiliar with many of the strains and requirements of civilian life. The small but essential things that prior to Shannon the Navy had taken care of, took a bit of getting to grips with: tax, insurance, medical matters. He constantly worried that he might miss something, not least how he would keep well enough attuned to Isla's needs to ensure that when the time came, she wouldn't get laughed at or left out at school. He remembered how Shannon had juggled to devote time to his rebuilding – she somehow managed to wipe all else clear during his periods of leave. His intention now was to find that flexibility within his own work, to do the same for Isla when she needed it. And he was certain she would need it.

His new venture, he decided, would be referral only. It gave him the leeway to choose what jobs he would take on and when; short bursts of work and plenty of time to be available for his kid. Charity, as he fell into the habit of thinking of her, had helped him find his way. Before he'd met her and thereafter Fran, he'd been lost for a real idea as to where he would fit into civilian society. Charlie brought income and pumped a little adrenaline back into his increasingly resting heart rate, but it also had purpose.

Jobs came in pretty regularly. It turned out Charity had

quite a network. Sam saw parts of Ireland he'd never even heard of, moving around, plucking women from apartments, houses and even caravans.

He was careful, always, but he knew the risk increased with every job. And as his confidence rose so did the potential to unpick all his good work. Aside from the inevitability of having been captured on CCTV at Dublin Airport, there were likely other occasions when he hadn't clocked a camera. He began using an old phone, a Nokia, as his point of contact, which was comparatively safe. But it was still a cellular device and therefore traceable.

He often liberated credit cards from the brothels he was sent to and used them to secure hire vehicles. It was all working well, but nothing could shake the lingering worry that the cops would eventually catch up with him. He knew he'd have to tighten his approach. He chose to tackle it at a handover meeting on a slip road just off Dublin's M50.

"It's just one woman this time – Chinese national in her twenties." Charity was ticking through the details and was just about to hand him a note with the address when he raised his concerns.

"Listen, we're going to have to stop doing this."

She looked up in surprise, disappointment crossing her face. "Why? I thought you saw the value in—"

"Not the extractions, the comms."

"The what?"

"The way we communicate – the handing over of notes with addresses on them, the phone calls – all of that can be ripped and gathered and used as evidence."

"Evidence for what?"

"For what we're doing."

"Rescuing people, you mean? What's wrong with that? It's not illegal."

"Look, you don't see what has to happen inside these places at times. It can take a bit of persuasion."

Charity looked at him for a long while. "Like when we first met?"

"Yeah." They both remembered the gangmaster groaning as he clutched his crotch.

"So what are you saying to me, Sam?"

"I need this to be more secure – no more meeting at the side of the road, no more calls that use phone masts—"

"What have phone masts got to do with anything?"

"You'll just need to trust me on that. I've literally been up and down phone masts and they're … intrusive."

She shrugged in acceptance. "Well, how do you want to do it?"

"I don't know, but Post-it notes that have been on your pad on your desk because of calls to your work, and texts and public handovers – all of that's a problem."

"I thought we were friends?" she said.

"We are?" Sam was surprised at her comment, but then again not. He found it hard to adjust to the civilian inability to separate the practical from the emotional.

"Then it's ok for friends to meet up. What could possibly be evidential about that?"

Sam struggled to find an answer. "They don't generally meet up at the side of the road and three hours later hand young women over for transportation."

"Well, are you saying we should go for drinks or what?" She tried to make it sound like a snipe but failed. "Or dinner?"

"Well, that would be better," he said. "Bottom line, the communications need to be tightened. I can't afford to go to jail."

Charity looked at him curiously then, and he realised

how little she knew about him. He wasn't about to elaborate.

"Ok," she sighed. "I might have an idea."

The unexpected solution came in the form of Charity's twin sister, who was some sort of tech guru working for one of the multinationals that had flooded Dublin in recent years. A week later, over drinks, he was introduced to Áine, the twin, and issued with a dual SIM smartphone.

"It's got one for the UK, one for Ireland," Áine said, regarding him curiously to see how savvy he was with the kit. She wasn't a carbon copy, in fact she was slightly smaller, but the similarities were there – same eyes, same cheekbones. "It's got an app on it, ok?"

"I know what an app is." He smiled. She didn't.

Looking straight at him, she tested him. "This is end-to-end."

"I also understand encryption," he replied.

"Do you now?" Her response was laced with scepticism. "You should be doing this yourself, so."

He relented to allow her to have her moment. "So what does the app do for me?"

"It will alert you every time an inquiry is made on a site."

"I don't want a website," he cautioned.

"Too late. But obviously I haven't put you WordPress or Squarespace."

"It's hidden?"

"Yes, Sam. It's hidden," she shook her head.

"The Dark Web?"

She heaved a deep sigh. "In layman's terms, yes."

Sam noted her permanent impatience. They may look similar, Sam thought, but they're different animals altogether.

"You wanted referral only, so the only people who can access this site are those who type in the exact complicated address. It cannot be searched for on Google or any other engine."

He looked at what she was showing him on the screen. It was simply black with a message: *This is Charlie. For inquiries, leave your details. We will be in touch.*

"Why Charlie?" Áine asked.

Sam felt Charity shifting slightly, curious. "Needed to call it something." Sam shrugged. He had no intention of getting into the background of how he'd met his wife, or that he'd had a wife, or that she was dead. "So how do I know when—"

"There's no banner or alert if that's what you mean. I built this app myself, from the ground up. The details aren't recorded on Confluence or anywhere and nobody else can get a version. It's unique to you."

"Confluence?"

"Doesn't matter," Áine said, her eyes narrowing very slightly, as if he'd just told her something through his ignorance.

"So how do I see when there's a message from your sister?"

"I am right here," Charity said, with a little wave.

Áine ignored her. "You have to open it, set a password, then swipe through and check for any new messages. Next you log in to the message area – different password, and make it a good one, not your date of birth or the name of your dog. Then you can retrieve the details."

"And what about location?"

"You mean tracking?"

"Yeah. How does it—"

"All cellular is off unless you turn it on. There's no Wi-

154

Fi hook-up when you go into shops but if you know the score, well …" Áine shrugged.

"Anything can be tracked."

"If the wrong people are looking for you."

"Then let's hope not."

"Yeah, but not the app – the app is safe. The phone, well, it's better than just about any other device, but …"

———

SAM KEPT the phone at a dead drop in Belfast. Still suspicious, he took to moving around a lot before he made contact – sometimes up to one hundred miles. He used a dongle, as Áine had called it – to draw down available data and turn it into a Wi-Fi bubble. Then he used the encrypted app to make calls. It seemed like the only way to mask mobile signals which, he knew from up-close experience, were exceptionally vulnerable to interception.

The next pressing issue was how they were living. Isla seemed to enjoy the adventure and freedom of the boat. It brought the advantage of constant proximity, which aided their recovery, yet he worried they would become overly dependent upon one another and she would become too accustomed to his company, rather than that of friends her own age. But he wasn't ready to return to land, and he knew in his heart that he was leaning on their circumstances to prolong their life at sea. He nearly persuaded himself that Isla needed that security. He reassured her that the bad man who killed her mam would never come back and that nobody could get to them if they sailed to different places, so they cruised the coast and settled somewhere different every evening.

For someone who'd always taken the harder path life

offered, he was ashamed that he was ducking one difficult discussion. His own rebuilding, at Shannon's insistence, had taught him one simple fact: reparation couldn't happen without acknowledging the past. He wouldn't repair without facing his own back catalogue of dreadful music, and Isla had not yet confronted her mother's death.

For a long period Sam just didn't know how. There were times while roaming an island or walking a beach when he nearly opened the wound. His logic was to try and disinfect it so that when it was stitched up again, it might heal. It felt as though infection could set in at any time, but that treatment could only be performed in a fresh, clean surrounding.

They were rowing in the dinghy the day he finally dropped it. Isla was behind him, facing forward, looking through the binoculars as he hauled on the oars. They were going to lift a lobster pot they'd left close to an island and she had a bucket in case they got lucky. She looked ahead, telling him when he was veering off course.

"Isla," he began.

"You're not going very straight, Daddy."

"Isla, we need to talk about Mammy."

"Ok," she said, brightly enough.

Ok, he thought, keep her steady. "We need to talk about the day she died, darlin'," he said.

"Oh-wuh," she replied, like she did when he told her it was bedtime – like she knew it was inevitable but wanted to delay it if possible.

"We have to, wee love. It's important."

"Why?"

Good question. He thought of what Shannon would say.

"Cos it's not good to have that memory in your head and not let it out."

"Like the memories in your head?" she asked.

"What do you mean?"

"Mam said you have bad memories in your head. That's why we had to leave you alone sometimes. She said that to me. She really did."

He could hear Shannon saying it. "Yes, wee lamb, the same as me. You need to get those bad memories out of your head so they can stay out as much as possible."

"I don't really want to talk about it," she replied to his astonishment. It was such a grown-up sentence for a five-year-old. Perhaps it was inspired by too much television; perhaps she'd been thinking about it.

"We have to, wee darlin'. It'll be ok, though. I'll mind you."

"Oh-wuh," she said again, and then adopted distraction tactics. "I can see the buoy!"

"We'll lift the pot in a minute, Isla. First, we just need to talk about that night, ok?"

"Oh-kaay," she relented. They were still not looking at each another, which he thought maybe helped.

"Can you tell me what happened?"

"I already told everyone, Daddy!" she protested.

She meant the police, he assumed, which had been before he'd got back from Bastion. He knew she hadn't spoken to his folks or Shannon's. "One more time, Isla. Please."

"The man cutted Mammy," she puffed in a big breath out.

"And you know why he did that, Isla?" he asked softly.

"Cos Mammy got mad with him, cos he nearly ran me over on my bike."

"Where, darlin', where did he nearly run you over?"

"On the wheel, it was all bended over and broken."

"I know, darlin', I mean where did it happen?"

"On the wheel, Daddy, I told you."

He gave up on that line of inquiry. "Ok, when did it happen, Isla?"

"When me and Mammy were going for ice cream. I had my helmet on, Daddy," she said defensively.

"I know you did, darlin'," he said, trying to soothe her. "What did Mammy say?"

"She said he was full up of beer," Isla said, which was the first time he had heard that.

"Did she?"

"He was smoking out the window and she shouted at his car."

He thought for a moment, the fog lifting a little. "What happened then?"

"He stopped the car and said really bad words to Mammy, and I shouted, 'Don't you say that to my mam!' and then Mammy told him to be quiet and she had a cross time with him."

"Were they close together?"

"No ... then we just went home," she trailed off, as if wanting question time to be over.

"What happened then?"

She sighed. "I think Mammy called the police."

Sam knew this was true from the crime log and the phone record. The solicitor had even obtained the call and played it to him. He'd listened to an agitated Shannon react with measured disbelief as she was told there was no police car available. She'd given the licence plate number, the man's address and full details of the incident, but it was clear on the phone call that nothing would be done. That was why she'd gone for the nuclear option.

"What did Mammy do then?"

"She put me in the back of the car and we went to the man's house."

The house of horrors built by the factory owner to accommodate his staff, who then paid him half their wages in rent.

"Ok, and what did she do at his house?"

"She didn't press the doorbell or anything. She just went inside." Isla sounded shocked, even now.

"And were you with her?"

"No, Daddy. She left me in the car seat."

"How long was she in the house?"

"Superfast," said Isla.

"She came back out straight away?"

"Uh-huh," she said. "Daddy, you need to go over this way." She tapped his left shoulder.

He kept rowing slowly. "What do you think happened in the house?" he asked.

"She took away the bad man's car keys so he couldn't drive when he was full up of beer," said Isla.

"Did she?" This came as a total revelation to Sam. "You didn't say that before darlin'?"

"Sorry," she said quietly. "I forgot."

"That's ok, you can't remember everything when you're five."

Isla said nothing.

"How do you know Mammy took the keys?" he pushed gently on.

"Cos I saw them," she said.

"But the police never found any keys?"

Isla fell silent.

159

Suddenly everything became clearer and Sam wished and wished and wished he could go back twenty minutes. He wished he had never started the conversation.

The rowing stopped. Sam looked over the side of the dinghy at their reflections. Isla sat quiet, her back to his, her head falling forward.

"That's why the man came with the knife," she said.

He closed his eyes, knowing what was coming next.

"He shouted at Mammy to give him the keys," her voice began to break.

"But you were in bed, weren't you, darlin'?"

"I heard the man shouting at Mammy."

"What was he saying?"

"He was saying, 'Where are the keys, you fucking bish'."

The shock of hearing his small child swear for the first time, even if only to repeat the words of an adult, made him feel sick.

"What did Mammy say?"

Silence.

"What did Mammy say, wee love?"

"I don't know. I don't know!" her voice cracked and he could hear the tears coming.

They were in it now. Sam knew in his heart what had happened. He knew she had been carrying it around for months and he decided it was time to purge her of it. "Did you get up out of bed?"

"Yes, Daddy."

"Why?" he asked, even though he already knew the answer.

"Cos I knew where the keys were." She began to sob deep, gulping cries and he pushed away the oars and turned to her, seizing her up and pulling her onto his lap, hugging her in tight. Her sobs became convulsions and her tears soaked into his chest. He willed the pain out of her and into him.

"I hided the keys in my bag," she gulped after it came out. He could see that it felt to her like an admission to a bold act. To him, it was a necessary pain that needed out, needed lanced and the blame directed where it was due.

"That man was a bad man, Isla." He brought her brow to his, lifting her chin, trying to look into her eyes.

"But—"

"Isla, that man was a bad man. He came to hurt Mammy and it didn't matter if he found his keys or not."

"No, Daddy!" she pleaded. "He just wanted his keys and Mammy couldn't find his keys cos I hided them," she said, pushing back from him. "Mammy looked every-where." She opened her hands, eyes now wide open in exclamation.

"Mammy didn't want the bad man to have the keys," he said.

"She did Daddy, cos the man had a big knife."

He held her back into him for a while. "You saw what he did, didn't you?"

"Mmmm hmmm."

"Did the man say anything after he hurted Mammy?"

"He was laughing," she sobbed, "and he went 'Aaagh-hh!' to scare me and he did scare me."

He thought of the man writhing in a cell in Vilnius and hoped it had taken days of roaring anguish.

"Did Mammy say anything to you?" he asked eventually.

"She was screaming at the man, 'Get out, get out, get away from her, get out'."

They rocked backwards and forwards for a while.

"I gave Mammy a hug and then I got the plasters. But she died."

They cried together for a long time, until the sun fell and the chill came. They were wrapped up, two sets of demons working hard inside their own heads.

"Isla," he said finally.

"Yes, Daddy?"

"You did the right thing, wee lamb. You were so brave. Mammy didn't want that bad man to find his keys. She was just pretending to look for them. She didn't want that man to drive with beer in him, cos he could have hurt another wee girl, and Mammy wouldn't have wanted that."

He waited as she seemed think about that, then she nodded into his chest.

"You did the right thing, Isla," he said. "Mammy was very proud of you."

"How do you know?"

"Cos I'm your daddy and I know stuff, wee lamb. I know. Sometimes I can hear Mammy talking to me."

"So can I," she said.

"I can hear her laughing," he said, not at all sure whether such confessions were useful or harmful.

"Me too," she said.

"Mammy is always with us," he told her, and with that a white dandelion blossom blew across the boat and stuck to the Velcro on Isla's lifejacket. She looked up at him and smiled, stroked it and rested again. As if there was the dawning of some sort of peace in her wee heart.

Chapter 18

S am could survive on very little, but he had learned that a five-year-old could not. At least once a week he came ashore to get the food shop over with. It gave the grandparents a chance to spend time with Isla, and him an opportunity to check the phone. He tended to shop in different places depending on what was required, and today was a supermarket day. He went to the dead drop, lifted the phone, got back in the car and drove for twenty minutes before firing it up.

The message on it meant little at the time – just a name, a request for contact and a number. He knew it wasn't from Fran or Charity, but that was the only unusual thing about it.

At a Tesco not far from the Irish border he pulled up as far from the doors and security cameras as possible and tapped the number.

"Yes?"

"This is Charlie."

"Yes. Charlie." The man's accent was southern. Leinster, Sam guessed, while thinking that his greeting was a bit weird. So he cut to the chase.

"Where are you based?"

"Dublin."

"Which part?"

"City centre. I have a job for you if —"

"Not on the phone," Sam said.

There was a pause.

"OK."

"When can you meet?"

"Up to you."

"Heuston, three hours."

"OK."

Sam closed the call, determined not to allow the man too much prep time in case he was a spook or a cop.

He then used his Nokia to call his folks and tell them, yet again, that a job had come in and arrange for Isla to sleep over. The drive ahead of him would take just over an hour. It made him curious: this could be his first client other than Charity or Fran. He sincerely hoped it wasn't some matrimonial and that he was wasting diesel by trundling all the way to Dublin. Nonetheless it brought a little excitement, some apprehension and a bit of suspicion.

Chapter 19

S am sat between two posters behind a Supermac meal, staring out of the fast-food restaurant onto the concourse. Dublin's Heuston Station was almost always busy, yet there was virtually no way for him to loiter surreptitiously. He didn't want to be identified without realising it and he was an easy spot. At six feet he wasn't particularly tall, but any time he stood outside a pub people automatically assumed he was the bouncer. Younger ones nodded to him with a kind of sheepish deference, and if he made his way through a crowd, it parted. He was aware he could look a little menacing when preoccupied - Shannon called it his "Halloween face". He wasn't wide, though, and hadn't thrown weights around since he'd left the service, now almost a year before. At forty-two years old it seemed pointless to maintain excess muscle that he wouldn't need outside the Marines. Besides, feeding muscle was expensive. But he did work his own mass: chin-ups, push-ups and squats, so his shoulders were stacked and his posture probably betrayed him a little. He shaved his head but seldom his chin. He looked like what he was: a salty, overexposed sailor with sun cracks round his eyes and paws like paddles. Concealment using a different dress code wasn't an option – he only possessed practical clothes. His shell jacket, heavy denims and cross trainers meant he couldn't have looked more like a demobbed marine if he'd tried. So he sat, staring out between the cracks in the super-meal adverts hanging from the window, hoping to see the man before the man saw him.

It didn't work.

Sam kept an eye on the door to the restaurant and flicked back to the space between the posters. He had sight of most of the station to his left and, rotating, could see the fast-food service counter and the constant stream of people seeking to use the toilets without buying burgers, given the state of Heuston's own facilities. As he swivelled his head back to the concourse his eyes locked on a man staring straight at him. Mid-sized with a tight lock of grey curls, the bloke had appeared from nowhere. He stood sixty feet away with his arms crossed, fixed in his stare. There was no smile, no nod, no wave. Even at that distance and through glass the man cut an unnerving presence. Sam looked left and right, seeing nobody in accompaniment. Despite feeling unsettled and angry with himself, he knew it was pointless to sit still and wait, so he rose, binned his tray and moved out. He met the man's stare as he exited the restaurant, but as he neared the man turned and they fell into a strange walk together, not close but not far from one another, a word yet to be exchanged.

"You'll need to tell me where we're going," Sam said as they left the station.

"Well if you're concerned, you're probably not the man for this job," the man replied.

Sam didn't know whether to be irritated or intrigued, so he decided to wait the man out. They walked west for twenty minutes, two feet apart, in complete silence.

The man was in his mid-fifties, dressed in a cardigan and jeans but with sandals. He represented no physical threat. Any unease slowly gave way to curiosity. They arrived at a tall Georgian terrace and he followed the man, creaking up old timber stairs to a small room. It was warm and in contrast to the rest of the building, soothing and pleasant. They sat in low seats positioned opposite one another. The man crossed his legs and stared at Sam for a long while.

"I think you understand evil," was the man's opening gambit. Sam stayed mute and his defences went up. "What I'm about to tell you will haunt you. You need to be sure you want to hear it." Sam then began to view the man as a drama queen intent on trying to shock him. "I have a job for you if you have the balls for it."

Irritation replaced intrigue. Sam didn't feel that he needed to have his courage tested and he didn't appreciate juvenile goading. This man wanted to grip him, to lock him in, and Sam had no intention of getting locked in to anything. He stayed silent and let the man plod through whatever pantomime he'd prepared.

"I was once a clinical psychologist in a large institution," the man said, which to Sam made a certain amount of sense – he'd never met a shrink who was completely sane. "Nowadays, I look after a very select few of the afflicted and tend to their wounds." He tapped his temple. "I want to tell you about a woman I have been counselling for some time." The man blinked but otherwise remained motionless. Sam mirrored his body language. "She had been held captive, in a manner of speaking." The man paused for effect, but it wasn't washing with Sam and he was forced to carry on. "Three years ago she came to me and told me about a group of twelve – a circle, a massively abusive circle. And at its root is the worship of darkness."

Now the man had Sam's attention, but not because of the tale he was spewing. Sam was considering the dreadful luck of a woman who'd allegedly escaped captivity only to end up in the care of a fruitcake.

"This woman is the product of a French mother and an English father from a union made here in Dublin." Sam idly wondered how she knew where she was conceived, but he let the man carry on. "Her mother gave birth to her in France. Her feet were skinned at nine months." Sam had already dismissed this bloke but that statement nudged him sideways. "This was the beginning of control over the child, who was then returned to Dublin."

Sam looked at him, thinking he could have had the bloody shopping done instead of driving a hundred miles to observe madness. If Fran had referred this man, he'd drop him in the tide the next time they hopped on a ship.

"She was the middle child of thirteen. She had an IQ of 168 and spoke eight languages by the age of three."

Ordinarily, when faced with a looper, Sam would simply remove himself – he was intolerant of nonsense. Yet still he sat and listened, and couldn't quite work out why. He thought it might be the man's rational appearance, or his soothing delivery. More likely it was the challenge of the man's menacing eyes. Whatever the reason, Sam found the circumstances bizarre enough to hang on in, oddly unable to zone out what was being said.

"The French woman's husband fathered the other twelve children, but this one, the heir, was to become the queen because the queen is always the middle child of thirteen."

He paused and stared at Sam, suspecting he had scored a point in his weird mind game. Sam stared back with less conviction. The man's thumb rested against his cheekbone, his finger at his temple.

"The girl conceived many children between the ages of eleven and eighteen, and each time the child was taken to a particular religious order."

He paused. Sam didn't move.

"Each child was sacrificed."

His eye lids quickly opened wider before resuming.

"She was systematically abused and ignored, indoctrinated and conditioned. Her lacerations were repaired by superglue."

The man's fingers fluttered then and just as a reformed smoker might habitually tap a pen, he almost stroked his cheek in an involuntary gesture.

"She cut herself and smeared her face with blood in an attempt to become a person – to be recognised. As punishment she was hung on hooks in the cupboard and coats were used to cover her face. She was brutalised and raped by the people in the group that controlled her. This group was made of distinguished people. A protestant minister in Dublin, a priest, policemen and some folk from England. The group is obsessed with numbers."

Sam sat and said nothing.

"She grew up being programmed and drugged to be mentored as the queen."

Sam spoke for the first time since entering the room. "I'd say their command structure needs work."

The man's head tilted slightly, considering Sam's

comment, and an almost frightening flicker of irritation crossed his face.

"She was then sent to kill the children of other heirs."

"Other heirs," Sam repeated. "So this isn't an isolated affair," he was aware that he could have sounded nothing other than dismissive.

"I'd expect you to doubt me," the man said.

Sam began to wonder whether there really was a woman and if the man had indeed spoken to her and believed her. He certainly seemed to believe what he was telling Sam.

"At times like solstice she was taken away. That's when the abuse increased, the mutilation. Forced to do unspeakable things."

Sam's concentration lapsed for a moment, questioning what sort of mind could conjure such dreadful fantasy.

"I didn't believe her at first," said the counsellor. "Just as you don't believe me now." Sam matched his stare. "But you will believe me."

Sam tried to concentrate on the man telling the tale as opposed to what he was saying. It felt easier to dismiss him that way. The man talked about trinkets left in specific windows as a means to tell her what to do, but Sam had had enough.

"What do you need me for?" He felt a sudden need for clarity.

"To keep her safe, of course," the man said, as if that were obvious.

"Charlie isn't a bodyguard service," Sam said.

"No," the man replied, "but you could help root out this circle."

"They must be old or dead, judging from what you've said."

"Oh, this is generational. If it isn't ended, it will simply pass on."

Sam shook his head, his decision made.

"How did you hear about me?"

"That's your concern?" the man leaned forward, his voice rising, suddenly displaying frustration.

"How?" Sam repeated.

"I've walked down streets with this woman when thugs have come towards us and tried to take her away. But so long as there is a semblance of good, there is no chance that harm can come to her. I and six others stayed with her over Beltane to protect her."

Sam had no idea what he was talking about, so he stopped listening. He gazed at the man's jeans and his sandals. He looked at his counselling couch, at his shelves, at his smug face, then got up and left.

He drove home but thought about the twisted story the whole way. Nothing rang true. He told himself that it had clearly been nonsense. Yet it lingered. Somewhere in the back of his mind lurked a logic that said it was too sick a story to have come from absolutely nothing. If there was a woman, her torture deserved better treatment than her counsellor could surely provide.

He made straight for his parents' house; shopping forgotten. He collected Isla, took her to the boat and cuddled her to sleep. He didn't let her go until morning.

Chapter 20

"That was some whack job you landed on me."

"Sorry?" Charity was clearly expecting a warmer greeting.

"That woo-woo with the story about the queen."

"Sam, have you had a bang on the head?" She sounded genuinely surprised.

"The man," he sighed down the handset. "He wanted an abuse victim protected. Just so you know, I have no intention of getting into that game. Short stints only. In and out."

"Sam, I have literally no idea what you're on about," she said.

"Did you not refer a man to me, to the ... business?" He remained wary, despite using Áine's magic app.

"I referred nobody to you," she said firmly.

Sam stalled for a moment. "I'm sorry, then," he said. "I just assumed it was you."

"Well, aren't you working for the little union fella, Fran?"

"Sometimes."

"Maybe he's your man, then."

"Yeah, OK sorry, ignore me."

"No problem," she said, before getting into her next request.

Charity had come to engage him about once a fortnight. The process was simple: she messaged to say she'd be calling and that was his cue to collect the fancy phone from the dead drop and drive somewhere he'd never been. They worked out availability, arranged a mutually convenient time for the handover and then she sent him an address via encrypted message. Sam hired a van, recced the address and decided on an extraction plan. Then he messaged her with details of a place at which he would provide the rescued people and she looked after the rest. He assumed that entailed booking flights or ferries or trying to get them asylum or resettled in Ireland.

The work itself wasn't well paid but Sam discovered that the spoils were generally pretty good. More often than not he found a bundle of cash in the flats, most of which he gave to the girls and a reasonable portion of which he kept. Even with a solid euro wedge placed in the girls' pockets, he could walk away with a handsome sum. He found it remarkably easy to justify given the risks he was taking – he had a child to look after, and although the work wasn't as dangerous as his previous job, it had the potential to be precarious at times and risk warranted reward. Regardless of the cash perks, Sam felt he was good at the work and appreciated that it had human value. More than anything, though, the extra income allowed him to spend more time with Isla than a nine-to-five life would have granted.

Sometimes there was a confrontation, which he didn't mind. Although reluctant to admit it to himself, he knew in the background that it satisfied something in him. Gnarly, shaven-headed pimps showed up from time to time. He thought of them collectively as horrible, selfish, callous bastards who were due a dose of their own medication. Word must have got around because at some point they stopped challenging him and ran as soon as they realised what was happening. On a few occasions he scoped out a place, only to find that they'd brought in extra security. He waited a few days until market forces kicked in, the pimps not wanting to pay the extra men, then he carried on as usual. There were times he rendered just enough pain to force them to take him to their vehicles, and their cash. Occasionally he liberated a weapon and slung it in the Liffey or some other deep river or lake. But he was always careful, ridiculously so. Anyone who could have followed him was left on the flat floor in bits, bleeding and battered and without their phone. The cars he hired using various IDs he'd picked up along the way. He secured them on spec, never in advance, using credit cards happened upon in the brothels. In the end, he always settled with the hire firm in cash anyway.

Fran pushed him lots of work too, which was cleaner and more in tune with Sam's skill set. The little union rep was a loyal friend and a committed ideologue, so Sam grew to trust him. But even after a pint and a yarn, Fran didn't know enough to ever place Sam anywhere. Fran couldn't yet be sure which jurisdiction Sam lived in, never mind his address. They'd shared a few beers and a few laughs after successful jobs, but Sam stopped drinking before his guard could drop and he managed to remain reserved. Neither Fran nor Charity knew he had a kid, or that he'd had a wife. Both contacted him through Áine's app, but other than that Fran joked Sam was a bit of an enigma and seemed to enjoy the secrecy of it all.

The trust he'd built up with Fran meant that the little man didn't even tag along all the time. Fran maintained that some shipping companies would never relent – the Greeks being notable examples. There was no point in trying to unionise a ship skippered by a Greek captain, he said. Even if they did sign, they were sure to tear up the papers as soon as it left the quay. The only option was to rescue any stricken seafarer and get the poor sod home. Fran's tendency to get a bit green around the gills at sea brought an arrangement whereby he organised the means to get Sam onto a vessel, and if the correct person could be extracted from the ship without Fran having to be there, he paid bigger bucks.

On one occasion, in Limerick, Sam took a bosun off a boat without the captain even knowing a stranger had been on board. It was a satisfying excursion, largely because the bosun refused to leave the ship without his papers. Sam was forced to creep onto the bridge in the middle of the night and break into the ship's safe. There he discovered nearly ninety grand in cash. They bailed over the side into a rigid inflatable and were in Galway by breakfast. He gave the bosun forty-five grand – his biggest pay day ever, and told Fran nothing.

Had things stayed like that, Sam could have had a rewarding enough afterlife as a former Royal Marine. He couldn't have asked for work more in tune with his talents, more helpful for his head. Apart from one nagging notion: he lay awake at night wondering about the madness of the story spewed to him by the counsellor. Countless times he tried to push away the memory of the encounter, but it resurfaced repeatedly. He knew it couldn't possibly be true, yet coupled to the uncertainty of how the nutjob had his details, Sam eventually sat up in his bunk and made a call.

"Hope this isn't a romantic call, I'm spoken for." Fran was groggy from sleep or stout.

"Did you refer anyone to me?"

"How d'ye mean?"

"Did you send a client my way? A client – a prospective client. Someone looking for my …"

"Your general assistance? No, Sam, I did not. I thought someone with your proclivity for privacy would not welcome such intrusions."

"Fran, how do you find these words so late at night?"

"It is but two of the morning, Sam. I am far from sparkling, but I thank you kindly all the same. Was that everything?"

"You're sure?"

"I am sure that I did not send anyone to you, brother. One hundred per cent, my friend."

"Ok, Fran. Thanks. And sorry for … you know."

"Asleep already, brother."

———

FOR A MONTH SAM PUSHED, without great success, the story from his head, but it just would not shift. His skull was already a crowded place and he knew the noise was unhealthy. He told himself that it was blind idiocy to entertain what the counsellor had said and dismissed it again and again. Then he lashed around for a while as it popped right back up.

The new Sam was based on the Shannon process: face

up to your fears and deal with them. He finally accepted that if someone had sent that weirdo his way, he needed to find out who. Without that knowledge, decent sleep would elude him for days.

Chapter 21

Amid the slapping and tapping of rigging and waves, a single creak was out of place. It was possible that an army of otters had clambered aboard again and he'd been roused by their tails hammering the deck. But somewhere inside, Sam knew.

A barely perceptible heave of the hull to port confirmed it: someone had boarded the boat. He lay silent, waiting for the next step to betray the visitor's position. The aluminium hull was solid, but only a ballerina would have the grace and balance to move undetected just a few inches over his head.

He knew from days of sweat and screaming with American SWAT teams that he should draw the intruder below deck and let his confined combat training kick in. But that carry-on had been aimed at protecting nuclear subs in Scotland – Sam had much more important things to look after now. He slipped from his bunk and opted for the rear hatch. The cover lifted silently; his emergence masked by both the half-moon light and the rubber dinghy he'd slung on deck before dinner. Half-in, half-out of the boat, he felt the same exposure his pals must have endured in the desert, gunning out the roofs of their amphibious Viking vehicles as he gazed at their bootlaces below. He lifted himself up, and that's when events got hazy.

He came-to in alarm, panicked. He jolted his face upwards, free from the slabber gluing his cheek to the teak deck, and his first thought was Isla.

He scrabbled onto his feet, touching his head, looking for injury as he rounded. What was behind him? He could find no evidence of damage, and had no idea how long he'd been out. Had he had another blackout?

And then his eyes fell on the outline of a body lying a few feet away. Sam rolled over the coachroof, landed on an enormous chest and struck down hard repeatedly. The lack of reaction made him pause to peer through the darkness. The person was belly-up, motionless and clearly gone – his eye sockets empty. Lying feet away, against the toe rail, was a Glock 17.

Sam tore below deck, through the main cabin and wrenched open the bunk door. His heart hit the bilges when he saw Isla's arm hanging loose and limp from her bunk, her face turned away. He fell to his knees and threw his arm over her.

She groaned, deep in sleep, and he heaved in a breath of relief.

He crouched beside her and hugged her tight, muttering his thanks over and over. She could sleep through a gale, his wee five-year-old.

"Hello, Daddy," she mumbled, not even half awake, and rolled back into the heat.

As she spun away from him, he noticed the blood on his thumbs, betraying the ugly method he must have adopted to despatch the man on deck. He climbed above scoured the surrounding sea, reluctant to fire up a torch for fear of attracting accomplices, but found nothing. He walked around the boat, eyes trained towards the waterline, looking for a dinghy. Still, nothing. How long had he been unconscious? Moving below in a hurry he fired up the radar and watched as it took its interminable time to acquire position and begin sweeping.

Nothing. Absolutely nothing.

He checked the time on the radar screen. Without being sure, he reckoned he was missing about twenty minutes of memory.

Returning to the body on deck he tried to reboot his memory as he searched the dead man. His eyes fell again to dark shape of the handgun and in anger he rose and kicked it straight over the rail to plummet into the mud thirty feet below.

They were anchored three hundred yards from land. If the intruder had been delivered by boat, surely the radar would have picked it up?

But there was no dinghy, the man had no identification and, worst of all, he was dry.

As dawn broke Sam worked through the contents of the dead man's pockets, which proved fruitless: a packet of Drum tobacco, papers and a wind resistant lighter, hardly enough to identify anyone. The haul was sealed in a small plastic sandwich bag. At least that told something – that the man had planned the excursion.

He looked at the face, such as it was after a fight Sam couldn't even recall. The features lacked the Slavic Eastern European angularity he'd half expected. Given the way he'd been occupying his time in the preceding months, Sam was sure that the incursion must have been ordered by an aggrieved pimp, a brothel owner or a gangmaster.

The plunged eyes were grotesque and made it hard to make any firm judgement but there was no hint of foreign origin; no pallor to the skin suggestive of warmer or colder climes. His shoes were from Next, the jeans were Diesel and the T-shirt could have been from any high-street store. The man's belt was equally unremarkable but that its circumference was tiny in comparison to his shoulders. The shoes had a tidemark, like he'd stepped in a puddle, but his feet hadn't been completely submerged. His knees too had damp patches the shape of a rugby ball, his back was moist and his T-shirt stuck to it. Everything else was dry. He looked fit enough despite the fags. Sam guessed he was about forty years old, but other than that the intruder's identity was a mystery.

That the man hadn't swum to their boat really set Sam on edge. He'd chosen the remote anchorage specifically for security and privacy. The breach was worrying enough but the absence of a boat or an obvious place from which to launch one was alarming – how did the man get on board? Sam took the binoculars and scoured the shoreline. There was a copse of trees to the east but beyond it lay only fields – no roads, no path down which to transport a boat of any sort. To the west was just sea, and small islands lay to the north and south. The spot had the added advantage of providing shelter from the gentle easterly breeze.

The closeness of the call exposed one huge weakness in Sam's plan: if he'd been killed and the intruder had simply left, his five-year-old would have been alone at sea, or worse. She'd have been terrified, called out for him and, eventually, have put on her life jacket to come and find him – possibly his corpse. If he'd been forced overboard, she'd have been stranded. If he'd been killed, she'd have been orphaned. He made a mental note that her next lesson would be using the boat's radio.

He looked again at the man. An island he and Isla had roamed a few days before came to mind. He'd found a natural fall in its centre – its marshy middle spouting bracken and reeds. The stagnant damp had struck him, even then, as a perfect place to dispose of a corpse. But he looked at the carcass, broad and long, and thought for the hundredth time that there was no easy way to transport a large body. Even small people seemed to weigh more when dead. Sam had learned that the hard way in Helmand when a tough little bootneck had bled out down his back. And time was against him. It wouldn't be long before the corpse stiffened beyond manipulation.

He wasn't prepared to take his daughter ashore with a body in the bilges either – whoever had accompanied the intruder might arrive at whatever dock he chose with a carful of cops. Isla had lost too much already and separation from her daddy was not an option.

The answer came gradually as he looked around the boat, assessing what he had that could be of use. He opened the deep cockpit locker and hauled out an enormous canvas bag that contained the old mainsail. He lifted the sail out of the bag, lashed it soundly, toppled it back into the locker and took the empty sturdy bag on deck.

Unfastening the main halyard shackle, he looped it around the intruder's ankles and winched the body into the air, cursing the deep bloodstain left on his timber deck. Drawing twenty feet of spare chain from a bucket in the bilge, he dropped it into the bottom of the canvas bag to act as a sinker. Then he opened the bag wide at the neck and drew it up and over the dangling body. It stopped just beyond his hips as he heard the man's head make contact with the chain. Sam let the cadaver down and folded the legs into the makeshift shroud. A rolling hitch with a loop secured the bag and he used the main halyard again to lift the whole lot over the side and into the water.

With the body in the bag secured about three feet below the hull and the teak deck scrubbed as clear as he could make out in the early morning glow, he did two things he generally tried to avoid. He sat in the cockpit and rolled himself a dead man's cigarette. Then he thought of the handgun and what its presence suggested, and worked backwards through his past in an attempt to fathom out who had planned to kill him. He needed to excise that threat in light of what that would have meant for his daughter now that her mam was gone.

Chapter 22

If it hadn't been for the presence of the Glock, Sam might not have run. The Glock was the only thing telling him for sure that the intruder had worse than bad intent. It was the only assurance Sam had that he hadn't messed up again and attacked an innocent man.

Had he not blacked out, he might not have been so worried about his ability to care for Isla. Twice now he'd shuddered into blackness without explanation, both times it seemed, involving violence. He hadn't remembered hitting the man in the shopping centre, but Isla had seen it. He didn't remember killing the intruder, but the evidence was all there. He feared it happening again. He worried that next time he might not come round.

Everything was telling him to get distance between them and the incident, the body, the gun. He needed familiarity; he needed good counsel.

Isla slept and watched her iPad on the long passage, the sails straining in a steady easterly as he beat into the Irish Sea before turning into the open fetches of water across the

North Channel. It gave him thinking time as he wound the winches and played the helm, coaxing the boat over the sea to make life below deck as comfortable as possible.

There was no escaping that he'd missed something. Never before had he been in doubt as to who wanted him dead. The enemy had always been obvious, and usually right in front of him. This time, though, nothing was clear. He had to work out who the dead man was so that he wouldn't die when they tried again. He had a child to mind, and a little heart to heal.

He'd started his new working life with Charity, so he pored over each job, every single scumbag he'd done over. Had there been any hint of foreign origin in the dead man, it would have made more sense that the threat was connected to Charity's work. Then he turned to Fran. Shipping involved big money, for sure. Someone like Sam operating in Irish waters represented an expensive irritation. Could Fran have shot off at the mouth about Sam's activities? Yet Fran knew nothing of substance about Sam. Even if the little man had blabbed about a bloke he knew who was raiding ships in the night, he could offer little more information than that. Besides, Sam was inclined to trust Fran, in so far as he trusted anyone. As the miles slipped under the hull, Sam became more convinced that the man who came for him wasn't connected to that work. There were too many shipping companies and no single one had been sufficiently stroked to hold such a grudge. Even if one of them had taken out a contract on him, he was difficult to pin down. Sam was under no illusions – anyone could be found, but the half-a-heads he'd been battering around Ireland had no such capability, he reckoned.

He looked at the chart plotter with its ability to tell him what way and speed the tide was running to within a few metres. The advances were extraordinary. If he wasn't so untrusting, Sam wouldn't need to consult a paper chart or use his navigational tools. He was falling out of date. Charity's sister Áine had laid that bare to him. He'd once been quietly confident that he understood tech, surveillance and all the sneaky beaky stuff known to man. Not any more. The tide had kept running while he'd been wrapped up in other things.

———

THEY SPENT a fortnight dropping anchor at various points up the Clyde. For Sam it was an edgy two weeks. No matter how secluded the bay he chose, sleep eluded him. Whoever had sent the man had managed to find him once before despite their nomadic and unpredictable existence. His ultimate destination was Scotland's Gare Loch, not far from the Port of Glasgow.

At Helensburgh he made a call to 43 Commando, stationed just a few miles north at Faslane Naval Base. The Fleet Protection Unit was a crack squad of Royal Marines deployed to protect the nuclear submarines that slipped in and out of those beautiful waters like enormous black seals. He felt stupid for the comfort that proximity to a few hundred marines brought. On the long nights sat in the cockpit Sam had been pensive, realising how difficult it was to maintain commando friendships in an civilian sense. Corps life had made him solitary, content to live without dependence. Yet bonds had been forged that could not be forgotten, even after discharge. Sam hadn't kept in touch with anyone since he'd left, save for a copy-and-paste exercise in response to the sympathy emails that had come his way. All the same, he knew with absolute certainty that there would be help.

Min responded to his request within hours. Sam made his way to a commercial marina, as directed, and heard rather than saw Min arrive on the pontoon.

"This what retired officers swan around in, aye?"

Sam smiled for the first time in many days. "Come aboard and see."

Like a monkey, Min swung on the rails and swept his two stocky legs over the dodgers that had shrouded him from view. Sam breathed out hard and nodded in relief at the sight of his best friend, who reached forward and gripped his paw before reaching up to cup his other hand around the back of Sam's head.

"How are you doing, pal? I am so sorry you've been through it. And I am so sorry I was'nae there. I didn't even get told till after the funeral."

"I knew you were deployed. I knew they wouldn't tell you." Sam nodded. "Part of the job."

"Part of the reason I need out."

"Nothing to do with age, then?"

Min smiled. "I'm as fit as a fox, but I won't miss it."

"So you're management now."

"Aye. Had to move up at some stage. Get the pension intae better shape."

"So I salute you now?"

"You should."

"You never saluted me."

"You never deserved it." Sam smiled and wanted to laugh, but couldn't. He just held Min's grip for longer than was normal.

"Thanks for coming."

"Don't be daft. I have someone with me, though." Sam

looked down the pontoon and saw a lanky man with a huge Peli case at his knee. Min turned towards him and barked, "Five minutes, then come over!"

The orders were typical of Min – a growler on the outside, a formidable and fearless leader. The men in any troop he led would have done anything he asked. Sam had often heard his Glaswegian accent barking at his team, and too many times he'd heard him counsel them with astonishing softness following the loss of their friends.

"So something's up aye? What's the story?"

Sam leaned down into the companionway to make sure Isla wasn't in listening distance and saw her cabin door was closed.

"Someone is keen to see the back of me. Caught a fella on the deck while we were at anchor a few weeks back. I have no idea how he got on board."

"Well, did you not ask him?"

"He wasn't much of a talker."

"Oh, right. Is he with Davy?"

If the topic hadn't been so serious, Sam might have smiled. Min's reference was one they'd used for drowned adversaries – Davy Jones' locker was packed with a fair few bodies.

"Pretty much."

"So who was he?"

"Good question. I don't know."

"Right. You're live aboard aye?"

"Yes. A while now. Pretty much since Shannon - " Sam tailed off.

"So how'd this bloke find you?"

"That's what I need a hand with. We've been touring around, never the same place twice, so that's the problem."

Min pursed his lips. "Why are ye livin' like this, pal?"

"To give the wee one comfort after, you know, what happened to her mam."

"Aye." Min nodded grimly. "So you think you've been elusive."

"I think we've done our best."

"But who'd be out for ye? You must have some notion?"

"I've been doing a bit of freelance work."

"Oh right." Min's eyebrows rose in interest.

"Nothing too strenuous, but I've been rubbing a few folks up the wrong way."

"And you think maybe it's one of them?"

"I don't know—not really—I just don't know what to think."

"Well, you know I've moved to 30 Commando?"

"IX? No. When?"

"Few months back. Still getting my head around it, you know. But, command position, nice steady slot, back in Scotland."

"I didn't expect you to go back to intelligence. Didn't end well last time."

"Let's not dig that up."

"No."

"I didn't expect to either, to be honest. But it's a type of different unit. Promotion, it's out of the bloody sand and it's actually really interesting."

"I thought the Exploitation Group deployed ahead of troops. How does that keep you out of the dirt?"

"I'm in Y Squadron – intercepts, comms."

"Back to your roots. Signals in the bloodstream, Min."

"Aye, lucky for you. Let me get this long wet streak of pish." Min turned. "Oi! Get your arse over here!" He turned back to Sam as the tall man lugged his case at a lollop beside him. "I dunno how he got through Devon but he's a wizard wi' the technology."

The man struggled up to the boat and heaved the case on board, his long, thin arms a wonder to Sam. He agreed that this fine-boned human had done well to make it through the commando training centre.

Min didn't stop to make introductions. "Spark up your kit and sweep everything. We're looking for any lumps or bumps that could give position, sign or signal." He looked to Sam for confirmation and Sam nodded. "Any of the navigational kit that's identifying the boat, anything out or in that could be exploited, I want to know. If you find something, don't be disabling it until we are told. Got that?"

"Sir."

"Right. We're aff tae the pub."

Sam smiled. "I'd better introduce you to someone."

———

SAM HAD NEVER SEEN Min interact with a child before. His friend had an uncanny ability to make Isla laugh in a way Sam yearned to do. Their interaction, father to daughter, always seemed either gentle or practical to Sam. To see her giggle and sparkle at Min's self-deprecating and deliberate stupidity would have made him a little envious had it not cheered him so much to see her happy.

"Right, we'd better shuffle back." Min looked at an enormous watch on an enormous forearm. Both Sam and Isla tried to mask their disappointment. Lunch had been the most enjoyable few hours since Shannon had been taken from them and Isla had benefitted from the company of someone other than her daddy.

Isla skipped ahead of them on the pontoons as Sam fielded questions from Min about Charlie.

"So how's it work, then?"

"I have this phone with an encrypted app. I keep it at a dead drop and only check in about once a week. Jobs filter in through two contacts and I take most of them. It's all pretty tight."

"Who are the contacts?"

"One's a shipping union bloke, one's a woman who runs a refuge charity thing. I think they're sound enough people."

"Is the encrypted app some off-the-shelf thing?"

"No, it's a bespoke build done by the charity woman's sister. I think she works for Google or one of the Silicon Valley big boys."

"And you trust her?"

"I think so."

"Really?"

"Maybe I'm getting soft."

"Sounds a bit like it."

When they got back to the boat the Peli case was open and the delicate kit was being gently replaced into dedicated foam slots. Min got straight to the point. "Well? What's the story?"

The awkward man frowned. "You've obviously got the usual traceable kit on board and a VHF radio, but I'm assuming from what the boss tells me that you know to keep that switched off most of the time, so the only signals coming off the boat are navigation – the GPS, the radar. The chart plotter could, conceivably, be followed, but it would take a hell of an operation to reverse a signal onto the boat and off it again. There's no tracker on board.

There's no unusual signature." He shrugged at Min, who turned to Sam.

"No matter what you think, you're not a hermit."

"I'm not trying to be a hermit. I'm just keeping my head down, for obvious reasons." He looked towards Isla. "You go on down to your cabin, darlin'. You can watch a movie."

They paused as she clambered down the steps and disappeared from view.

"If you had literally kept your head down, you would have stood a chance, but what you don't appreciate is how much of you is recorded – images, photos, social media, you're there. All someone somewhere needs is a tagged image and you're bloody nailed." Min's colleague got his orders. "Go on up to the vehicle. I'll not be long."

"I avoid cameras." Sam shook his head as the man wrestled his cargo off the boat.

"You avoid snappers with an SLR," Min dismissed him.

"I avoid people with camera phones, I avoid selfie sticks – I'm not even in family photos."

"You're on camera all the time. Whoever it is that's after you, all they need is your service record mugshot that matches your image to your name and you're banjaxed. They can input that image and search and find where you were last recorded."

"I haven't even been on CCTV." Sam thought of Dublin Airport but tried to persuade himself that it was in a different jurisdiction.

"Yeah, you have, and most of it is streamable some-where. You know the kit we used to have in the Det."

Sam nodded. Their secondment to 14th Intelligence Regiment felt like a lifetime ago.

"Well, pal, those toys are commercially available nowadays. Hackable, shareable. They'll let anyone have that stuff. World's gone mad."

"None of that is used near where we've anchored, though."

Sam really struggled with Min's suggestion. He was convinced he'd been careful: turning off location settings, refusing the laptop access to data roaming or anything that could ping him or where they were moored or headed.

Min sighed like he was talking to a dope. "You come ashore occasionally, right? For food or work, aye?"

Sam nodded.

"Where do you launch the dinghy from?"

"Mostly a sailing club," he said, content that it was isolated enough to defend himself.

"Which one?" he asked.

Sam named a few as Min lifted a phone from his pocket and stared into its enormous screen. He tapped. "This one of them?" He turned the screen to Sam.

"Yeah," he said.

He turned it back to himself and tapped once. "A weather cam live streamed."

"So?" Sam doubted whether anyone ever looked at the thing. "That's just to tell members whether the tide is in or out, or what the sea state is."

"It also tells them who's walking across the boat park, and if someone is recording it, this allows them to take your image."

"Bollocks." But Sam began to realise the extent of possibilities. "So if they can access an image that is verifiably me – one from a military database, they can then search around the internet to find where I am?"

"If they've got the right software, which is restricted stuff mainly, they can tell where you were recently recorded," he said. "It probably wasn't the bloody sailing club, pal, but it could be. It could just as easily be the local post office or the petrol station. Man, it could be someone's home if they have security cameras linked to their Wi-Fi. Anything can be hacked. Anything."

"And it what ... it maps your face?"

"It takes a kind of fingerprint of your face and keeps it. Then all they need to do is hunt around the area you were last pinged or they sit at their computer and nail your position using one of these." He wiggled his phone at him.

"But I'm meticulous with that yoke," Sam said. "I've the privacy settings nailed down, and—"

"Yeah, yeah, yeah," Min dismissed him again. "Then why do you have it? There's a GPS in there – there's a signal to switch off. When you power-down you tell the system where the thing is. No matter what your settings are your provider and the phone maker know where you are, or at least where you last were. Don't believe anything else. And better than that, there are people who can turn the bloody thing right back on again. They can listen, they can even watch through your camera. Only when the power source is totally and utterly exhausted, way beyond shut-down, are you really on your own."

Sam stared at him. It took a while to sink in. He was hunting back through all he had done, all he had said. All those private moments consoling Isla, the pair of them crying and hugging and promising to look after one another. He got more and more despondent.

He turned to his friend. "But it would take some doing, wouldn't it?"

"Aye," Min said. "This is probably government-level stuff or super hacker. This is special ops capability or a freelancer with skills like that bollocks." He nodded in the direction the tall guy had gone.

"This isn't great."

"Whatever you've got into, pal, it looks like it might be pretty serious shit."

Sam deleted the few contacts off his phone, changed the access code and handed it to Min. "Could you find a place for this? Preferably on board some ship headed for foreign waters."

Min smiled. "I will. It may or may not be the phone, by the way. It could be your ugly phizog."

With one hand he took the phone. With the other he grabbed Sam's hand, pulled him down to his shoulder and gave him a bump.

"You mind yourself," he said. "Call me any time you need."

Then he turned heel and peeled off. Sam didn't need to thank him. He just watched his little colleague's Neanderthal gait as the broad low structure made its way up the timber walkways. Eventually the steel shutter slammed in the distance and Min was gone. Sam found himself lamenting the time they'd lost together since he'd been busted back to the Marines and in the months since he'd left the navy. It was the first time he was aware of missing anything or anyone other than Shannon.

He reached into his pocket for the boat keys, keeping his eyes on the marina gate, suspecting that years might pass before he saw Min again. To the right, from a small Caddy van he noticed two men emerge and walk to the gate, one looking behind him, the other shaking the stockade gently, curious as to how to gain entry. Sam could tell by their clothes that they weren't boat owners – most yachties conformed to an irritating dress code: boat shoes or gratuitously expensive wellies, red trousers, branded jackets. These men had none of those. Nor were they contractors, their dress being marginally too smart for manual work. But they were large and fit looking and completely out of place. Sam stooped to place his key in the ignition and rose to keep an eye on them. He couldn't be sure but the second man had turned from the direction Min had travelled and was looking straight at their boat.

Sam wished he had a phone to call Min and ask him to take a look at the men, but his phone was in the pocket of the very person he wished to contact, which made him worry a little for his friend. He considered confronting the men but dismissed it as paranoia. That suited him well because he didn't want Isla alone on the boat. Instead he stepped over the rail, slipped the lines, turned tail and took his surveillance-free boat with its clean bill of health back out to sea.

Chapter 23

One uneasy month after visiting Min, Sam checked on the resting place of the man who had come, uninvited, to their boat. To go at night would have been impossible as torchlight stood a very good chance of being spotted from the mainland. He'd towed the makeshift body bag to the island in darkness, removed the carcass and hefted it over the rabbit-hole riddled surface with no small measure of difficulty. During the day it would be easier but because he refused to take Isla to that particular island to exercise any more, he built a cover of sorts by dragging his dad's dog along instead.

The deep shuck he'd deposited the man into was reasonably well hidden. It was hollowed into the centre of the island and covered in overgrowth and briars. He'd been counting on the local wildlife, rats and birds, to assist with the decomposition, and when he got to the grave he was pleased to find that there was no easily detectable sign of the corpse. It had all but sunk and even the dog showed little interest in investigating. It would be up to the bugs now and the body's exposure to humid moist air would help strip it back quickly. He reckoned another month would make life properly difficult for a forensics team.

Sam scoured the press every day for stories of a missing man but there was absolutely nothing from any part of Ireland that fitted the intruder's description. He found that curious – surely someone somewhere would miss a hulk like him? He'd roasted the man's clothing and was confident that once the final rashers of flesh were gnawed back, the corpse and he could not be connected.

That didn't solve his issue, though, and it certainly didn't mean that Isla was safe. The uncertainty and suspicion were, he knew, in danger of getting the better of him.

AT NIGHT he forced himself to consider other possibilities from his past. He had long accepted that not all of his behaviour had been entirely justifiable, besides the possibilities were many and varied. The man who had been sent to kill him could have been anyone. A dissident Irish republican trying to kindle the dying flame of the IRA perhaps. It held a certain logic – he'd served in the UK's armed forces after all, and military personnel were considered a target to the dissidents. Yet it didn't feel plausible. They were distinctly non-participatory extremists. Car bombs, random shots fired from a distance and urban back alley beatings were more their bag.

He considered whether it could have been an attempt at revenge for poisoning his wife's killer, but he doubted anybody would care enough about that scumbag or that the dots of that escapade could be joined.

The factory owner's departure posed a possibility, but nobody on the planet had liked him enough to care about his demise.

The more Sam reasoned it out, the more he came to believe that there was something desperate behind the intrusion. Nobody chooses to kill at sea unless they have to. There are too many variables: how to get aboard or ashore, how to dispose of a body, where to leave a dinghy or how to approach without being spotted. Stainless steel and gelcoat surfaces leave traces too, and boats are seldom exposed to heavy footfall, so forensics have few individuals to differentiate. Admittedly, that part of the whole assassination attempt – as he was convinced it must have been – still baffled him, but the facts were pretty clear: the man had come with a gun and it must have been drawn when he boarded otherwise it wouldn't have spilled onto the deck. So someone had a serious issue with him. Someone wanted him dead and they didn't care or didn't know that he had a child on board when they came to do it. No matter how Sam rationalised it, he felt that it wasn't about prostitutes, politics or seafarers; it wasn't about revenge either.

With no obvious strings to pull, he decided to excise another nagging irritation that he'd still not been able to shake. He dropped Isla off with her grandparents, drove thirty miles and hunted for a phone box. Eventually, in a village close to the east coast, he found one.

"Hello?" Charity answered after a long wait.

"It's me," he said, ever reluctant to use his name.

"Well I saw the northern number so I kind of guessed," she said. "You normally use the app?"

"Yeah, well, I don't have that anymore."

"Really? Why?

"Long story."

"That explains why you haven't answered any of my messages."

"Sorry, I had to… anyway, it's gone. Ehm, how are you?"

"Oh," she said surprised. "I'm grand thanks, and you?"

"OK. I eh, wondered if you could help me with something. I don't really know where to start."

"OK?"

"I'm looking for someone who might know about bad stuff. Ehm, like social services stuff, but at a convent. I think probably quite a long time ago. Maybe forty years, but I'm not sure."

He could hear Charity blow her lips out in. "That's a tall order. Can you be more specific?"

"Not really," Sam said.

"A convent in Dublin, I take it?"

"I don't know. Maybe. Probably. I don't know."

"But in Ireland?"

"Yeah. Pretty sure. It's to do with babies being brought to a convent. Unexplained and, ugh, I dunno."

"Unexplained and?"

"Harmed," Sam tried. "Horribly."

"Oh shit," Charity said.

"You've heard of this?"

"Not really, but I'm not surprised. How did you get drawn into that stuff?"

"What stuff?" Sam said. "Is there stuff?"

"Look," Charity sighed. "I work alongside nuns. They're pretty closed, you know? They don't say much at the best of times. But here have been times, things, rumours." She paused.

"What do you mean?"

"Well, sometimes a woman might get sent to them. I've only seen it a few times. They're not introduced or anything and the only explanation anyone's given is that these women are damaged and need spiritual guidance. Like a retreat."

"Who are they?"

"Well, they're nuns, like. From other convents."

"How do you know?"

"Cos they dress like nuns."

"And have you spoken to any of them?"

"No, I was never really allowed. Not that I was told not to. It just seemed that I shouldn't. Nothing to do with me, you know?"

"Right?" Sam's tone was coaxing.

"It was a while ago, going back a good bit. But there was a younger nun, a novitiate in the order that's here all the time. She and I were a similar age, I didn't think her heart was really in it. We chatted a little. She came to me once after an oul' one was brought in. She said the poor woman was haunted."

"By what?"

"Well, it was about babies. This young nun claimed the older one mentioned a graveyard somewhere out west."

"What sort of graveyard?"

"A graveyard, graveyard. I don't know. Where bodies are buried."

"But how do babies fit in?"

"I don't know. But whatever happened, the young one never took her final vows." "Where is the old woman now?"

"No idea."

"What about the young one?"

"Don't know."

"Did she mention anything unusual about babies? Were they buried in this graveyard?"

"I hope not. I didn't get any sense the babies were dead. I assumed it was their mothers had died. Childbirth or something. Like a mother and baby home, or the Magdalenes. A laundry or whatever. Is this about dead children?"

"Not sure," Sam said, staring through the glass of the call box at the sea.

"I think they all thought she was mad. But whatever, it wasn't long before the young one packed it in and left."

Sam thought for a moment. "Can you find her? Put me in touch?"

Sam heard Charity blow out into the mouthpiece again. "No, it was a few years. And she was old even then."

"I mean the younger one?"

"I can try," Charity said. "But, I don't know. The nuns here don't really respond well to questions. They'll want to know why I'm asking."

"I'll call back this evening," Sam said.

"That's a very generous window you've given me. The speed you work at is unhealthy you know?"

"Speak to you later, and thanks."

———

SAM WAS NEARLY FLAT PACKED by a Luas tram on the North Quay. He turned onto a street he thought he knew well only to find the silent menace trundling towards him. It had a bell like a pushbike, hardly a fitting warning, he thought, as he reversed at speed and nearly killed a horse pulling a carriage full of tourists. The coachman's reaction reminded him that swearing is a national pastime in

Ireland. It isn't spoken – or roared, to be offensive, it's simply common parlance, but it made sailors like him sound dainty. He decided to abandon the car and make the rest of the trip on foot.

He'd allowed himself a day away from Isla. To do that he either had to make money or make it worthwhile, and he already knew there would be no cash return on his task today. This was an exercise in exorcising the doubt that was keeping him awake every night.

Charity had come through with a number for the young woman who'd abandoned her vocation. After an obscure description of what he wanted and why, followed by a further check call made back to Charity, the woman reluctantly offered up an address.

"Now go easy on her," she'd warned. "I think she's been through a lot."

Sam hadn't pressed for detail; he just hit the road.

He crossed the river and wandered through into the south side where the accents became more refined and the streets more leafy. Moving east he crossed the Dart line and, under the flickering reflection of Lansdowne Road Stadium, he found the address.

The woman who answered the door was everything he could have imagined: old Ireland, right there, staring at him with suspicion. She was small, gaunt and dressed like a 1950s schoolteacher wearing hard, uncomfortable shoes, a grey dress and cardigan. No colour and no humour. Sam had done some reading and was gradually gathering a sense of the old-style care system in Ireland – reliant on the church, no smiles, no hugs, be grateful you're getting the nothing that you're given. The would-be nun had warned him the woman would appear austere but assured him that inside a tough exterior beat a heart of gold.

"I'm sorry to disturb you. I was given your name by a woman who used to know you a bit at…"

"Yes," the old woman looked him up and down. "I'm aware."

He filled her subsequent silence with blether. "It's ehm, it's a bit sensitive and a bit odd. I was hoping you might be able to spare me a bit of time and an open mind. It's not a conversation for the … for the street, really. Can I take you for a coffee? Cup of tea, maybe?"

She stood aside, apparently persuaded that he was genuine. "No sense in spending good money on tea when there's water in the tap," she said.

He walked through a tiny porch into a doily dreamland. It was fusty, dark, decorated for the blind. Wallpaper peeled from the corners of her living room, the carpet did not meet the walls. The cold was striking and the furniture ancient. There was little sign of any means of entertainment – no TV, no radio, few books. Sam wondered what this old woman did to amuse herself in her retirement. Prayed, perhaps.

"I need to ask you about something a bit bizarre, I'm afraid," he told her.

She stared at him. "You don't need to ask me anything, but I am quite sure you will go on regardless."

She didn't offer him a seat, so they both remained standing.

"It's about a convent in Dublin – I think - well, partly. Not the same one where you met the woman who called on my behalf. This might have been a children's home? An orphanage, maybe?"

There was a tiny shift in her eyeline as her gaze flickered from his to the barren mantelpiece behind him. "I wasn't told you were coming about that." Her tone was one of offense and he realised she felt she'd been misled, engaged under false pretences.

"I wasn't able to tell the woman what it was about because of … well, because of the nature of what I've been told."

The woman's eyes clicked back to his and he saw suspicion – maybe even anger. He thought he might lose her, so he consolidated: shit or bust.

"It's about a crazy story really. I don't know whether to… it's ritual abuse, possibly somehow connected to the seasons."

She slumped backwards, crumpling, and he jolted forwards instinctively to catch her, but she somehow gripped the arms of her chair as she sank, barely cushioning what sounded like a surprisingly heavy blow into tired springs. He stood back. She eventually looked up at him, both shocked and resigned at the same time.

He pressed on. "You see, I've been told a terrible thing and I need to know if it's true or if it's just a horrible fantasy. It involves a child – well, an adult now – a person described as 'the heir'."

"Oh, dear God, forgive us." The woman spoke indiscreetly for the first time as she crossed herself.

Sam didn't take his eyes off her as he moved slowly across to crouch and sit on her sofa. He waited while she stared at the wall until eventually her head rotated back towards him. "Who told you of this? Why would they tell you of this? What did they want?"

Although Sam didn't realise it until much later, that question betrayed an awful assumption. He ignored her query. "Is it true?" But he already had his answer.

She made an unusual gesture, contorting her fingers a bit like the scout salute but backwards, and placed the tips against her forehead, masking much of her face. The slack skin on her bony fingers was a little unnerving and stirred some distant fear from a childhood nursery rhyme. He swiped it aside and sat silently.

"It's true," she said after a time, raising her gaze to meet his, her stare hardening. "And my advice to you is to drop it."

Chapter 24

He didn't feel foolish. Certainly his instinct had been to disregard the crazy counsellor and his hallucinogenic horror story but, in a way, that put him at ease with himself. There was a sharp relief that his view of human life had not darkened to the point of blindly accepting that such things were possible. If Sam was to reinvent himself and emerge as a civilian and a father, that he'd originally dismissed the story gave him hope that he might see the transition through. Still, he'd sought to disprove the counsellor's tale through an independent source and it hadn't gone as planned.

Once he'd prised open the crack in her conscience, the old woman treated their encounter like confession. The surroundings were appropriate enough: cold, claustrophobic, no eye contact. She'd turned from him and stared straight ahead at the mould on the wall opposite. Enormous tears leaked down her cheeks; their deep crevices filling like tributaries. In the end the truth flooded her face with peace, as if those years spent suppressing the horrors had wizened her and left her incapable of laughter, of life. He took his leave; exiting with her in deep exhaustion and him with his mind racing. There were gaps in her knowledge but her story kept driving at one thing.

"You are not safe."

She said it three times and each time it sent an unwanted shiver through him. He didn't care if he wasn't safe – he hadn't been safe since he was twenty-two. Isla, however, was another matter.

"You have no possible idea what you've got yourself into."

The way she described what had happened made him wish he was a decade fresher and fitter for the imagined fight she was sure was coming his way.

The old girl had grown up in an orphanage in Galway, but from her account it was nothing short of a workhouse and the children were treated as free labour. From her language he could tell that her view of the world was limited – her references were almost childlike and her experience of life had been curtailed by dreadful hardship and the constant threat of punishment. She described coming of age in the dormitories and how she was told repeatedly that she had no ability to live outside the convent walls, that her skills were washing, cleaning and reading and that nobody would want any of that on the outside unless she married and nobody would want to marry her. She explained that she hadn't even wanted to leave; her life in the echoes and shadows of that cold, hard environment was all she knew.

At some stage, when she was old enough, she'd been given the task of looking after babies. They came in quite often but she didn't specify any regularity. Her job was to feed and wash them only, and she was scolded for amusing them in their cots. The first time she encountered a child who had been skinned, she looked alarmed at the nun who had carried the child in. "Bathe the feet and mind your business," was all she was told.

And that's what she did. She fought the infection that set in and asked repeatedly for a doctor who was never summoned. Over the years the process was performed again and again and the little unmarked graveyard at the back of the building filled up with tiny corpses.

"You become numb to it." She explained – as if her mind was a million miles away. "You, God forgive me, you just learn to accept that little children are going to die. You try to take away the pain for them, you try to stroke away their cries and their screams. My mind is filled with them, my sleep is filled with them. You never recover. All those babies ..." She drifted back into her torment.

"Who brought them to the convent?" he asked.

"A man from America," she said. Her pronunciation of the continent made it sound like some exotic, untouchable land.

"How do you know?"

"I heard him speak once, to the sister. She asked him how things were in New York. He was giving her money. 'God bless your good work,' he told her. He was a small man. He had hair at the sides and he tried to make it cover the top. He'll be dead now, I expect."

"He was old?"

"Much older than you, and that was a long time ago. In the nineteen and seventies."

Sam thought about the timeline and what the counsellor had claimed about the horrors being passed through generations.

"How do you know the American brought the babies?"

Her eyes narrowed and she turned to him for the first time. "Because he had one with him?"

"I'm sorry," he said, "I'm just struggling to understand how anyone could do that to babies."

"You understand nothing," she spat, before turning back to face the wall. "You do not realise who you are dealing with. These people will stop at nothing to keep their secret. They even killed a nun."

"What?" was all he could muster.

"She challenged the sister – told her she would go to the Guards after a child was brought in and infection took it. The sister said nothing, turned her back to the nun, and the next day the nun was dead."

"Dead, how?"

"Dead in her bed! A young, fit woman – she wouldn't even have been thirty years old. A woman that age dying in the bed. Sure, who would ever hear the like of that? She was buried in the graveyard, the marked one. Her family came, a brother and a cousin, but there was n'er a doctor allowed near her. No police. Nothing. She was just dead and that was that."

"Do you think she was killed?"

"Of course she was killed!"

"How do you know?"

"Because her face was purple and her bed was … soiled, terribly soiled. And the smell from her poor throat when they lifted her up. They must have poured poison into her." The old woman simply shook her head.

Sam was no pathologist but he bought her diagnosis.

"It was to be a closed coffin," she continued. "Her brothers made an almighty fuss but the nuns would not have it. A priest had to quieten the brother, and she was laid to rest without any more to-do." The old woman stared at him. "That's what they'll do to you if you don't get a bit of sense for yourself."

"Who? They must all be dead?" he probed.

"This kind of evil never dies," she said. "They'll go on."

"Who? Who are they? Is it a group? A cult?"

"Well, I couldn't tell you that," the woman said, indignant again. "Sure, how would I know? And what is it to do with you? You don't say who told you."

Sam debated for a moment. "I don't know how they found me," he said truthfully. "I don't know what to think."

"Perhaps you should go back and ask whoever led you here to my door to open up about this horrible stuff. I don't know what you were thinking at all."

"I didn't intend to upset you, he told her, "but I'm in it now."

"Well, if you're in it, I suggest you get out of it as soon as you can for these are dangerous and powerful people and they will do anything to keep their dreadful secrets."

There was something about the elderly, Sam later thought as he drove home trying to think of the word to describe how the woman had issued her warning. Chilling, he settled upon. The woman had been chilling. Perhaps it was her frailty, the slack skin showing her skeletal future, her proximity to the grave; a head start towards decomposition. Perhaps it was her experience, the corners she'd turned long before him. Either way, the old woman had unnerved him in a way that he had never before experienced, and it was in stark contrast to his reaction to the counsellor. Unlike when listening to his story, he believed every word she uttered.

———

HE TUCKED Isla into her bunk, settled in the cockpit, rolled a cigarette and worked through possible scenarios. If there was a victim, and if the nutjob was her counsellor, then her abusers could well have placed him under surveillance. They may then have pinged Sam when he met the counsellor at Heuston Station. The two of them may have been followed, in which case the tail was pretty good – Sam hadn't seen them, despite being wary. When he'd met the counsellor he'd had the smartphone with him, an oversight he now realised. His eagerness to get the meeting over may have proved fatal. It seemed possible, if not plausible, that they could have somehow traced the cell phone or its GPS. That pointed again to reasonable sophistication, and if they had that sort of tech, they might have been able to discover Charlie. If they knew the right people, they'd have been able to hack into databases and find his service records. If they knew where he'd served, and in what unit, they would likely have become concerned. Nervous enough, perhaps, to decide he was best removed.

Sam had sat through countless intelligence briefings and during surveillance training it had been hammered home – *the target rarely predicts the lengths to which we are prepared to go*. That was the strength of the UK intelligence services – its cunning. It appealed to him, frankly, that those who work hardest and think more than anyone else get results. If any target were to try and expose the type of intrusion and eavesdropping they'd endured, nobody would believe it. It was too devious for civilians to accept. That's part of the reason he worried that the people who were on to him were professional, well connected and dangerous. If they were on to him at all. If … if … if …

He inhaled deeply and heard the crackle of the tobacco burn. He looked at the ember and shook himself for his ridiculous imaginings. Then he looked out to sea and blew the plume of smoke into the black air. Miles beyond it, in the darkness, lay the island on which a corpse rotted. Whatever its intention, the intrusion onto their boat had become serious business with catastrophic effects.

He threw the butt into the tide. It was no use. Something in his bones was telling him to run the notion into the ground. He knew he wouldn't sleep properly until he'd put his suspicion to rest. The next day, he decided, would be used to find conclusive evidence, or in its absence to settle on another line to pull. If they'd got to him through that bloody counsellor, he reasoned, they must have assumed Sam was working for the crazy bastard. And if that was their thinking, there would be no way such a dreadful group – if such a thing really existed, would ever leave him and Isla in peace.

He wondered who was crazier: the counsellor for his story or him for half believing it.

He thought fleetingly about going to the police, but there was a dead body now for which he'd been responsible. He knew they would simply listen to the tale of feet skinning and seasonal abuse rings and have him committed. He could send the plods to the counsellor but the police would just take the man's weirdness as confirmation of their scepticism. The counsellor would probably refuse to speak to them anyway. The victim, if she existed, would be dismissed as damaged or institutionalised. In any event, if this ring was anything like as described, it would surely have the capacity to close down a fledgling investigation. The police had handled his wife's murder appallingly, so he reckoned there was just no point. Even if they did act, it would take too long, and they wouldn't keep Isla safe.

Chapter 25

"So now you understand what evil is," the counsellor said gently. He'd woken calmly, despite Sam having entered his bedroom uninvited and shaken him awake.

Not here, Sam motioned to him with a metronomic movement of his free forefinger, staring at the nefarious smart speaker sitting beside the counsellor's bed. Sam had long ago learned not to trust any device that could pick up voice commands. If the companies that made them weren't recording, someone else probably was. What a gift to those involved in surveillance, he thought. Nobody need ever go to the trouble of placing a bug in a home again. People were doing it all by themselves by selling their souls to convenience. Finding the counsellor's home had involved little more than a short tail from his office.

There followed an odd arrangement whereby the counsellor, wearing aged pyjama bottoms with a gaping convenience, was beckoned into the en suite to sit on the lid of his own toilet while Sam perched on the edge of the bath. The shower was set running as an extra audio precaution and they talked as the steam built up.

"I understood evil before we last met," Sam said. "This is not evil alone, this is perversion."

The counsellor smiled at him. Sam didn't know whether the grin was smug or seedy, but the whack job seemed to be enjoying it until he realised that Sam was equally relaxed, and then he scrabbled for a foothold.

"I take it you confirmed what I told you."

"Some of it."

"How?"

"I second sourced it."

"With whom?"

Sam knew he had the counsellor on the hook then. This man didn't like the notion of others revealing his secret story. He wanted exclusive rights to its telling and the power that came with it. Sam ignored the question but hoped he'd ask again.

"I'm prepared to take the job. How do you want to pay?" Sam delivered the lines he'd rehearsed. He needed the man to believe that his interest was primarily commercial, but the counsellor wasn't past his previous question.

"Did she tell you about the others?"

Sam knew the crafty bugger was fishing but held the line. To ignore that query too might tip the counsellor over the edge. He'd be forced to show that he knew more than Sam's source or risk becoming irrelevant. Nonetheless it was interesting that the man had chosen to guess the source was female.

"Cash only."

"You'll get your money," the counsellor cast an arm to the air dismissively, as his trunks yawned.

Sam stared at the steam condensing on his enormous

mirror. Something caught his attention then – something visual, unusual. "When?" He tried to keep returning to the cash. It useful distraction to conceal his real motivation - fear for the safety of his daughter.

"When you deliver." The counsellor smiled, a leer to his grin.

Sam began to reassess the man. "What is delivery to you?" He adopted a phrase he'd heard some plummy officer once use with his poorly trained troops.

"Well," his hands opened like his jocks, "that's up to you, but we can't have these people abusing anyone else, can we?"

It was then that Sam saw his weakness: his desire to be respected. Such people were often incapable of commanding regard so they clung to tufts of power as if grabbing at roots when sliding down a cliff. The desperation of a jobsworth. The counsellor sat on his bog lid and treated Sam like a pupil. Sam loathed him.

"I need to meet the woman, the victim."

"Oh, I can't let you do that."

Sam was in sync now – the counsellor's condescension was about retaining control.

"Why?"

"Trauma. She's deeply unwell. She needs protection. If she knew I'd spoken to someone about it, a huge amount of the work I've done to help her would be undone."

The man's vanity was staggering. This was all about him. Sam thought of his designer ripped jeans, his age-inappropriate affectations. Something Sam had seen since entering the house was niggling at him and it was time to leave. A lead was required, though, so Sam poked him enough to provoke one.

"You don't even know where the abusers are, do you?"

The counsellor's eyes darted in irritation while his hands movements tried to appease.

"Let's not—"

"You claim to protect her, but you can't. You don't know who they are, the people she's afraid of." Sam laced his observation with utter contempt and made to leave.

Despite possessing the intelligence to realise what Sam was doing, the counsellor's heart ruled his head and he reacted to the slight before he'd thought it through.

"You'd wouldn't believe the half of it," he blurted out.

"You don't *know* the half of it."

"People in high places."

His aim was to draw Sam back but Sam needed more from the man's anger before it ran out.

"Riddles and nonsense." He slammed the bathroom door for effect.

It opened immediately, and turned to see that the counsellor's pecker had finally found its exposure.

"Close to the president," he said, desperate. "Part of the special envoy's team."

And with that Sam turned to face him.

It wasn't until the drive home during which Sam's mind plotted through his next steps that he realised his oversight. He'd forgotten to ask how the counsellor had found Charlie.

———

SAM TRIED to break up the sickening fear that was clotting inside him. He was incapable of doing anything while worrying about his daughter. With her at his side he'd constantly operate at half power, always conscious of the risk to her. She was doing so well and he refused to let what he was about to do mess her up.

He took an enormous amount of cash from the bilge of the boat, handed it to his dad and pleaded with him not to ask any questions. They'd seen a lot of life themselves, his folks, and Sam's occupation had taken its silent toll on them; the worry, the fear that every time a military death was reported it might be his. They knew where he'd served and what unit he'd been in but had learned to ask fewer and fewer questions as he grew older. Their attention and care instead turned to Isla, into whom they decanted their love. He'd often wondered at the shift in their devotion. It was beautiful to watch, the mutual pleasure of simply being in the company of the third generation of their existence while Isla reciprocated with simple contentment. She would reach for them without thinking, placing her tiny hand in theirs and in so doing gave them purpose and a sense that their lives had rounded in some sort of natural order.

His dad knew by the way Sam asked him that the task simply had to be carried out. He frowned a little as Sam talked him through the need to pay for the convoluted journey in cash, but he accepted it. The only thing he argued over was whose cash it would be. Eventually he took the money and booked the ferry, and Sam knew that when his parents got to England they would secure flights and the three of them would spend a few months in the sunshine. Sam thanked God for their early retirement and their good health.

Then he turned to the task at hand. Much as he'd tried to dismiss the counsellor, it now seemed depressingly clear that so long as the members of the abuse ring remained at large, he and Isla were in serious danger: him from them, Isla from being orphaned. He believed that the men at the marina in Scotland had been somehow connected to the threat. Disposing of the phone felt like it had been a sensible move, as there had been no discernible observation since. But the fact remained that they had been able to follow him, even across the Irish Sea. And so they were organised and had reach. If there had been a hiatus in their interest, he felt it inevitable that it would end. He sensed a looming confrontation. Rather like many situations he'd found himself in before – he knew his choice was to take them out or be taken out. After what he'd learned from the old woman, truth be told, he'd have gone after them even if his life hadn't depended on it.

Chapter 26

S am detested wasting time and hated things remaining unresolved. He much preferred to deal with matters as they arose. Issues that lingered irritated him beyond what many would consider reasonable. He also preferred straight-talking to bullshit, which contributed to his detestation of the counsellor. The conceit, the acting, the desire to play with people and the dramatic delivery. With the counsellor it was all suspense and the suggestion of higher power. As far as Sam was concerned, the group of people he was looking for could be boiled down to what they were – a bunch of abusers who had managed to merge their horrible fantasies into collective action. If he despised the counsellor, though, he had a feeling he would hate the colleague the counsellor had put him in touch with.

Flying out of the States was easy: once you were gone, you were gone and nobody cared. Flying into the States, however, proved to be a tricky business. Sam had found no way to do it without being tracked. Dublin offered the best route in because travellers could clear immigration before they left Ireland, and Ireland and the USA were buddies. Sam had been sent to America countless times on NATO-related deployments and his visa was still valid, so he rolled through, but his nervousness around his recent display at the terminal door was through the roof. He wondered whether someone somewhere was watching his progress from a computer screen. Until the plane stuck its nose in the air and the G-force pressed his head back into the cushion, he fully expected to get lifted. His destination was New York and then a bus trip, in the hope that at least some of his journey remained unobserved.

The rest of his plan was pretty vague, which annoyed him. All the counsellor had given him was a mobile phone number and the message that the contact was in New England. Sam knew it was the counsellor's way of maintaining the mystery around it all and of keeping his hand in the game. Such was Sam's repulsion at the time that he simply took down the contact details and left. He couldn't face the prospect of posing further questions. That would have given the counsellor the pleasure of holding court and talking in misty-eyed circles.

Sam was grateful for the cash he'd amassed on previous jobs because it removed the worry of how to fund such a trip. Marines and special forces were not particularly well paid and since leaving the service he was better off than he'd ever been. The only plane seat he could get at short notice was in business class, so it made for a pleasant flight. He had no phone with him, nothing that would allow him to be followed on foot without significant effort. When he arrived he jumped on a bus and crossed the river, headed for Manhattan. There he strolled around a bit, jumped on and off the subway and eventually bought a burner phone to make contact. The text he sent was brief: *In country. When and where? Charlie.* It took two hours to receive a response: *Tremont, Boston. I'll be ready when you're here.*

At Grand Central he queued at a ticket booth and dropped the burner phone into the handbag of a transvestite in front of him. She ordered a one-way to Connecticut, which was well short of Boston, so it suited Sam fine. He hopped on the bus and slept a while, as confident as he could allow himself to be that he'd avoided being followed. He always mustered some peace of mind from knowing he'd done his best. If he got caught, it would likely be the contact's fault, not his.

He trundled around on the T beneath the streets for a while and then found digs in Southie, where the bars looked more Irish than those back home. He tried to beat the time difference by sleeping immediately, to leave him alert early morning. The neighbours, however, had other ideas.

The guest house was pretty rough. There was a family in the next room, presumably in the process of being rehoused from some project. The mother had only one eye, and one of the sons was chasing the dragon in the corridor as Sam left the next morning. The tinfoil rested on his knees and he crouched, wedged, foetal, between the carpet and the wall. He looked up, startled, when Sam emerged. The way his hand fluttered towards the small of his back made him note that the youth could be useful, but for the moment it was recce time and he battered on.

He eventually got on Dorchester Avenue and walked towards town. As usual he was drawn to the sea and the harbours. There was a more direct route but not, he thought, a better one. It gave him time to think about the counsellor's contact. The person seemed confident that he'd be available whenever Sam arrived. He wondered what that meant. Was the contact retired? Did he work in the area, and if so, what sort of hours would make him accessible all the time?

It was still too early for the shops to be open, so Sam had to wait before picking up another phone. It worked in his favour because he wanted to walk Tremont and get a feel for the area and its landmarks. In the service they'd called it "an appreciation" – working out the ways in and out, the risks and the opportunities. The big disadvantage in plodding the streets so early in the morning was that he would stand out on CCTV and could be accosted by a cop. For that reason he had on a pair of runners, tracksuit leggings and a baseball cap. He popped in some head-phones, linked to nothing, and made out like he was exercising.

Tremont was long and pretty by city standards, but coming from the eastern coastal side was initially disap-pointing. The city hall, usually a centrepiece, looked boxy for such an old town. The architecture rapidly improved, though, and he allowed a little respect for the speed at which America had been built. There was a small church right bang in the centre of the metropolitan area, then countless banks and chain cafes. He admired the planners' willingness to preserve green areas and he could see the sky without looking straight up, which was unusual in some downtown US areas. The window of an armed forces career centre caught his eye, but his attention quickly turned to the park where he imagined the meet would happen. He expected it to be predictable. If the contact was anything like the counsellor, he would choose a park bench where neither man would look at one another. It staggered him that every movie happened the same way. Why on earth would anyone meet in a public place, potentially observed by thousands, when they could do it in an office or a toilet or a lift?

Eventually the cosmopolitan gave way to the ordinary – hotel and cinema land, which then became residential, and it terminated without glory at what Bostonians would probably call an intersection. Still, it had all he needed: countless ways out, countless ways in, and he had options for exit north and south. There was nothing at the guesthouse he couldn't do without if he needed to extract, and through the recce he had identified the means by which he could get to the airport quickly and unobserved. In fact, he looked straight at it and it made him smile.

———

SAM SAT by the Frog Pond in Boston Common and slapped together the parts of a new burner phone. The battery wasn't particularly well charged, which suggested it had been sitting on the shelf for a long time. Hardly surprising given that nobody really wanted phones for phone calls any more – they wanted computers in their pockets.

In place. What next? Charlie, he tapped, and lapsed into a thousand-yard stare, working logically through the possibilities and the connection he was trying to make.

He had no idea what the background of the contact was, but it seemed reasonable to assume that the person had an interest in stopping the abusers. Sam didn't believe all of what the counsellor had said but he saw no logic in connecting him to someone with opposing goals. By extension, there would be little point in connecting Sam to someone involved in the abuse.

The American angle was odd and Sam suspected the

claim of someone close to the president had been spewed out so as not to lose him. "Part of the special envoy's team," the counsellor had said. Sam knew that the White House had maintained a Special Envoy to Ireland, or more specifically Northern Ireland, since peace had broken out. The aim had been to secure business and economic prosperity but also to wade in with the boots when negotiations between the factions got tricky. Sam's broad sense was that it had been a success, but an attaché involved in an abuse ring? He neither knew nor cared except for the fact that cover-up required power – and the ability to keep something covered up for a long time required a special kind of influence.

Sam knew that behind every public leader was the person with real clout. It had been such in the corps and in the military, and his various secondments to other units, including those close to government, had confirmed that politics was no different. The colonels and the cabinet ministers were often just needy extroverts who possessed the ability to string a sentence together. They also had enough arrogance to wade through any media onslaught because they needed the attention. He'd seen at close quarters the good reasons why the back-room boys and girls didn't like the limelight. They were people who enjoyed power so much they wanted to hang on to it. The cyclical nature of politics ensured that failure for the elected was guaranteed. When it came, the breed that lingered behind the politician simply crowned another king or queen and sanded them into shape. Such people could draw their fix and their finances from power yet remain unseen. When Sam's friends had protected politicians in London and abroad they'd been issued intelligence briefings that went with any principal. On two occasions they'd been told to be more wary of the advisor than the cabinet minister because unspecified proclivities could pose a risk.

The phone chimed. He'd forgotten to put it on silent. The message suggested an American: *Come back tomorrow, noon. SMS me then.*

Sam deleted the contents of the inbox and sent folders, rubbed the phone hard to get rid of fingerprints and hurled it angrily into the middle of the pond. On the long walk back he bought a third phone from a dingy little corner shop and charged it at the guest house. He got between the sheets and waited.

The neighbours – the sons, at least – had been fighting when he'd climbed into bed, but Sam woke to silence and darkness four hours later. The jet lag from the time difference had worn off. He lay and listened, hoping he'd been roused by movement in the adjoining room. Ten minutes later its door opened quietly, which suggested that some of its inhabitants were asleep. Sam gambled that one of the sons was on the move and slipped out of bed. He heard steps in the corridor too heavy to be the one-eyed woman, so he dressed and followed.

The son turned heel into an alley fifty metres from the house and must have been needy because he didn't venture far up it. From the street Sam could hear his preparations: the crinkle of foil, the telltale Zippo flip, the strike. Sam didn't know what the kid was cooking up to suck but he hoped it was good stuff. He walked off and by the time he came back the teen was just as he wanted him, curled over his knees. He couldn't have been more accommodating if he'd tried. Sam lifted the back of his jacket and his belt practically handed him what he'd come for: a 9 mm Beretta. But there his luck ran out – it was in shit shape, rust in the barrel and the slide was sticky. Worse still, Sam could tell by the weight of it there was nothing in the magazine. The kid must have used it for show or for robberies. America was awash with such sidearms skimmed from the military and available in most unfriendly exchange stores. Still, he took it anyway and went back to his room. There he replaced the plastic wedge he always carried with him on such trips and kicked it tightly under the door. Simple but enormously effective: key or no key, an intruder's only option was to break the door down to get in. That and the weapon gave him enough peace of mind to get some more sleep.

———

SAM MADE CONTACT AT MIDDAY, as directed, and tried to take the reply in good humour. *Go to where the Puritans lie, by Philips.*

He'd assumed that the contact would want to take a look at him before he stepped forward, so a runaround was to be expected. He began walking, same route, same pace as the day before, with a reasonable idea of where he needed to go. The little church he'd seen yesterday had a graveyard, which pleased him. In any other major city anywhere else in the world, they'd have paved over it and thrown up a Starbucks, but the Americans had so little history that they hung onto every tale and title.

There was a sign indicating he was on the Freedom Trail, at the oldest burial ground on the outskirts of a Puritan settlement. Lovely, he thought. He waited a while to see if the contact would hit him up and when he failed to do so wondered whether he was being followed at all. He lifted the phone and composed a text: *Ok, I'm here.* The response was immediate: *I think not.*

Sam tried to suppress his irritation and looked again at the first text. *By Philips*, it said. He began to dander around the gravestones: Deacon Robert Gardner, Simon and Mary Rogers, Mary Seymore. Many were hard to make out. They'd been standing in the same spot since the seventeenth century, eroded by smoke and later fuel emissions. Isaac Merrion, Piebec Merrion, wife of Isaac, William Hallowell. Three hundred graves and not one Philips. His patience was wearing. Perhaps he'd missed something the day before? He ran the recce through in his head as if replaying a tape. He vaguely remembered another church but with no graveyard, and decided to carry on up the road. As he walked another message buzzed his balls. He lifted out the phone, imagining the contact was watching him do it.

Go first to Franklin, then Philips.

This told him the contact was impulsive, changing his mind. That, to him, suggested he was excitable, which was frankly not his favourite trait. Sam disliked him a little bit more.

It happened as he passed the Last Hurrah bar. He'd been alert, so he saw it coming even though he didn't quite believe it. A vagrant lying by the side of the main street begging had picked him out at a hundred yards and was giving him the eyeball. He had a note scrawled on cardboard, identifying himself as a veteran. Takes one to know one, Sam thought. The beggar leapt up but wasn't keen on a greeting.

"Fucking fag!" Anger roared in his eyes.

Sam moved aside and had to pivot and turn when the vagrant followed him. The man was fit enough and not for letting go, trying to shove his face in Sam's. "Fucking faggot, fucking faggot!" he yelled.

This was attention Sam could do without, and like the

ripples made when a stone hits water, people circled wide but stared towards the commotion. The rabid scruff wouldn't let up. Every time Sam moved away from him his hands groped out while screaming and hurling his shoulders towards Sam's upper body. Sam quickly tired of the intrusion and the attention and made the poor choice to drop him. He placed his weight on his aft foot and using his moment, bent his forearm to drive through.

As he connected something of interest registered out of his peripheral vision, but then it was all about withdrawing. Sam upped his pace and listened to what was going on behind him. Someone was trying to help the man and he turned a little to catch the beggar lashing out at the Samaritan with his legs. Then there was a patter to the rear and he knew the man was determined to follow up. This time, Sam had no choice. He timed it by the sound of the approach, swivelled and put an end to the debacle. Had he punched the man, Sam would have injured himself and the man would simply have got up again. Instead, he'd caught the man just where he wanted – palms up under his eye ridge. His head flew back, his feet rose and he hit the pavement with his skull. Even at that the man wasn't entirely knocked out, but he'd certainly lost his grunt.

One woman stared at him and hustled away. "So unnecessary," she muttered, but she didn't stoop to help the bleeding man.

Sam crossed the road and hunted for whatever had caught his attention. He got sight of it as his heart rate returned to normal. Surrounded by high buildings, apartments perhaps, was another ancient graveyard. The beautiful steeple of a clock tower stood to its left, a real *Back to the Future* type structure. He had to move on but he could see that the centrepiece of the graveyard was a cenotaph on which he could clearly make out the word "Franklin".

He walked two blocks and then coasted back to the area, removed his shell jacket and took the sunnies off his head. He skipped up the steps through wrought-iron gates into the graveyard. A man in period dress was addressing two Asians and he had to pan between the tour guide and his captivated audience to see the engravings. He caught the largest headstone, "Philips", and took note to thank the vagrant with a little cash if he passed him again. Without him he would have walked the wrong way and missed it altogether. This sort of mystery and suspense nonsense would normally have made him contrary but he was buzzing like a brothel's doorbell. "First Mayor of Boston" read the inscription on closer inspection. Then the phone rang.

"You could have just called in the first place," he said.

"Well, you certainly know how to make an entrance." The voice was muffled but was American for sure.

"I think it's time to stop pissing around," he said, in his best command voice.

"Come in, pull up a stool. You could probably do with a drink," the man said.

"Where?"

"Right beside where you drew blood, my friend," he said and hung up.

Sam looked across the street. There was a classy sign made of bulbs: Beantown Pub • Cafe. Sam was quite thirsty and a little tired of bullshit.

Chapter 27

S am tended to walk into a pub as some women might a jewellery shop. But this time he tried his best not to linger on Jack and Jim twinkling at him from behind the bar. They were part of the reason he didn't do as much drinking as he would like to.

"Diet Coke, please."

He met the barman's gaze and received a nod with an odd hint of approval. The barman placed the drink in front of him and stood for a moment. Sam hadn't been expecting to pay right away, so he looked up from his first sip, from the man's apron to his face.

"On the house," the man said. He discreetly motioned to the lower darker part of the pub where multiple TVs were showing sports. "I finish in a half hour. We can talk down below."

Well, there you go, Sam thought. A barman. He lamented the time he'd wasted doing a recce and took a seat enabling him to watch the contact out of the corner of his eye. The man was late thirties, lithe and confident, capable and comfortable. Sam told himself to not appear overly hostile, but was pissed off about the unnecessary confrontation on the street. Exactly thirty minutes later the man shook off his apron and strolled down to sit opposite him.

"How was your trip?"

Sam ignored the question. "So where do you fit in?"

"How do you mean?" The man shifted uneasily on his stool.

Sam just stared at him, hoping he wouldn't have to play any of his cards.

The bartender relented. "It's a long story," he sighed. Sam thought of the counsellor and rather imagined it would be. "I'm not sure where to start."

"How do you know our friend in Dublin?" Sam tried.

"Survivors' network," the man replied. "I met him at a gathering here in Boston. He was in a closed seminar about healing. We shared."

Sam tried not to bristle at the phrase. He knew it was only a matter of time before the man began to talk about closure.

"Shared what?"

"Umm, how should I address you, sir?" He spoke respectfully, even though he clearly had the upper crust.

"Not as *sir*, anyway. Charlie will do."

"Ok." The man shrugged. "I'm from money, Charlie. I had what we call here an Ivy League education, grew up in a big old house in the Hamptons – the whole nine yards." The man looked at Sam and it was his turn to shrug. "My family and I are … not real close any more." He got up then, walked a few paces and reached over the bar to grab a coffee pot. He poured himself a mug and sat down again, waiting for Sam to ask a question.

"You're going to need to keep going, I'm fresh eyes on this."

"Well, then, you'll need to be very, very careful because what I've got to say to you is exceptionally dangerous."

Sam hissed a breath out, trying to mask his frustration. "Exceptionally" didn't feel like a word people used without rehearsal. "So people keep telling me."

"I went home unexpectedly one night — to New York, from here in Boston. I was at Harvard." He paused and stared straight at Sam. Not a flinch did he receive in return. "I was gonna surprise my folks. I went around back and there were big cars in the space the staff would normally park, which was weird because visitors usually pull up out front. There were no cars at the front, not even my mom and dad's. I kicked around some and then I went to the dining room." He pulled a chug on his coffee mug and then cradled it again. "Our dining room is kind of like a library, Charlie. It's a big old room with a balcony all around, two doors attached to that and two stairways down to the dining area."

Sam nodded.

"The house was quiet, so for some reason I was moving around kind of quiet too, and when I opened the door to the balcony nobody in the dining room heard me."

Sam followed his logic and had an image of the layout in his head — old dark timber with a ladder on wheels to reach the books.

"Down below there were some real bad things going on."

Sam remained silent, and the man was forced to press on.

"There was a female at the centre of things. She was… being abused."

233

"A child?"

The man looked surprised. "Oh, no. A woman. A kind of, older lady. Maybe a little older than you?"

Sam ignored the implication but narrowed his eyes and tilted his head, waiting for more.

"They were taking it in turns, and there was some kind of reading. Not a prayer, but like a script. And I knew who was doing the talking. I stood frozen, afraid and watched. Things is, nobody was clothed, Charlie. It was bad. There were sheets, and there was blood."

Sam shook his head a little and held his hand out flat. He didn't need to hear any more of the horrors.

"Just tell me who was with your father," Sam said.

The barman's head jolted in surprise. "Oh, my dad wasn't there. These were friends of my mom."

That shocked Sam. Yes, he'd been told women were involved but he hadn't anticipated a mother being associated with something like that.

"Did they catch you? Is that why you're estranged?"

"No. They don't know I know. I just, well, I picked something up and I left. Quietly. After that I just withdrew. Dropped out of college, stopped taking her calls and her money. Started tending bar." He gestured at his surroundings. "She thought it was a phase or that I was doing drugs. She hasn't tried real hard to patch things up."

"You said you could identify these people?"

"I can identify one of them," he said.

"Your mum?"

"Well, sure, but I knew someone else down there."

"Who?" Sam couldn't help but shake his head as he struggled to keep the exasperation out of his voice.

"My tutor at Harvard. Well, he was back then – that's why I never went back to college. He's in politics now. He worked in the State Department, then he moved to the White House. He's like an advisor. I've seen him on CNN stalking around in the background. He's Irish and he's over in Ireland a lot."

Irish to an American could simply mean his name was Seamus. As it turned out, when Sam pressed the Harvard barman, the man was a third generation American.

"And you didn't go to the police?"

"No. But that's complicated."

"Yet you shared this ... this experience with the Dublin man, the counsellor?" he asked.

"I was at a seminar, all about healing. I shared. Not everything, I mean, I left my mom out of it and kept some parts vague. But it felt good to off load. Afterwards he came to me, and we talked. He came right out and described what had happened to some poor woman in Ireland and it fitted right in with what I'd seen in my mom's house. To hear someone else describe that sort of evil, I felt like I wasn't insane, you know?"

Sam nodded. The link was tenuous, though. The man was offering nothing to connect the abuse in Dublin to that in New York, and Sam knew there were twisted bastards all over the world.

"But, you're not suggesting that the Dublin thing and your thing are connected?"

"Oh sure they are," the man said, again surprised.

"How do you know?"

"See, Sir... Charlie, sorry. When I spoke privately to our mutual acquaintance from Dublin, he asked who was in the dining room that night."

"And you told him?"

"Sure. He looked up my tutor right there on his phone. He said straight off, that's the guy."

"And how did he know?"

"Well Charlie, I guess he's been helping the poor woman at the centre of the whole thing. And I guess that's how he knows. He told me it had been happening for a real long time."

"Where can I find this tutor, this advisor?"

"The Big A. There's an office on Lexington. It's close by some Irish folks who wine and dine big business people to try and get them to invest over there. It's part of the deal with the peace process."

There was a certain amount of logic to that. American business had been crucial to the rebuilding and rebranding of Northern Ireland after decades of violence.

Sam wanted to wrap it up and go. "What's his name?"

"Professor Marcus Agey."

"Is this tutor the only thing that makes you think that the Dublin abuse and what you saw are the same?"

The barman shook his head. "It's the same. It's the solstice, and the shaving, and the skinning. From what our Dublin friend described and what I saw, it all happened exactly the same way. The head, then the feet, on different sides of the pond. The old country and the new. This has probably gone on for generations."

Sam sat still for a moment and thought. Whether the two events were interwoven or not was almost beside the point provided the barman was telling the truth. Sam remained suspicious. The counsellor, as links went, was far from reliable and it crossed Sam's mind that there could be other motives at play behind this dreadful story. Perhaps the barman had grown to dislike his tutor for other reasons. Maybe he'd returned home to find the professor shagging his mother. He seemed to sense Sam's scepticism.

"There's something else," he said, his hands now inter-linked, one squeezing the other as if wringing it out.

"Go on then," Sam said.

"My dad," he said.

"I thought you said he wasn't there?"

"Well, no. I didn't say that. But as it happens he wasn't there."

"So?"

"So, I looked into a few things. I'm not real proud of this, but…"

"Probably best just to tell me it all now," Sam sighed.

"I took his check book. I was upset. I was gonna run and I needed some money. I couldn't ask my mom for it, not after…"

Sam nodded.

"I saw the stubs, you know? Of the checks he had written. My dad is kind of old fashioned."

Sam had no idea what was coming next, so he just shook his head in bewilderment at the pace of the delivery.

"This check book had been used for only one thing. It was for a separate account, I think. Not the one he used for my allowance. Not the business account. Different bank, different city."

"Right. Well, what had it been used for?"

"Every six months my dad wrote a check for twenty thousand dollars. It was made out to a convent. In Ireland. In Galway County."

Sam closed his eyes and sighed. "They were adopting children?" he asked.

"Oh, no," said the man. "The other way about. I can't be sure, but I think the convent was taking children, from the abuse of the woman. The person our Dublin friend calls the heir."

"Fucking hell," Sam muttered.

"I'm not sure my dad knows everything. I'm not sure he knows anything. It just, doesn't fit with him. He's kind, you know? A lot older than my mom. He's a bit of a sucker. Rich, but, impressionable I would say. But a good man, you know? He maybe got persuaded by my mom, or my grandfather to make donations or something. He's all that's stopped me going to the police. But I thought about it. Many times. Many, many times."

"What about your mother?"

"My mom is different. And her dad was a piece of work. My grandfather. He was always going to Ireland. I never felt comfortable around him. He was a creepy guy."

"I've heard of a man bringing children to a convent in Ireland," Sam said.

"When?"

Sam blew out, trying see if the timeline fitted. "The seventies, anyway. But this guy wasn't a young man then."

"Do you know anything else?"

"I was told he was a small man, maybe from New York. He had a comb over."

"That kinda fits with what I remember, but..." the bartender shrugged.

"Could have been anyone," Sam nodded.

"Look Charlie, I think it's the same. I can't prove anything, but that's just what I think. Somehow, it's been passed on."

Sam couldn't think of anything else to ask that he couldn't verify independently, so he shook the barman's hand to end the conversation. It was strong and sincere and came with a dramatic request. "Sir, you stop these people. You wipe them from the face of the earth."

Chapter 28

I f Sam harboured any real doubts as he emerged to the dazzle of the day, they were quickly extinguished. Wrapped in his thoughts at the start of his trek he didn't pay enough attention to what was happening around him and it took some minutes of walking to realise that the vagrant was back, only this time his stoop wasn't so low and his gait was livelier. The vagrant made his way through the buggies and shoppers, moving fast and determined, darting from side to side on the outside of his feet. Sam watched him with a growing realisation that the man was not what he had seemed. He moved too well, he was gym fit, and he had an eye on Sam that was no longer as crazy as it was determined.

With just enough space between them to sprint through his options and he knew there were two ways to deal with such a situation. His preference was to meet force head-on – that way the issue was dealt with and finished one way or another. The other option was to turn and run. He didn't think it through consciously but instinct told him that the earlier fracas with the vagrant had been a fishing trip to determine whether Sam was armed. The man headed towards him would not have gone down so easily otherwise. Physical confrontation would have confirmed to the supposed beggar that Sam had the Beretta tucked into the small of his back. Because the vagrant knew he was carrying, Sam knew the man wouldn't be alone. That he was prepared to confront Sam more than suggested he had backup, which meant Sam had to turn and run.

Sam hated running, always had. Not just running away, which he loathed, but actual physical running. He did it, of course, but not well and not particularly fast. "By Strength and Guile" was the service's motto. At his age he preferred the second bit.

Sam's slow start was hindered by a hankering to fight and by some stout, short Americans warbling around like bowling skittles just short of a strike. He cut down Beacon, and from then on was cursed by the sun directly overhead. He needed it to find east and keep on going. His navigation was on his wits and his eyes hunted as he ran, trying to find a means of cutting back to where he'd started in the hope that those following him wouldn't think to return there.

As he moved he caught sight of some vans marked "Suffolk University". He turned into a car park muttering a prayer of thanks because he knew that students would provide what he was looking for. Sure enough, chained to a lamp post were four bicycles. Mercifully, one was secured through the front wheel, another through the back and both had quick-release nuts. He left the front wheel of one bike chained to the post, set the frame aside and then took the free wheel off the bike chained by its rear. It wasn't a perfect match – he had no front brakes, but he didn't plan on stopping.

Sam slung on his sunnies, ripped a Red Sox cap off a shopfront display as he cycled past and made for the sea, instantly anonymous. They were hunting for a man on foot – bikes wouldn't enter their field of vision. No one ever expects someone to escape on a pushbike, but bicycles are like low-hanging fruit – ripe and plentiful and people naturally look at the machine, not its rider. They were, in his estimation, ideal for extraction.

Ideal if you know where you're going. Sam reckoned he could get to Logan International Airport in about twenty minutes. All he could think of was east and as his legs pumped he plotted the geography in his head. There was a bridge, which wasn't perfect – a bike would be out of place on a flyover and if he got caught, there was only one way to escape. He didn't fancy a dip in the Mystic, which made him think of a Van Morrison song. But the river was shaken from his mind by the sight of two athletic types and the vagrant standing together on a street corner. They looked around urgently. Perhaps it was arrogance, perhaps it was to test them, but he cycled straight by and they didn't even register his passing. The two strangers were dressed like they meant business: rugged trainers, strong canvas trousers that looked casual but had purpose, and windcheaters over body armour. Sam wondered just what sort of wasp nest he'd disturbed.

He kept the wheels turning and eventually saw signs for ferries. Long Wharf was the first option he noticed so he ditched the hybrid bike and started to walk, trying to slow his heart rate. As the boat pulled away from the quay he looked back on the city and dropped the Beretta overboard. He was glad not to have needed it, even as a deterrent. Next thought, New York.

———

THE BIG A wasn't much of a peg to hang a hat on. Other than that the only steer Sam had was the barman's mention of the Lexington office. He couldn't imagine how many tens or hundreds of thousands Manhattan hosted every day. He was tired and a bit belligerent and so threw caution to the breeze and phoned New York's Northern Ireland office and asked for Professor Marcus Agey. The receptionist was surprisingly helpful.

"Oh, he doesn't work from this office, sir," she said, and duly gave him the correct address, which, as the barman had said, was on Lexington. Sam checked into a hotel by the same name and got some sleep despite some unnerving artwork on the walls.

The professor's office was a skip up the street, hidden behind a glass affront to compassionate reflection. Beneath it was a Pret a Manger, so he started there. After an hour he realised it was useless. He could be on someone's doorstep in New York for a year and never see them.

Five cups of wishy-washy coffee later, he settled on a plan. Perhaps it was the upped caffeine intake, perhaps it was irritation at the rigmarole he'd managed to get himself into, but he decided on a direct approach. At a RadioShack he bought the closest thing he could find in place of a GoPro camera – a barrel-like device for sports action shots that would normally be fixed to a helmet. Then he bought a fancy leather binder and writing pad to conceal the camera in the spine.

He made his way back past the Pret and into the reception where he asked for the professor, again, by name. Americans, he mused, could be so polite when you're white and show some authority and manners. The security man consulted his computer, directed him to the sixteenth and used a pass to authorise the lift, which, typical of all skyscraper lifts in the US, reminded Sam of being at sea in a trawler plummeting and hurtling on the waves of a storm.

He had to make like he was meant to be there, so when the doors pinged he waltzed forward, hoovering in the surroundings and selecting one of three further reception desks. Once close he leaned forward and quietly asked an elderly woman for Professor Agey. She responded in kind and in a whisper asked if he had an appointment.

"If you could tell him I have an update from Dublin, please," Sam said conspiratorially, momentarily raising his eyebrows.

She nodded inscrutably and hobbled off to an office on the left. Sam, meanwhile, pointed his fancy binder at her back.

His heart rate increased slightly at the ease with which he seemed to be obtaining access. He suppressed his shock that he'd managed to get upstairs, never mind into the office.

The old woman emerged ahead of a bloke who couldn't have been more academic if he'd tried. A tweed three-piece with leather elbow patches hung unflatteringly from small shoulders. A dicky bow wouldn't have looked out of place around the man's neck, which supported a chin with a patchy beard. When the professor's eyes met Sam's, his face frowned in a mixture of suspicion and alarm.

"Come in, please, Mr …"

"Charlie is fine," Sam said, worrying again that he was getting cocky. He knew he should be more careful yet he found his caution evaporating. He checked himself. He should be worrying – he had been seen by so many people.

The professor turned and his little legs carried him back

across the large room to his office. He moved in a little and held the door open, glaring warily at Sam. Sam walked past into a roomy office with a large window over which venetian blinds tilted to keep out the reflections from surrounding skyscrapers. There were tall plants and book cases filled with tomes. The professor closed the door behind Sam then hurried around him to the shelter of an enormous desk, and they both sat. "How can I help you, Mr ... Charlie?"

Sam noticed the worry fall away from the tutor and the semblance of a snigger curl on the edge of the query. He positioned the binder nonchalantly on the desk between them and came right out with it.

"Do you know who I am?"

"Well you didn't make an appointment, so..." he opened his hands and raised his eyebrows as if to say, what am I to tell you?

Sam couldn't decide whether the man was panicking or posturing. His head offered a barely perceptible shake, the tiniest of tremors but the man didn't take his eyes off Sam.

"I know about Dublin." Sam paused. "I know about the convent. I know about the Hamptons. I know that you are part of a group that abuses children, that skins them, that locks them up, that kills them. I know what you did."

The professor started making an odd sort of noise and stretched his mouth open as if flexing the muscles in his jaw. Sam noticed a fidget in his fingers until he eventually composed himself. Beady little eyes widened and retracted. The man looked at the wall, then at the desk, then at Sam's binder as he gradually settled on a course of action. Sam watched an epiphany, like the professor had always known this moment would come. The man seemed to work through pre-prepared motions as he summoned some protocol. Then there was a faint chuckle before the professor eventually raised his gaze. He leaned forward, as if possessed by a new confidence, their eyes locked and he spoke.

"You know nothing, Sam."

Chapter 29

S am had nobody to blame but himself.

He tried to calm down, to turn the anger and shock into some sort of useful action. Immediately he thought of Isla, of what they might know and that fear brought an explosive urge to smash the man's face in. Instead he found himself rising, desperate to make contact with her, to know she was safe.

He lifted the folder, his mind reeling. He couldn't understand why he was so surprised. He knew he'd been placed under surveillance. He also knew in his heart that it had somehow been triggered before he'd even taken on the counsellor's job, which was a measure of how good their intel was and of their paranoia. The irony, though, struck hard. If they hadn't sent that goon to his boat to kill him, Sam would never have become involved. He simply hadn't believed the counsellor or had any notion of taking on his job. But he was where he was.

Sam turned back as he left the outer office to catch a glimpse of the professor flipping open a laptop. He was familiar with the make – a MacBook Air. The thin black cover made it look like any other machine but Sam could make out the glow of the Apple symbol through it. It gave him an idea as he'd carried on past the old receptionist and into the lift. He was itching to check the small camera to make sure it had recorded the conversation.

Sam didn't bother concealing his return to the hotel; he wouldn't be staying. There, he got his stuff together and consulted a concierge map of Manhattan. Back on the street a yellow cab shuttled him, deep in thought, to the Apple Store on Fifth Avenue. Thirty minutes later, using a brothel-stolen credit card he bought a MacBook Air, a black cover and was getting various pieces of software installed. The whole lot went into a new ruck with zips and pouches for passports and camera bits. The order provided by the little bergen would normally have pleased him, but he didn't have time to think about anything other than his next move.

At H&M he bought a full set of clothes and bundled his old ones into his original canvas bag. More wit was required. He was worried there could be residue on his clothing from the old Beretta he had stolen from the kid in Boston and if his plan was to work, he could afford no slip-ups or delays at airport security. With new Nikes and the subway he made his way back, leaving his old bag on the train.

On Lexington he took up a position opposite the Pret and watched the doors. He couldn't be sure the professor was still in there, so he decided that if the secretary came out first, he would go with her. If her boss beat her to it, all to the good. Either way, by nightfall he intended to be outside the professor's house. At 1730 the avenue was mobbed. A tsunami of commuters drained down into the subway stations and he began to panic that he would miss them both. He fought through the wave to stand in the arch of the Pret where he waited an uncomfortable but determined twenty minutes before the old receptionist emerged from the door and joined the current. She was slow, which made it more difficult to keep pace, but by bus and by foot they got there together, to a nicely kept little street in a Jersey suburb. Her house had handrails screwed onto the walls either side of the door and a ramp, which indicated that Sam might find leverage inside. He waited, gathering bearings, making sure. A few minutes later a young woman emerged. She was wearing a tunic, plain trousers and trainers. Sam pulled on a pair of gloves.

Ten minutes after the receptionist entered her little house, he knocked. She wasn't so much surprised as alarmed when she opened the door and recognised him, but to his shame her alarm was about to escalate. There was no room for apology for what he was about to do – he needed her to be scared, for a little while at least. She remained silent as he bundled her back inside and when he got into the kitchen he saw why. In a motorised chair was an older man, Sam assumed her husband. He was frail and curled, with saliva dropping from his lower lip. Dementia, he imagined, which made what he was about to do harder to justify but easier to achieve. She would protect him at all costs.

"I need the address of your boss," he told her.

She stared at him. He could see she was a tough enough nut and on a different day, in a different place, he had no doubt she would have defied him. But she was a carer, and that meant the well-being of someone she loved depended on her own health and safety. That was something he could identify with in that moment; it was his advantage, and his leverage.

"If I don't get the address, this won't end well." He

spoke in a low, steady tone – factual, cold, detached. "He'll watch you die," Sam pointed at the man in the chair, "then he'll be left alone with you dead on the floor. He will starve to death."

Sam's cards were good. He was aware of his capacity to appear menacing, but if she saw him out, he knew he would have to fold and leave. He stared into her eyes but found he couldn't read her.

She broke. Lifting a small pad from beside an antiquated telephone, she wrote down an address and handed it to him.

He looked at what she had written. "If you talk to the police, I'll be back. If this address isn't correct, I'll be back. Do you understand?" She didn't answer but he could see the debate churning behind her glare. "Am I going to have to come back?"

She pursed her lips and turned to the pad again. She wrote something on the top sheet and ripped it off. Handing a new address to him, she said, "This is his place. Now leave us alone!" She moved in front of the old man as if to shield him.

Sam walked around her and removed scissors from a magnetic strip on the wall before snipping the curly phone line. The old woman shivered as he passed, which felt awful and ideal at the same time. He needed her to remain afraid. "Write down the phone number of the home help," he told her.

"Who?" she asked.

"The woman who left a few minutes ago – she's a nurse of some sort."

"Why?" she cried, as if faced with some fresh hell.

"Because tomorrow's the weekend. I'm assuming she doesn't come on weekends because you're here. I'm going to lock you in a room for one day and when I've spoken to the professor, then I'll call the nurse to let you out."

He watched as proper panic set in. Her jaw dropped and tears welled in her eyes. She opened her mouth as if to say something but firmly shut it again, her lips thinning, her eyes darting from side to side. Eventually she lifted the pad and wrote a number down. She tore it off and handed it to him. He cut from her glare to look at the note. There was a silence for a full minute as he waited for her to verbalise whatever was alarming her. "He's not at home," she blurted. "My boss. He's flying. Tonight. From JFK."

The idea of being locked up until he found the professor was evidently too much. Sam kept the pressure on. "Where's he flying to?"

"Belfast, but through London – I couldn't get him a direct flight."

"When did he ask you to book it?"

She was shaking now, rapidly becoming a blubbering mess and he knew he was going to get all the information he needed, grim as he felt about it.

"About five minutes after you left his office."

"Did he make any calls?" Sam strove to maximise this rich flow of information.

"He used Hangouts. I never make those calls for him. He does it on his computer, with earphones."

Sam knew she was telling the truth. "Do you know what this is about?" he probed.

She paused for a moment. "I know it must be something to do with Ireland. You're Irish, he's over there all the time. You could be IRA."

Sam actually snorted. "Get some food and whatever medication he needs," he told her before walking into the hall.

There was a box room, which seemed cruel, but he had no choice. If he locked them in a room with a window, she could summon help in an instant. He turned back to find her holding a Tupperware tub and a plate heaped with leftovers.

"Who does your boss speak to? Who are his contacts in Ireland?"

"I don't know," she said, firmly. The old woman was gathering a bit of composure and Sam could tell his time was running out in all sorts of ways. "He flies in two hours. You should get out and leave us be," she said.

"One last thing, where did you book him in to stay in Ireland?"

She looked confused. "He stays at the apartment?"

"Where?"

"Belfast. They all stay there."

"They all?" Sam exasperation crept into his voice.

"Just who are you?" she countered, now as curious as he was.

"Well, I'm not the IRA. Your boss is into some pretty sick stuff. That's what this is about."

"What sort of stuff?" she asked, moving closer, peering up at him, suddenly more curious than afraid.

Sam registered her interest and was taken aback. "Abuse," he said, intending on leaving it at that. To his surprise she nodded. "You knew?"

"You never *know*," she said, "but I *do know* how malicious he can be." She turned to walk towards the man, looking lovingly at him. "And I'm wise enough to know how well connected he is, for no apparent reason. How a man like that got a job advising government people." She shook her head and tutted as she stroked the man's hair. "I'm in no position to challenge someone like that." She rounded her gaze onto him. "And I've been around long enough to know that if you're going to stop him, then you're not like him, and that means you're not going to hurt me or Hans." She wiped his chin as a mother might an infant.

"Tell me who the others are, those who stay at the apartment?" he pressed.

"I don't know. He deals with all of that directly. I have no contact with any of them."

"So how do you know there are others?"

"Because I organise the cleaning. The laundry bill lists five sets of bed sheets. I book the transfers to the airport. Why would one man need a seven-seat vehicle to pick him up?"

Sam nodded. "I'll let you out just as soon as I can," he said.

"What – but what about the bathroom?" The surprise on her face told him she thought she'd done enough to not be banged up.

"Get a bucket," he told her, and took the plate and tub from her grasp and placed it in the box room.

She got a bottle of water and wheeled the old man inside the tiny space. She was utterly compliant, no longer out of fear but perhaps because of a feeling she was doing it for the greater good. Then she retrieved a bucket from a kitchen cupboard. Sam didn't want to consider the logistics of its deployment; he felt bad enough as it was. The door was hinged favourably and it took no more than a broom handle broken to size and levered against the hall wall opposite to incarcerate them.

Chapter 30

Sam missed the professor at JFK. He stood at the check-in desk and tapped his hand irritably on the counter. He wanted to call his parents, check on Isla, but he was wary of being watched, of someone seeing him make a call from a public phone and using it to find them.

"Can I pay extra?" Sam tried to keep his cool.

"I'm really sorry, sir. The seat price doesn't change a thing. There's no room on the flight," the clerk sang to him.

He held a wedge of notes before her, most of it sterling. "I'll pay whatever it takes," he said.

"Sir, I am sorry but that's just not how it works." She shook her head and glanced at the queue behind him. "I have you right here on the reserve list and if a seat becomes available, you're welcome to it."

It wasn't until ten minutes before the gate closed that Sam was approached by the same young woman, who delivered the good news that someone hadn't turned up for the flight and the seat was his. She encouraged him to get to security "real quick".

He prayed he could board from the rear and get a seat behind the professor. There was nothing more conspicuous than a late arrival to an aircraft tacking up the aisle like a sailmaker's stitch.

Sam couldn't see the tutor as he took his seat, but it was a big plane. He made sure the man wouldn't recognise him, even on a trip to the toilet, by keeping his head down and his hat on. Sam put in headphones, took out the Mac and camera and used them to play back the media.

The conversation with the tutor was audible and in frame, but his hopes for it were quickly dashed. His intention had been to send the professor's admission to *The Boston Globe* but Sam was the one doing all the talking. No amount of editing would prove the tutor guilty. Worse still, he'd identified Sam by name. Sam was hazy on the particulars but conscious that the law around secret recording was much stricter in the USA than the UK, so he gave it up as a waste of time and thought the flight would be better spent trying to get some kip. Then an idea began to form and he returned to the computer. He fumbled about with editing software to ensure he duplicated only the part of the parent file where he levelled the allegations at the tutor and watched the reaction. Then he erased his own voice and the parent file, ensuring the original media file had been properly trashed and emptied. As the computer was new, there was nothing else on it but the exchange between them – no documents, no media, no photos. He relaxed. It had taken half of the seven-hour flight to perform the task but he had achieved something. And now he could doze.

Sam knew Heathrow well. There was no other way to get on the domestic flight to Belfast except through Terminal 5, so he hurried to get there ahead of the professor. On the Heathrow Express he connected to the Wi-Fi and used WeTransfer to send the video file to himself. The progress symbol ticked round interminably but completed before he hopped off the carriage, with just enough time to erase the rest of the hard drive.

His plan required proximity and that made him jumpier than usual. Tiredness had exacerbated his paranoia. That the professor knew his name and whereabouts suggested that he might also be looking for Isla. Sam couldn't shake the pestering fear that the professor's people might already know where she was, even if *he* did not. Sam was therefore out of options – the tutor's sick group of friends had to be dealt with in its entirety.

Sam needed to get through to the departures area, which meant another cash transaction at the British Airways desk, another flash of ID, another risk taken. His main problem, though, was security. Heathrow, he knew, was tight. He watched the lift for fifteen minutes, willing the professor to come through, and just as Sam believed he'd missed his mark, a green tweed three-piece ambled into view. The tutor was fumbling with his rucksack, a throwback to the fifties, academic in appearance and made of beige canvas and brown leather. His distraction allowed Sam to fall in behind him, have his face scanned and be waved into the queue for X-ray at the tutor's heel.

They stood silently, edging forward by pace and pause, the professor no more agitated than most travellers. Sam had the chance to see him prepare and re-prepare for the conveyor and the machine. Out came a little bag of toiletries, toothbrush, aftershave, toothpaste and floss. Then he remembered something in his inside coat pocket and after much fiddling produced an e-cigarette that he tried to fit into the clear plastic bag. As they neared the top of the queue and a security guard with his hand on the retractable belt barrier, Sam shuffled with insistence behind the professor to avoid being funnelled off to another team. The tutor didn't appear to notice Sam watching his unpacking like a hawk.

"Please remove any liquids, computers, tablets, Kindles and place them on separate trays," called the woman with the plastic tubs. She sounded like a town crier.

The tutor wrestled with the buckles on his bag and hauled out his MacBook to place alone in a tray. Sam made sure he set his in the same way in the tub beside it. The tutor fiddled and flustered, unfastening his belt and stooping to unlace his shoes, which was probably unnecessary. Sam had taken the time to think it all through and was better prepared, so he filed around the tutor's back and walked though the scanner tube, urging it to render him clear. He got out of the machine with a nod from the security personnel and tried to subdue his adrenaline as he made for the MacBooks. The professor's tub came out first, ahead of his, and Sam's heart fluttered when he saw how battered the computer casing looked compared to his own. But it was take or break, so he lifted it and willed his bag to emerge without further scrutiny. Sam grabbed it just as the professor came through the arch. One movement disposed of the tray and the target laptop was stowed and zipped in before the tutor had time to compose himself. Sam sidled off as the professor hopped around in his socks trying to replace his brogues.

The Belfast flight was two hours away, which offered Sam another opportunity. He watched his mark wander off, gazing up at the shops and eateries. The tutor paused at Wagamamas, where there was a queue for tables, before moving on. Sam followed at a distance until the little man turned back, apparently having changed his mind. Sam had no choice but to keep going, waiting a good ten minutes before returning to join the queue for Japanese food. He used the enforced break to wash his face and buy some sticking plasters at a pharmacy. The queue had emptied in his absence and he was ushered to a spot overlooking the concourse. The professor was at the bar, not far away. They were seated back to back, two single travellers eating in silence. Sam could see him, but only just, in the reflection of the glass in front of him. He had no idea whether the professor would do what he needed him to do, but he couldn't take his eyes off him and happily accepted the waiter's recommendation, whatever it was, and ate it without looking.

When he'd finished the professor started fishing around at his feet and drew out the laptop. If he noticed anything wrong, he didn't show it, and Sam began to move. The start-up chime was Sam's cue to whip his phone from a pocket and he stroked it into video mode and swivelled his stool to aim the camera at the stainless hood above the tutor. The shot, however, was rubbish, so he was forced to take the risk of getting in close. Putting the phone to his ear, he walked over and reached in between the professor and the woman beside him to grab a basket of soy sauce and forks, loitering longer than was decent. He had no idea whether he had what he needed, but he'd run out of reasons to stay longer.

Back in the toilets he sat on the pan, phone in hand. Turning down the sound, he consulted the video, convinced that his good luck was sure to have run out. There he watched it all back: his clumsy attempt to catch the reflection above the professor's head, the meandering stretch for the sauce and then, in the bottom left-hand corner of the screen, the flutter of the tutor's fingers on the keyboard.

Sam caught five letters, VISIT, before the image moved out of shot. On repeated playback he heard the stroke of three more keys.

Sam opened the tutor's laptop and wondered what on earth the little man must be thinking – the screen saver wasn't even the same. Sam stuck a plaster over the webcam and paused. The possibilities were pretty much endless. He strained to remember the briefings they'd been given on observation training – the old DET instructors revelling in their connivance and cunning. Breaking passwords had been mentioned but he couldn't recall anything specific. Sam sat on the shitter and went for the obvious, simply adding ING to the password box. It vibrated to indicate a mistake. ORS he tried instead.

He was in.

Chapter 31

I t turned out that they weren't on the same plane to Belfast, but it didn't matter to Sam. He knew exactly where the tutor was going. The drop-off address was in the taxi confirmation email sent by his secretary, who was wedged in a box room with her dementia-suffering husband three and a half thousand miles away. Sam could make the call to the couple's nurse in a while but there was one more task to perform before he could release them. He hoped she would understand, even if she never knew the extent of the guilt setting in.

He could feel the doom building now that he was back on home turf. It took the same path as previous attacks. On tour he was able to focus on the job, on killing and not being killed. It wasn't until he got leave that the horrors began.

When he got to Belfast City Airport there was no escaping the remorse, or the fear. He pictured the distress of the old man in his wheelchair, his wife stroking his withered veiny arm. The noise in his head grew as the magnitude of the responsibility he'd heaped upon his parents dawned on him and the uncertainty he had around their safety increased. He knew they would protect Isla with everything they had, but they were civilians, and kind, gentle people to boot. They were also blissfully unaware of what was really going on.

He hired a car at the airport and on the Newtownards Road stopped at one of the few phone boxes left in the city. There he dialled his dad, then his mum but got no answer from either. He ached to hear Isla and had to work hard to lower his heart rate and purge the panic. He reminded himself over and over that his folks didn't always answer their phones and didn't carry them in their pockets. He imagined them having their evening meal at a beach restaurant, their phones buzzing in a car or a hotel room. But the squeal was returning; he could feel the start of its whine. It started somewhere in his inner ear and although it felt as if it had been there all the time, he only became conscious of it when that bottomless foreboding crept in.

He dialled again and again, each time becoming more agitated. He allowed himself the anger. He knew it had to surface before it could be purged. Before long there was blood everywhere and the handset was in pieces and his jeans were torn from what remained of the glass walls of the phone box. The frenzy slowly subsided as he slumped in the cubicle, utterly helpless to protect his daughter or his parents from a threat he couldn't be sure they faced.

He knew such outbursts weren't down to PTSD alone. He'd experienced anger attacks before he was forced into the corps and, ironically, the trouble they got him into became the reason he ended up in the military in the first place. But the service just channelled the violence and gave that occasional anger a grip that his teenaged years couldn't have imagined.

As he slowly calmed, his attention shifted from what he couldn't do to what he could. He made his way back to the car.

———

THE APARTMENT WAS on one of Belfast's finest roads. Trees lined the wide avenue that had pillars at either side of the entrance: one way in, one way out. The car he'd rented was easily the least expensive of all parked on that road. Even the children of its residents drove more upmarket models. The lit-up apartment was the top floor of the four-storey building. There was a balcony and Sam could tell that the professor was home because the tutor came out after a few hours to puff on his vape. Sam worried that there might be someone inside who was objecting to his habit, hence why he came out to smoke, but he saw no evidence of company. If there was nobody else there, it simply suggested routine.

Sam looked up at him from the anonymity of his parked car, musing that less than eighteen hours had passed since he had confronted the man in New York. He wondered how the professor would react if he could see him now, sitting beneath him. Sam knew he would have watched the only media on the Mac. He wondered how the professor had reacted when he saw the exchange, his own response to the allegations. He hoped it had been deeply, deeply unnerving, and that the confusion as to how the computer swap had come about had disturbed him beyond his ability to sleep. Psychologically, having the upper hand was important. Sam would have preferred that the tutor imagined him still in

Manhattan scrabbling around for a lead. The computer swap may have disrupted that but it was worth it. The professor's inevitable agitation gave Sam a certain degree of comfort, but not as much as the realisation that he could see the man's legs quite clearly – the base of the balcony being made from reinforced glass plates. Sam decided to wait a while longer to establish the little man's routine. An hour later the tutor appeared again in a plume of vapour, gnawing on his pipe before sliding the door across once again to return inside.

Eventually another light came on, followed by the first light going off, and then a softer glow beneath a blind. The time watching had given Sam an opportunity to think. He knew from the receptionist that there were at least five bedrooms in the apartment but there was a light in just one. Sam felt strongly that the professor was alone, for the moment.

But it was too soon to deal with him. Sam needed to interrogate the man's computer properly first. His worry was that the tutor may be able to locate the missing laptop as soon as it was connected it to the internet and Sam needed the internet to get any new emails or messages, which he felt were sure to be relevant.

Sam needed expert help.

Chapter 32

He drove straight to Dublin and appeared unannounced at midnight on the doorstep of the charity woman. She was, of course, enormously impressed.

"Sam?"

"I really need a hand."

"Of course. But now?"

"I'm afraid so."

"What is it?"

"Can I come in?"

"Yes, sorry. Of course. Are you ok?"

"Yeah. Is your sister here?"

"You can wake her but you'd need the heart of a lion."

By 1 a.m. her twin's growling face was aglow with the reflection of the professor's computer. Within minutes there were wires going into and sticking out of it as she copied the entire contents onto a stick the size of his finger.

"Ah, bollocks," Áine said about twenty minutes into the process.

"What is it?" Charity asked.

"He's got an MDM and it's wiping."

Sam knew broadly what that meant – some sort of mobile device manager. He just closed his eyes and prayed.

The twin worked furiously with the keyboard and the cables. "Ok, now we see what the diddly dory is," she said as she untethered the tutor's computer and slotted the drive into her own laptop. "Ah, it's grand. His hard drive's all there, that's it cracked too. There shouldn't be any files you can't see."

Sam was tempted to ask for her help to navigate around its contents but he needed to do something else while it was still dark outside.

"Can you find a number for him, a contact number?" he asked her.

"Of course." She looked at him as if he was a dope. "It'll be here in his text messages." She stirred two fingers around the trackpad.

"Oh, an American number," she said, and read it to him. He wrote it down on the back of his hand. "Is it stolen?" she asked.

"It was picked up by mistake," he said.

"This is all totally illegal, like," the twin snapped, accusingly.

"I'm sorry. But I really appreciate it."

"I didn't do it for you. I did it for her."

———

TWENTY MINUTES later Sam bought yet another burner phone from a service station on Dublin's M50. It was a tiny place, cheap as chips, and its security cameras were dummies. He then roasted up the road at over one hundred miles an hour. At his dad's workshop he threw a wrap of Pozidrivs, a socket set and a suction handle into a tool bag and headed for Belfast. He gave a lot of thought to the practicalities of his next move and virtually none to the implications. His mind craved relief and implications wouldn't bring the succour he desired.

Sam thanked God for the affluence of the people on that Belfast road. That type of wealth could purchase privacy through influence on the city's planning committee. The apartment block occupied by the professor had been designed with meticulous attention to detail. No balcony was visible from the windows of any other flat, and the lush trees gave him just about enough cover to clamber up, his tools swinging precariously from his belt.

Four o'clock, he reckoned, was the time when virtually nothing happens – the decent period between asleep and awake. He knew this from countless dreadful hours on surveillance in gutters, in refuse sites, on cliffs and in cars, watching bad people get rest while his limbs seized. By four thirty he had unfastened the glass floor of the small balcony and raised it against the balustrade. By five a.m. the professor was dead.

Suicide seemed to Sam to be the best option. Murder would invite vigorous inquiry by the police, but of greater concern was what the professor's friends would make of it all.

He tried not to be pleased with himself but it had gone incredibly smoothly. All he'd had to do was phone the man. Sam debated briefly what to say, but nothing seemed fitting – nothing that would achieve what he wanted, so he chose just to let the tutor know that he was close by, to spook him and place him under enough pressure that he would move, hopefully in the right direction, without thinking. The phone rang three times before it was answered.

"Hello?" The tutor sounded like he hadn't been asleep.

"You're in Belfast, you're in an apartment and you're finished," Sam said and ended the call. Then he watched.

No lights came on, which didn't surprise him. He imagined the tutor lying there, stock-still, computing. He wasn't a physical man; he would interrogate the silence and worry that someone was inside the apartment. He might stay in bed and wait for daylight, which was alarmingly imminent, but he might eventually take a look around. Fifteen minutes passed and Sam knew that his window to make this clean and easy was closing. He stared at the balcony doors and ground his teeth.

Suddenly a tiny blue dot appeared behind the glass, which confused him initially, until it partly illuminated a small fog and he realised it was the vape working furiously. The professor was looking out. Sam swore at his own stupidity – of course the man wouldn't go outside when he was afraid.

He hunched over in the car seat and held the burner phone under the steering wheel and between his knees. He removed the caller identification in settings and composed a text: *You have been compromised. He's coming to the apartment. Find a back way out.*

It did the trick. Sam sat up and saw the glow of the tutor's phone as it received his message. Then he caught a glimpse of his face as the door slid back, and a flash as the phone's light twisted and plummeted downwards. Then nothing. Silence. Sam didn't even hear the impact. He fumbled for the car's internal light switch to make sure it wouldn't come on when he opened the door and walked over to where the professor lay. He didn't need to crouch down to make sure – the man was dead. His shoulders had somehow hit the ground first and his head was stove into his chest. Sam found his phone a few feet away. The screen was covered in cracks, but incredibly it still seemed to work. He used a warm dead thumb to unlock it and took it behind a set of bins to reset the password. The last attention he gave it was to place it in airplane mode before dropping it into his own pocket.

The climb to the balcony was made easier by the injection of adrenaline. The risk had been heightened given that he was now a killer; previously he'd been just a burglar. The glass was replaced with greater care than it had been removed. The post-mortem examination would show no evidence of bruising or pushing. There were no fingerprints, and it would be assumed the professor had jumped. Sam was gone by five o'clock.

It was enormously satisfying, and the biggest mistake he could have made.

Chapter 33

The burner phone was flung out the window into the Lagan as he crossed Shaw's Bridge, closely followed like a frisbee by the professor's laptop. He was freezing because he was tired and he needed either coffee or sleep. He wanted to get to the boat, fire up the Eberspacher heater and interrogate the tutor's files.

Once aboard he realised how big his error had been. It took an hour to erase his own laptop and replace it, in its entirety, with the professor's files from Áine's little drive. Sam couldn't do it all without connecting to the internet, which he imagined came with huge risk, but he had no choice. Eventually he was able to tap his way through the tutor's folders that were frustratingly bereft of detail. Much of it was work-related – strategy for investment, advice for media communications, copies of speeches. His email was regimented, factual and perfunctory.

There was an application on the desktop he was unfamiliar with that appeared to be a video-conferencing tool. Sam hammered around it for a while looking for a record of conversations, but it looked like a live-streaming hook-up app, probably a bit like Skype, he imagined. However, there was another application that appeared to have the means to capture and record whatever was shown on the screen. That seemed like an exciting prospect but he struggled to find evidence that the professor had made any such recordings. He went back to the hook-up software, opened the professor's profile and found the last number dialled. He scribbled it down on the now shabby piece of paper the receptionist had given him. Looking at the scrap of paper, he became distracted by guilt: the old woman and her husband were still locked up.

Sam made his way ashore to make the call. If the professor's friends were tracking his phone, he wanted to confuse them as much as possible. He drove fifteen miles before stopping and pulled out the handset. What harm? he reckoned. Using it would only serve to blow more smoke around the place. If some copper did manage to piece the crazy pattern together in years to come, he deserved to get caught.

Ten in the morning in Belfast was 5 a.m. in New York. He dialled the number the receptionist had given him.

"Yes?" The nurse answered abruptly, concerned.

Sam affected the best North American accent he could. "I'm calling about the old lady ..." he paused, realising he didn't know her name, "and her husband Hans."

"Hans is her brother," came the curt reply, which taught Sam not to make assumptions. "It's the middle of the night. Who are you? What's going on?"

"They're stuck in a room inside their house. They need help to get out. Can you go to them?"

"Sure, of course. Are they ok?"

"They're fine." He imagined the best scenario.

"How do you kn—"

"You need to go now. They need help."

"Uh-huh, I'm getting up right now."

He tapped the big red button.

The receptionist and Hans had been banged up for a full day and a half. He had caused them pain but he could live with it. It was time to move on.

Sam was about to swipe the phone back into airplane mode when something occurred to him. Someone involved in the professor's brand of grotesque behaviour might want to maintain some form of insurance policy. He was part of a group after all, and groups often argue, individuals fall out. If one of them was compromised, what was to stop that person from betraying the others in return for some sort of leniency?

He stared at the phone and put himself in the professor's place. The tutor was, by definition, a clever man. If he'd made any sensitive or secret recordings, it would make sense that he wouldn't keep them on his hard drive. Computers are cumbersome, you can't take them everywhere with you, they break, and the man had learned the hard way that they can get mixed up at airports. So, if not on a computer, where would he keep an insurance policy? On a pen drive or an SD card? Probably, Sam thought. But drives and cards can be lost or stolen more easily than computers, and in any case you need a computer to view the contents.

Sam tempered his expectations. He had no reason to get excited. It was a very long shot but the phone in his hand offered an opening. Staring at the settings option, he wondered whether the tutor might keep his insurance on hand, or actually *in* his hand.

He punched in the new code he'd assigned to the

professor's phone and swiped through to his photos folder. It was empty. Sam's heart sank a little. Then he opened iMovie, which was also empty. He thumped his head back against the headrest and allowed the frustration to pass. Realising he'd left the phone live, he went back to trigger airplane mode once more. In settings, in haste, he nudged the screen and the option for iCloud caught his eye.

While he understood the premise of cloud technology, he wasn't a regular user. Sam knew that everything was stored on a server somewhere. It saved space on devices until the user dragged down whatever music or movies they desired. He messed about in the options for a while but it didn't seem obvious to him how to view the contents of the professor's cloud. Sam wondered about third parties – about using the cloud to share with others. If the professor did have any photos or videos, he might have shared them with someone else. Assuming any had been kept on the cloud at all.

Sam could only remember a few email addresses by heart: his parents and that of his dead wife, and, of course, Fran and the charity woman. He had no desire to involve anybody new, so he put out an appeal to Charity.

"Hi," he said when she picked up.

"Have you even been to sleep?" she began.

"I need another favour," he said. "Is your sister there?"

"She is."

"I want to share some photos with you but I can't see them. Maybe she can talk me through it? I'm sorry, it's complicated. I don't even know if they're there."

"I have no idea what you're talking about, so, here, talk to her."

The phone rumbled as it was handed over and he could hear a few mumbled words of explanation before the twin came on the line. There followed a list of instructions and actions he knew he'd never be able to retrace, but after five minutes he was back on to Charity.

"So I think that's the cloud account shared with you. Can you have a look and see if there are any videos or photos on it, please? I'll call you back shortly."

"I'm tied up all morning. Will this afternoon do?" she asked.

"No, I'm sorry, it's really important. Can you have a look, please?"

"Right, so. I'll call you back as soon as I can, and, Sam?"

"Yes?"

"I'll help you any time, just like you helped me. But I'll …" he heard her walking, "get it in the neck if there are any more late night visits."

"Understood," he told her. "But, again, this is really important."

"Is it dangerous?" she asked.

He hadn't the heart to lie to her. "For me, yes. For you, I don't think so, but, honestly, I don't know yet."

———

HE DROVE to the closest town and thumbed coins into a public phone like rounds into a gun belt. His forehead rested against the glass and his eyes closed as ring after ring became a dead tone. At least he knew his folks' phones were charged, which suggested they were ok. But then if everything was grand, why would they not answer? The sickness in his gut grew and grew and he debated whether to buy another burner phone and text them its number to get in touch. But in his tiredness and subsequent twisted logic he feared that someone else might be keeping their phones alive in the hope he would do just that. That would allow such a person to back trace his movements and potentially leave him unable to achieve anything.

Sam had no clear idea of where Isla and his parents actually were. He raked through possible scenarios to find them. The next call he made was to a naval base in Scotland.

"Min, it's Sam."

"How you getting on, pal?"

"Not great, Min. I need another favour."

"What's it?"

"If you trace mobile phones – old ones, not iPhones – can other people see that trace being activated?"

"The short answer is I don't know, mate, but I can find out."

"How long will it take?"

"Well, the long fella you met at the marina, he's the boffin. He's on exercise, but I could get in touch. Are you in big diffs?"

"Isla could be."

"Right," was all he said, understated as usual, but he got it.

"If nobody else can track the trace, can you do it for me? The phones belong to my parents. They're minding Isla, and they're AWOL."

"Right. It'll be at least twelve hours before I can do anything, pal."

Sam read the numbers of his parents' phones to his friend. "Thanks, Min," he said, and hung up.

Having made what felt like a positive move, Sam's service rituals surfaced. "When you can realistically achieve nothing," he muttered, "rest or eat." The time, he knew, would come when he'd need energy. He went back to the boat, rolled onto his bunk and closed his eyes.

———

THREE HOURS later he woke in a panic, not having intended to sleep for more than an hour. Paranoia gripped him. He looked at the professor's phone and shook the temptation to use it. Even in desperation he didn't want anyone to know where their boat was moored, so he used the boat's VHF radio to make a ship-to-shore call routed through the Isle of Man.

"Where have you been?"

The last thing she sounded was charitable. He ignored the question. "Is there anything on the cloud?"

"Yes, and it's fucking frightening. For you, and now, I think, for me."

Chapter 34

C harity steadfastly refused to email or transfer any of what she'd found, and Sam heard her sister in the background instructing her not to say anything further on the line. She told him to meet her at the usual place, so he hit the road and parked outside the Applegreen on the M1, just north of Dublin.

Ninety minutes later he watched Charity hurry over to his rental from her hairdresser's car. Her twin, behind her, climbed into the back seat. Both looked harassed.

"What the actual fuck have you got us into?" the sister barked at the back of his head.

Sam twisted to glance at her and decided to deal with Charity, who looked more terrified than cross. "What's on the cloud?" he said, flat calm.

"Show him," the twin said. "I don't fucking believe this," she muttered.

Charity pulled an iPad mini from her bag. "We've watched three recordings so far."

The twin chimed in. "They're encrypted and it takes

ages to process them. I have special software – it's churning away in the background."

"Videos?"

"Kind of." Charity held out one hand, palm down, fingers spread, willing herself to slow down.

"It's not …" Sam's heart sank, fearing they'd sat through some vile ritual.

"Just show him," Áine snapped.

Charity gripped the edges of the screen, braced.

"How many are there?" he asked as the screen lit up, startling Charity.

"That's another one cracked," said the twin. "Play it, sis."

Charity shook her head. "No, he needs to see them in order otherwise we'll all be as confused as each other. They're dated. Here's the first."

She tapped the screen and two boxes appeared, one larger than the other. The heads and shoulders of two people could be seen as they would appear on their own webcams. On the right was the professor, and on the left, the main talker, was a man with a refined English accent. He was well groomed, not a hair out of place, a club tie around his neck and a golf tan. "How can they be sure this man, this stranger, knows anything about us?"

"The keeper said he seemed to know a lot," the professor replied.

"And how does the keeper know this?"

"He is well connected," said the professor.

"Well, what does the keeper intend to do about it?" sighed the Brit impatiently.

"He'll move the heir … in case any of us are compromised."

The Brit grunted. "I'll get this stranger looked into. We may be best to nip it in the bud."

"Agreed," said the professor.

"And he's Irish, this chap?"

"Apparently," said the professor.

"I may need you to go over there," said the Brit.

"Whatever you need," was the reply, and the recording ended.

Sam had a horrible feeling that he might be the stranger. He also had questions. "So who is the keeper?"

"Who are any of them?" demanded the sister, exasperated.

"I know the one in tweed," Sam said. "He's an American university professor who was involved in an abuse ring. I don't know the posh English one."

"You need to keep watching," the twin said.

Charity tapped another file. There were three squares this time: the Brit, the professor and a younger man – skinny, in a T-shirt, in his forties. The Brit was running the show.

"This is our investigator," he introduced the new man to the professor. "He's been looking into the stranger. I believe the news is not good."

"Oh?" said the professor.

It was the investigator's turn to talk. He sounded French. "The stranger is a dangerous man. He is a kind of bounty hunter and was special forces officer for some years."

Sam shifted uncomfortably in the driver's seat. He had no desire for the background he'd tried so hard to conceal to be discussed openly in front of others. He understood they'd already watched it, but it still made for awkward viewing.

The Brit broke in with incredulity. "Irish special forces?"

"He is Special Boat Service and Royal Marine commando."

"Oh, dear," said the Brit, understatedly, in typical British fashion.

"Like a US Navy SEAL?" asked the professor. "I'm not following the accent."

"He's Belgian," spat the Brit. "And SBS is rather worse than SEALs, if such a thing were possible," mumbled the Brit. He closed his eyes and his face took on a look of resignation.

"He is retired. Not long ago, actually," offered the Belgian.

Sam wondered where the little twerp was getting his information.

"So how much does he know and where can we find him?" asked the Brit.

The professor took the first part of the question. "The keeper's information is that he knows enough, but, uh, perhaps that's for a discussion offline." The tutor was coy in front of the investigator. That suggested to Sam that the investigator was hired in rather than being a member of the abuse ring.

"He lives on a boat," said the Belgian.

Sam's heart sank.

"Of course he does," said the Brit, exasperated. "But where does he keep this boat?"

"Nowhere. He moves around. He sails from place to place. Mostly he is in Northern Ireland. Sometimes he just," the Belgian searched for a word, "vanishes," he said with a flourish.

"What does he want? Who's he working for?"

The professor broke in, keen to show that he had something helpful to contribute. "He's working for a group that helps trafficked women – some sort of charity."

Charity paused the recording and looked up at Sam. "I can't understand this bit. This has nothing to do with us, does it? I never asked you to look at an abuse ring. What have these people got to do with my organisation?"

He looked back at her. "I genuinely haven't a clue," he said. "Keep it running, maybe it'll become clear." She tapped the arrow.

"The keeper described him as a kind of mercenary – a freelancer, if you will," said the professor. "Rescuing women from pimps. The keeper didn't know anything about his background, though."

"I still don't follow how that fits our picture," said the Brit, "but we can't have him vanishing." He addressed the investigator. "We will need to know where he is at all times."

"Is possible. Lemme see what I can do."

"That's all for you for now."

The investigator took the hint and dismissed himself. Once his image left the screen the Brit and the professor kept talking, the Brit looking deeply concerned. "Could the heir have contacted a charity?"

"I don't know," said the professor. "I doubt it."

The hairs stood up on the back of Sam's neck. The question seemed to confirm the counsellor's story – that the heir had come to him for help. He looked at the Brit and imagined he was staring at the leader of the abuse ring.

The professor looked uncomfortable. "The keeper suspects we have a breach."

"Are you suggesting someone within."

"It's ridiculous, I know. There has never, ever, been a breach."

The Brit stared hard into the camera. "A breach would be unthinkable."

Chapter 35

Sam found it bizarre listening to strangers piece together a picture he had been trying to build for weeks. He wanted to watch the other videos but Charity needed clarity.

"So they think *I* engaged *you* to help this heir person?"

"Who is the heir?" growled the twin from the back.

Sam exhaled then reeled back. He spoke quickly. "About a month ago I got a request for work through the website you set up for me."

"Yeah," said the twin. "I know. I checked."

He held out both hands, index fingers pointed upwards in concentration. "So I went to see the bloke who wanted this job done. He told me a cock and bull story about a woman who was being abused. It was grim stuff – involved the seasons and all sorts of crazy stuff. He called her the heir."

He looked to Charity for a reaction but got none. "I assumed at the time that you had referred this bloke to me."

She shook her head. "I told you, no."

Sam looked back at the road. "Well, that's when it all started. I didn't believe the counsellor bloke at all, but then someone came to the boat one night. I don't know how he got aboard but, anyway, he came to kill me—"

"Sweet and gentle—" the sister in the back began.

"And after that I got a bit twitchy."

"Twitchy?" growled the sister. "Someone comes to kill you and you get twitchy."

Sam ignored her. "Then I came to you looking for someone who might help explain what was going on – remember? And through the jigs and reels you put me in touch with the old woman from the convent."

"Who's now dead," said Charity.

"What?" Sam flicked his stare to her.

"Yeah. She got killed during a burglary."

"Fucking hell," he said, his mind racing. "She knew about the cover-up of an abuse ring. What you've just shown me just confirms what I already knew – that it's the same ring that the professor and this Brit seem to run."

"Right," said the twin from the back seat. "So they're killers. They think my sister tipped you off about some heir person, and now we're under threat – thank you very fucking much – and you, you've endangered the very person you're supposed to be protecting!"

"What d'you mean?" He turned to face her. "Who am I protecting?"

"Well, Sam," said Charity. "Apparently you have a daughter."

———

FEAR IS A MENTAL STATE, yet Sam knew from others' experiences that it could also be physical. Fear had never made him sick before but he threw open the car door and vomited hard, his darkest terror realised. He panted out the door, conscious of the twin swearing in disgust at his back but unable to care about what she was saying. As the fug cleared, he wiped his eyes and regained a little composure. He drew himself upright again and hauled on all of his reserves to focus his concentration. He'd been here before, albeit without Isla in danger. He boxed away the exhaustion and zeroed in on what he needed to do.

"Play the next one."

Charity was so taken aback by his reaction that she complied immediately. The third recording drew his mind in so tight that he managed to finally zone out the fractious twin completely. He worked through what was happening, listening intently. Every word spoken took on a fresh importance.

The investigator was speaking.

"The stranger has taken a flight from Dublin, Ireland."

"Yes, we know where Dublin is, thank you." The Brit's impatience was back with bells on. "Where did he fly to, please, or is that some sort of secret?"

"Is not a secret?" The Belgian looked confused.

"Then bloody well tell us where he flew to, then!" shouted the Brit.

"New York." The investigator looked more confused than afraid.

"New York?" The professor was perturbed.

"Yes. He has been buying mobile phones. I monitor a little but he is ..."

The Brit and the professor stared at him, waiting for the next word, which the Belgian struggled to find. "Trash them," he said eventually.

Sam wondered how the hell the investigator had worked

that out but he had no time to dwell on it because the conversation moved on.

"Where is he going?" the professor asked.

"He is moving north-east," the Belgian replied.

"We thought someone was going to deal with him on his boat, didn't we?" said the Brit.

"Well," said the professor, "they still don't know for sure what happened there. The man they sent didn't actually—"

"I know!" yelled the Brit. "He bloody vanished, like this bloody commando keeps disappearing."

Charity looked at Sam. Sam shook his head. It wasn't the time to get into more explanations.

"You could wait for him to collect his daughter," offered the investigator.

Sam tried not to pant but his chest heaved at the mention of Isla.

The Brit placed a thumb under his jowly chin, a finger resting against his cheek and exhaled loudly. "His daughter? Why am I only hearing about a daughter now?"

"His wife, she is dead. He has a young girl," said the investigator.

Sam felt two pairs of eyes on him and an odd silence filled the car. He stayed fixed on the screen and waited for the Brit to finish his exasperated huffing and puffing.

"And where is his daughter?"

"I don't know," said the Belgian, and Sam sucked air into his lungs for the first time in what felt like minutes. He knew the video was a few days old, but still it offered hope, for a few seconds. "But I can find out."

"Then do it." The Brit had calmed and was able to contain himself again. "If this bloody commando disappears again, things will get very uncomfortable for you."

"I will deal with it," said the investigator.

"Get off the line," barked the Brit, and the Belgian vanished.

"If the stranger gets away," the Brit addressed the professor, "I need you to get the rest of the circle, travel to Ireland and tidy things up. Immediately."

"But what about the keeper?" said the professor. "He's not authorised to allow anyone near the heir between Beltane and Samhain."

Sam looked at Charity, who paused the recording and shrugged.

"It's pagan shit," the twin broke in, reading from her iPhone. "The first one's about fertility, the second one's about … death and stuff."

Charity pressed play.

"Leave the keeper to me," the Brit said. "I have a task for him. I'll make sure he's not around."

The professor's head fell into his hands, his voice becoming muffled. "The Irish police – how do we navigate that?"

"We have people where they need them. You know that. You just get done what needs to be done."

The professor nodded and the recording finished.

Sam's heart hammered like a mortar drop.

Chapter 36

E verything slowed down a little.

"Is your daughter safe?" Charity asked, not looking at him.

There was silence for a long moment. Even the twin managed to keep her mouth shut.

"I don't know," he said.

"When did you lose your wife?"

"A while before I met you."

"You never said," her delivery was gentle.

Her sister's less so. "Umm, sorry to butt in, like, but we have an issue here. There was a new recording cracked, remember? So maybe we should, like, watch it?"

Charity came to. She fumbled around, bringing up the fresh film. Three people were on the screen.

It had an immediate tone of urgency – the professor obviously having started the recording after the video call had begun. The Brit was shouting.

"So where is he now?"

"He's leaving my office building," the professor replied.

"To go where?" the Brit screamed, the sound distorting.

Sam realised he was watching the call the professor made straight after the confrontation at his office in New York.

"I don't know." The professor was shaking his head in panic.

"Well, hadn't you better find out?" boomed the Brit from the top right of the screen.

"Is ok," interjected the investigator. "I can pick him up, is no problem."

"But how? I thought you said he was dumping his phones." the Brit blurted out in frustration.

"I can get him again. Soon probably." The Belgian shrugged. "Phones are good but not reliable, really. They are sometimes discarded or broken, and many people know they are compromised." There was flippancy to his delivery, which suggested complete confidence in his ability.

"How, then? How can you be sure you can track him?" asked the professor.

"Same as how I found him in Boston," said the European. "He has one thing with him almost always."

"Which is?" yelled the Brit.

The Belgian snorted. "Look, I do not ask who you are or what you do. I provide this service and track the persons of interest to you. You have no need to know how I do this."

The Brit was silent for a moment. Sam could see his tremor, like an incendiary on the cusp of detonation. Suddenly his face loomed large in the screen as he leaned in.

"Listen to me, you little Belgian bastard," he spat. "Do you think we can't find people ourselves? The only reason I chose you is because I don't currently have a tech in

Ireland. I know everything about you – your little rental home on Achill Island, where your wife works, where your children go to school. You are not indispensable, you little twat."

Sam could see the veins in the Belgian's eyes. He'd been completely blindsided.

The Brit's voice lowered. "If you cross me, I will fuck … you … up. Do you understand that, or shall I speak slower!"

The Belgian didn't move or make a sound.

"Now, let's start again, shall we? What is it, this thing the commando has with him all the time?" The Brit paced his delivery, enunciating each word, crystal clear.

The Belgian's eyes fell.

"He has the key to his boat," he replied softly.

The Brit nodded sagely.

Sam felt the sister's head hit the back of his car seat and heard her groan. Charity paused the recording and turned to him.

"Tell me it's not in your pocket now, Sam."

It was in his pocket. He looked at her, and nodded.

"Ok," said Charity, "we need to get out of here."

"We need to get away from him," said the twin, incredulous.

"I need to know what else is on those recordings," Sam said.

"Eh, yeah," said the twin, "that's the priority, yeah. Not a bunch of fuckers looking to kill us!"

Now he understood why Min's boffin hadn't detected any tracker on the boat – he'd gone to lunch with the key in his jeans. Sam worked through his recent history.

"Wait a minute. If they had me in Boston, then why did it come as a shock that I got to New York?"

The twin looked at him. "Well, was it a shock?"

"The professor was definitely not expecting me," Sam said. "And I was... elsewhere in New York too. They could have picked me up in New Jersey."

Charity's face looked incredulous. "You were in New Jersey?"

"And they could have got me in London too. I had the keys the whole time."

"Show me," the twin snapped. Sam fished his keys from his pocket. "What's the fob for?" she held up a small black cannister the size of a pen lid.

"It opens a key pad at a dock we use to get in the gate."

"And when did you last use it?"

"Weeks ago."

"It's the only place the tracker could be. Maybe the battery's gone flat. Or the airport security scanner mangled its signal."

He looked up. They were in a section of car park for articulated lorry drivers to park up and get some sleep. Nobody was looking at them; the hauliers were all appeasing their tachometers by lying in their curtained bunks. Sam watched a small dog pad over and sniff his vomit. He looked at the collar and wondered about fixing the key to the fluffy wee yoke but dismissed the idea when he caught sight of two children playing on the grass swinging the dog's lead.

There was a refrigerated container and cab to the rear. Sam watched a sleepy-looking driver climb down from the driver's seat and head for the shop. Wake-up time. Coffee probably. Sam motioned to the twin to give the keys back, then pushed open the door, stepped over the puke and walked to the back of the load. He used a key ring to bind it to the lorry's security cable. On his walk back he saw the driver returning with a paper cup. The reg was Polish. If the signal did come back, the Belgian would have fun tracking that.

Sam could see the twin shaking her head in the back seat as if trying to work out what the hell was going on. He climbed back in the driver's side.

"Am I getting it right – you actually met this bloke?" she said. "This tutor?"

"Yes."

"When?"

Sam thought about that, unsure of what day he was now in. "Day before yesterday, I think."

"Where?"

"Manhattan," he said.

"So we need to go to the police, get him picked up," said the sister.

"Afraid not," he said.

"Why not?"

"He's dead."

"Eh, what?" The sister was struggling with the news and shouting.

"He killed himself. Long story."

"Unbelievable."

It was now plain to him how monumental an indulgence killing the professor had been. He'd missed an opportunity to round up the circle at the Belfast apartment. Sam doubted anyone would go near it now that it was the scene of a police investigation.

"How long until the next recording is cracked?" he asked her.

"Depends on how long it is." She sighed and slumped back into her seat like a teenager.

Sam started the car and pulled out. If the Belgian was looking for Isla, he needed to find the Belgian.

"Oh, so we're going with you now, are we?" The twin shot forward again, her voice thick with Dublin attitude.

"We need to get to Achill Island," he said.

Charity had been churning the information in silence for a long while and spoke for the first time. "We're safer with him for the moment, sis, honestly." She turned her head to the back seat. "I've seen him working and we're better off with him."

"I am not going to the west of Ireland with ye," barked the sister. "You can let me out now."

Sam swerved to the hard shoulder.

"No, no, no, sis! We stay together," said Charity. "They know who we are and probably where we live. The only way to sort it is to deal with them. Sam can deal with them."

"The Guards can deal with them!" yelled the twin.

"You heard the man – the cops are on board. Let's get away from here. If they've tracked him this far, we need to keep moving."

Sam looked in the rear-view mirror. "Get out if you're getting out. Otherwise the next stop is Achill Island," he said to the twin.

She slumped down petulantly, her arms folded across her chest. He took that as confirmation, pulled into the traffic and headed west.

Chapter 37

He knew that many people loved the barrenness but bogland, for Sam, represented one long grim reminder of freezing wet nights yomping across desolate countryside, the mud clinging to his boots, the earth trying to lay premature claim to his sodden, aching carcass. Those months of training were far from fun, and similar to the drive to County Mayo. He was tailgating, speeding and hurtling ahead, despite the swearing and gasps from his passengers who clearly thought they were destined for deliverance. They swept through the flat black gorse brush, Heaney's turf, where much of the country's brutal history was embalmed and concealed.

In the past he'd sailed by Achill Island but he'd never been on it. Neither had his passengers. The twin, with her Google maps and her iPhone, became his consultant. At least it gave her purpose beyond criticising his driving.

"There's not much there," she said. "There's, like, some villages and a good few pubs, mostly holiday cottages. And a beach."

"What about access?" Sam asked. He hadn't a clue whether getting to the island involved a ferry.

"Well, far as I can see there's one bridge, but that's all. It looks pretty tight." She looped her phone around the headrest and he glanced at it. She made the image bigger. He grunted. It seemed like good news.

He scrabbled around for ideas about how to locate the Belgian. From the little they knew of his line of work, the investigator would almost certainly require good bandwidth. "See where the broadband connection is best."

Áine began tapping. "Seems ok in the villages," she said, "but I'd say he's not hardwired – that's too volatile way out here with the wind and probably power cuts. I'd say he uses a dish out here for when the electric goes down in winter."

"Would he not just ride it out until they connect it back up?"

"No way," Áine said, no doubt countenanced.

Sam glanced at her in the rear-view as she stared into her phone. She was probably a good judge of the techie mindset. "If you're right, he'd need a generator too."

"Yeah."

"So a garage, or a shed."

"For sure."

The twin may be a pain in the arse, but her reasoning and skills were on the money. A small supermarket loomed ahead, close to the bridge. Sam decided there was no point in wasting time and pulled over, turning to Charity.

"Can you take a screenshot of the Belgian from the iPad and enlarge it?"

She shook her head. "Technically incompetent."

"Here, give it to me," said the twin reaching forward. Sam heard a camera shutter. She handed the iPad into the front again, job done.

"Right," he said to Charity, reasoning that she was most likely to get the desired response. "Can you go inside and ask where he lives?"

"I can try," she said, "but they'll think I'm a cop."

Sam didn't care what they thought. They could either tell her nicely or have him wreck the place.

She returned fifteen minutes later, during which time he had twice considered the strangulation of her sister as she banged on about the mess he had dragged them into.

"Sorry, took a bit of plámásing."

He raised his eyebrows.

"Sweet-talking," explained the know-it-all.

"He lives in Keel, up a hill. I have rough directions but they only go so far."

The drive shouldn't have taken long but it was slow going at times because of sheep dodging.

"There's windswept and there's ravaged," Charity said. "I can't work out whether the village is beautiful or battered."

Sam passed a final solo sheep and tore around the island, up lanes and roads, until the place they were looking for revealed itself. At the back of one falling-down house loomed a dish NASA might have been proud of. He wondered what the locals thought the Belgian was up to in there.

He stopped hard, wedging the vehicle across what passed as a driveway with a battered jeep parked in it.

"Stay put," he muttered and threw the door open. He marched up a small overgrown path and without breaking stride put his shoulder to the front door. The whole frame gave way, falling like a tombstone with an almighty clatter.

Inside he heard scuffling as someone took off, but it was useless. The inhabitants could tear into the surrounding terrain but it was home away from home for Sam and nobody would get away. He caught the Belgian wrestling with a broken PVC door at the back of the house and used his forearm to pin the man's face against the glass. The Belgian's feet raised off the floor, lips slabbered the windowpane, heavy panting steamed up around his face.

In that moment something came to Sam – as if he'd taken a round in the trunk. It nearly took his own legs from beneath him, but he had to remain standing. He had to see this part through before he reasoned out the rest.

"You've been looking for me," he whispered into the investigator's ear. "So here I am."

"He's choking Sam, put him down!" Suddenly Charity was at his back. Sam ground his teeth in irritation, unable to shake the knowledge that the Belgian had volunteered his daughter as leverage. He determined to damage him.

"You might actually need the little shithead," he heard the twin say as the shithead began to expire.

Sam dropped him. Killing the professor had been a mistake, he decided not to add to it.

Ten minutes later they'd looked through the small house, confirmed he lived alone and were sitting in a studio surrounded by monitors and stacks of servers, cables pouring out like meat from a mincer. Lots of little dots flashing.

"Cool," said the twin, admiring the Belgian's set-up.

"You've a choice to make," Sam told him, speaking evenly. The investigator rubbed the back of his neck and looked up at Sam in fear. "You tell us what we want to know or I will beat you to death."

Charity was looking everywhere but at Sam. He knew what she was thinking and he wished she'd stayed in the car. It was one thing to commission someone like Sam, it was quite another to see how that commission was carried out. But he couldn't afford to tone it down this time.

"If I help you, they will kill me," the Belgian said, which to Sam sounded like a reasonable assumption.

"If you give me enough information, I'll deal with them." To Sam it was all starting to sound a bit ridiculous. Whether he realised it or not, the Belgian had little choice: die now or die later.

"Just tell him, please," Charity pleaded.

Sam glanced at her. She had heart and had evidently inherited the entirety of the compassion gene in the womb. Her less sensitive sister was already playing with the computers.

"I reckon I could give this a crack if you want to just do him," Áine said over her shoulder.

That's the ticket, thought Sam, and leaned forward to catch the investigator by the hair. He dragged the small man off his seat towards the door of his den.

"Please, no," said Charity.

Between the sisters, they made a bloody convincing pair.

"Ok, ok, ok," the Belgian screamed. "Ok, ok."

Sam gave him a kick and dragged him up to his desk, which half encircled the user. He dumped him in a chair and leaned forward, lips close to the man's ear. "If at any point you tell me a lie, I will make sure the group of sick bastards who employed you get to know where I got my information from. Some of the questions I am about to ask I already know the answers to. Some I do not. If at any point you piss me around, I'll let her do the work," he nodded his head at the twin, "and you and I will take a walk, ok?"

"I get it, I get it."

"Who is the American?" Sam said.

"He is dip-lo-mat," the Belgian's accent proved tricky through the tremor in his voice. "He, umm, makes business for Nortzen Ireland, for econ-om-y," he said.

Sam found his delivery mildly irritating. He'd been clearer on the recordings. Fear had heightened his pitch. "Where is he from?" Sam asked, establishing the man's commitment to the truth, as his old agent handlers had taught him.

"He is not so important," said the Belgian. "He is academic from Boston. He is living in New York."

"Who is the Englishman?" Sam asked, expecting a quick answer.

The Belgian looked terrified. "Whish Englishman?" he said, his eyes fluttering all over the place.

"This one, you fucknuckle," the twin said, thrusting the iPad in front of him.

The man's jaw muscles clamped when he saw a screen grab from the recording. "I donno," he muttered. "I am not joking witz you, I do not know who he is."

"But you know *where* he is, don't you?" said Áine.

Sam glanced up at her and thought she was making a better job of the interrogation than he was. The Belgian gently rocked his head as if to say maybe, maybe not.

"You had a hook-up with him. You have the kit here to trace his IP, or at least the one he used for the call."

Again the Belgian remained silent, staring at her with real fear in his eyes.

"Ok, I'll find it myself," she said, turning to the middle of three keyboards and hammering the keys.

The Belgian leaned forward to protest. He evidently didn't like the idea of someone looking through his files, particularly when his system appeared to be live and therefore open to inspection.

But the Brit wasn't Sam's main concern. "What about my daughter?" Sam asked him.

The Belgian turned to him, cowering at the same time; a dog that knew it was about to get the stick. "The Englishman has arranged to send someone to find her."

"Who?" Sam growled, gripping the man by the ear and placing a thumb over his left eye socket.

"The keeper, they call him!" panted the Belgian. "But," he held up his hands, "I don't know, I don't, I don't know who this keeper is."

Sam increased the pressure on the man's eyeball, knowing there was little more frightening than the prospect of losing your sight. Reluctantly, he believed the man was telling the truth.

"Where has he been sent?" he asked.

"All I find was your parents' phones registered to a mast. They make no calls and they do not answer calls."

"Where!" Sam thumbed down, this time on both eyes.

"L'Estartit," the man said, trying to slump deeper into his seat and keep his head away from Sam's grip.

"France?" Sam inquired, genuinely shocked.

"No, is in Spain."

The twin was working on one of the other keyboards. "Costa Brava," she said. "Very nice. Your folks, they must be using some pretty old devices, yeah?"

"They don't have smartphones."

She pulled up a map on a screen. "You didn't get very close, did ye?" She turned to the Belgian, then back to the screen. "SIM-based tracking is pretty shitty," she said. "He only got to within a few miles."

Which seemed far too bloody close for Sam. "When was the keeper sent?"

"Three hours ago," he said.

"From where?"

"I think Dublin."

"You think? Why do you think Dublin?"

"Because the professor is coming for the heir. And he has come to Belfast and is to meet people in Dublin."

"How do you know that?"

"The Englishman," said the Belgian. "He tells me to start to track the professor. He wants to know every place he goes."

Sam dropped the Belgian's skull. He was ready to leave, but two things occurred to him.

"These women will be needing your jeep," he said. The Belgian had covered his eyes and was sobbing. Sam turned to Áine. "Get all you can from that computer then destroy everything."

"Wicked shame," she said but turned dutifully back to the screens ready to comply.

Sam looked at Charity. "I'll leave you a rucksack. There's a couple of grand sterling in it. Get yourself somewhere safe and I'll send you an email when all this is sorted."

She had all the wherewithal of a car wreck.

"You," he grabbed the Belgian by the hair, raising his head from his hands, "where was the Englishman's IP? Where was he when he dialled in?"

"I have it here," said the twin.

When Sam looked at the screen he understood why the Belgian was so terrified.

Chapter 38

Three hours was a hell of a head start, particularly given that Sam was four hours' drive away from Dublin Airport. Depending on what flight the keeper caught, that gave him as much as seven hours' grace. Sam tried to convince himself that he had things in his favour: he knew his parents' habits and he had a rock-steady friend in Min. That didn't stop him cursing himself for not getting Charity or her sister to book him a flight as he left Achill Island. He then debated whether to stop and buy a phone or push ahead and get to the airport. In any event, he badly needed fuel, but the bloody garage didn't sell mobile phones.

Three hours and twenty minutes later he abandoned the hire car in the same spot where he'd fought with a pimp less than a year before and ran into Terminal One. Scouring the departure screen for a flight to Spain, he racked his overly exhausted brain for a sense of the geography. There was a flight to Barcelona, which seemed like a good option, and another to Girona, but he had no idea where that was. The woman at the Ryanair desk showed him a map and he paid in cash.

Seven hours and forty minutes after he left Achill he stood in the warm heat of Girona Airport. It was dinky but it had everything he needed – including hire cars with integrated GPS. Twenty miles later he had set up a Spanish SIM pay-as-you-go mobile. Dog-tired, he called his old base at Faslane and asked for Min.

"Where have you been? I've been trying to reach ye."

"I had to ditch my old phone, Min."

"Y'alright?" Western Scots, like the Irish, manage to weld all their words into one.

"Yes, mate, how did you get on with tracking my folks?"

"Aye, we have them. They're in a Spanish town near Îlles Medes—"

"L'Estartit?" Sam cut in.

"Aye?" He sounded surprised. "You're way ahead of me, are ye?"

"I'm about half an hour from there. I need a fix, though, Min, please. Close as you can get."

Min's voice lowered and became softer, apologetic. "They're no GPS phones, pal."

"Min, I know, just give me your best, please."

"Looks like a wee peninsula, round the corner from a beach, kind of private, like." He sounded frustrated and Sam could almost see him shaking his head. "It's about a mile long, there's coast to the east, so no masts at sea to triangulate for sure. The phones hav'nie moved in hours, mebbe even days."

Min read out what coordinates he had and Sam punched them into the GPS.

"Thanks, Min. Really, mate, thank you."

"Let me know how you get on, when ye can, like."

Sam debated calling the Spanish police but he didn't know what he could say to them. He rehearsed the details of a possible conversation: two Irish adults, one child, at risk from an unidentified person. Can't say who, can't say whether that person is definitely even there. He wouldn't be able to identify himself or elaborate on the background. He couldn't even speak Spanish.

Another irritant was the aftermath of whatever he was heading into. Think ahead, Sam, he told himself. It's not just the next move, it's the move after that. Lurking in his thinking were the ramifications revealed by the Brit's location. Sam now knew where the Englishman had been when he'd made the hook-up calls, and that meant that if the keeper made it into custody, he would be protected. He also knew the circle wouldn't rest until all evidence of them was destroyed, which would make an orphan of Isla. He chewed the situation over for so long that he arrived in L'Estartit before he'd made up his mind on his next steps.

The GPS took him through a bustling little town shortly after afternoon siesta. The traffic was at a standstill and all he could do was clench the wheel and rock in his seat in impatience; both completely pointless. Nothing would move quicker because of his frustration, so he zoomed in on the little console screen, took a mental map of the peninsula Min had referred to, abandoned the car and started running.

He glared into the face of every person he passed. He listened for the three voices most familiar to him as he cantered past restaurants and bars. Awnings were being wound out and tables set for evening service. He prayed like he'd never prayed before that his mum would be following her usual routine.

He must have stood out like a snowman on a beach as

he raced through the town while everyone else sauntered at a retirement pace. Life in L'Estartit was obviously generous. Nobody showed any urgency. He began to panic that he'd become disorientated – he'd been expecting masts of a boat marina before now – but he should have known better, that the flat visual of the map confused the actual size of the place. Eventually he saw the tips of rigging as he emerged from a pedestrian street and headed towards the rocks. He was adding things up in his head: the previous flight had been from Belfast, an extra two hours' drive from Dublin for the keeper. That made the keeper three, maybe four, hours ahead of him. But for all Sam knew the keeper could still be in Ireland. He reached a road about five feet above a short beach.

His parents were predictable in some ways. They liked a drink in the evening, just one or two before dinner, and they liked to feel they'd earned it. That might involve a walk, some work in the garage or garden, or when the sun was on their backs, a swim in the sea. He scoured the sand for them but it was crowded with broad white floppy hats and broad white floppy British bellies. They'd not go for that, he knew. They'd seek out space. He kept running in the full knowledge that he was acting in desperation with little structure or hope of success.

Beyond the sand he saw what appeared to be a road that rose slightly and curled around a bend. Above and to his left were apartments, beautifully appointed, stylish, with generous sun covers and sand shutters. He wondered whether their phones were sitting inside on a table charging. He tried to close out notions of the three people he cared about most lying face down, dead upon the marble floors.

He hammered up the incline, swearing at himself for believing he would find them alive and well. His legs burned and began to slow as his initial optimism wore off. He cast around more in hopelessness than confidence. The place was all but deserted, apart from two local kids clambering onto bikes at a bridge, their day fishing off the rocks over. He grabbed the timber railing and lowered his head between his shoulders to catch his breath, chest heaving, acutely aware of his increasing vintage, his lack of energy and his fear. He looked up slowly, sweat steaming his vision.

And then he saw her.

She was standing with a plastic rake in her hand in a swimsuit and crocs, less than forty feet below him. She looked amazingly happy and brown and was pottering about with sand stuck all over her. He hunted for his parents and saw a woman swimming in the cove further below. He could tell by the stroke it was his mum – chin high, short, strong strokes. Then he found his dad in his shorts and sandals twenty feet to the right of Isla. The relief would have been enormous if he hadn't been standing there talking to the keeper.

———

SAM URGED himself to act smart, but it was a grave situation. His dad, true to form, was just shooting the breeze with who he must have thought was a fellow Irishman abroad. Sam knew he wouldn't have given a second thought to the city shoes the man was wearing in a rocky cove or the jeans and fleece round his waist despite the heat being above thirty degrees Celsius.

Had Sam managed to get some proper sleep in the preceding week, things might have worked out better. As it was, his approach was too fast. It was a mistake he almost knew he was making when he thundered down over the rocks, bounding and sliding down the incline. He could have – should have, predicted Isla's reaction: she looked up, immediately overjoyed.

'Daddy!' he heard her yell, but he was looking at her grandfather and the man beside him.

His dad looked up with the beginnings of a baffled smile forming on his lips, and then he realised something was very, very wrong. Sam was still too far away when the keeper turned to face him. Sam watched the man's face snarl in recognition, a shoulder stoop and a hand reaching for the pocket of the fleece jacket round his waist.

"Dad, get out of the way!" Sam screamed.

But dads were dads no matter what age they were, and children were more important to them than anything no matter how old they might be. His father must have realised that the man he'd been chatting to was no friendly stranger. He stepped back and stared in shock as the keeper produced a short knife, jabbing it into his chest before turning it towards the oncoming Sam.

Despite the puncture to his chest, Sam watched his father refuse to let go of the keeper, protective instincts giving old arms strength and returning them to the gorilla-like power he'd had when Sam was a boy. Sam reached them as those enormous freckled forearms locked around the keeper's wrist and elbow, gripping him as he tried to wrestle the knife free.

Sam had no choice: he had to flatten them together. He left the surface about eight feet above where they stood and hit them midship, toppling them down onto the sharp rocks below. The fall could have done as much damage to his dad as the knife wound, such was the jaggedness of the cove.

Sam never wanted Isla to witness another death. He never wanted her to see another violent act. Her recovery from the murder of her mother was far from complete, and yet here she was on the cusp of watching her grandfather die too.

Sam could hear his father panting to his left, reaching for air, but incredibly he still had his hands around the keeper's wrist. Sam grabbed the keeper's free arm and twisted it backwards to open the assailant's ribcage, then fell on it with his knees.

Time paused as he gripped both ears and stared into the shock of the man's eyes. Under him, terrified, was the counsellor.

Sam lifted his head and smashed his skull onto the rocks beneath him.

Chapter 39

Isla was in a desperate state, heaving with tears and wanting to hug him, but Sam couldn't allay her tears – he was soaked in his dad's blood as he worked on him. His mum, having cut her feet to slices tearing from the sea and running up the rocks was behaving as calmly as his dad had. Despite her distress she saw the sense in keeping Isla turned away while doing exactly what Sam asked of her to keep her husband alive.

"Daddy, stop shouting at Granny," Isla sobbed as he barked directions at her grandmother.

Sam knew there was a puncture in the left lung. He taped the sticky flap from a pack of wet wipes above the entry wound to make sure the cavity didn't fill with blood. If that happened, his dad would drown. Placing the makeshift flap above the incision acted like a draught excluder, sucking flat to the chest on the breath in but bellowing out to allow the exhale. There was no catastrophic bleed. The messiest wound was on the back of his dad's head from the fall, so Sam packed it, then turned to the counsellor.

He found the man's phone in his jeans pocket and handed it to his mum. She hadn't only good Spanish but she knew exactly where they were. She called an ambulance.

Sam couldn't put his dad over his shoulder because of the wound in his chest, so he had to lift him in a cradle, which was awkward. Even then his father managed to speak.

"It's ok, I can walk, son."

Sam laughed at that but appreciated his dad's hardiness. The tough never show the depth of their resolve until it is required, he thought. The gentlest of people often turned out to be the ones who not only survived, but who pulled others through when the going got tight. He prayed his dad's age wouldn't overcome his gristle.

His mum, too, showed her mettle. Isla was far too heavy for a woman her age. Regardless, she was swept up in a piggyback and carried bare foot to the bridge. There Sam sat his dad down and explained what was going to happen.

"You're not going to like this, Mum, but it's the only way."

Isla stared up at him and he turned to her.

"Look, wee love, you need to listen to me really, really carefully, ok?"

Her big eyes were still filled with tears but she nodded.

"I have to leave you—"

"No, Daddy," she cried.

"Just for a little while, I promise. Not like last time – not for days and days. Just for as long as a movie, ok? Just for as long as *Ghostbusters*, I pinkie promise."

Isla nodded to him, her little finger smearing in her grandfather's blood.

In the distance he could hear the whoop of an emergency vehicle. He turned to his mother. "This attack happened on the rocks. You were approached by some mugger who saw you guys alone. He stabbed Dad and ran off. He didn't get anything. Don't let Isla out of your sight. Take her into the interview booth if you have to. Don't let any plod talk to her on her own. She's on holiday with you. Tell them you have called me and I'm on my way from Ireland."

"What are you going to do?"

Sam looked at Isla. He didn't want to say anything that she could regurgitate in front of anyone. He leaned forward and whispered in his mum's ear. "I need to deal with yer man." He nodded below to the rocks. "He got far too close."

She looked at him in stunned silence and eventually nodded. "So … are we ok, then? There's nobody else to worry about?"

"No, I don't think so. We're ok now. How will I find you?"

"There's only one hospital round here," she said. "We had to take your dad there last week for an ear infection. He's not allowed to swim," she said as she stroked her husband's head.

"Ok, I'll find it. Stay there till I join you. Have you money? You'll need clothes."

"They're in the bag down there." She nodded to the cove. "I'll ask the police to bring them to us when they arrive."

He put an arm around his dad's shoulders. His breathing was steady-ish. He looked at the two women in their swimsuits and the blood. He kissed Isla and told her not to tell anyone she had seen him, and not to talk to the police, and then he leapt over the railing and hopped down the rocks once more.

———

THE COMMOTION above had removed all attention from the tiny cove, which meant that dragging the counsellor into the sea was straightforward. The man was still unconscious and his breathing was laboured. Sam moved into the water pulling the body in with him and keeping the face above the lapping waves. He lay back, drawing the counsellor's head onto his own chest to keep it up, and felt the gristle and bone of skull fragments rub against his shirt. There was virtually no wash and he was thankful for the negligible tidal pull of the Mediterranean. They swam tight to the rocks towards a jutting headland. Sam reckoned that it was so steep it would be impossible for anyone to see them from above.

Once they reached the outcrop he found a small shelved inlet. It wasn't quite a cave, but it was covered and impenetrable by land. Kicking hard and using a doggy paddle with one arm, he guided them in. Then, using the counsellor's arms with his upper clothing hooked over a rock, Sam suspended him with his mouth above the water, Christlike, head hanging between his shoulders. The water around them gradually filled with the counsellor's blood. Sam gently trod water, preserving as much energy as possible. He had a long haul ahead.

As darkness fell he swam out around the headland and looked for a vessel of some sort. The wait in the cove had given him time to think about what he needed, both practically and from the counsellor. He looked to the lights ashore where a few hundred yachts and motor cruisers sat elegantly in the marina. However, twenty feet beyond their owners cavorted merrily in the restaurants and bars that decorated the harbour. The way his luck was going, he was sure to steal a boat owned by someone within spitting distance of the theft. There was no choice, though, so he swam towards the lights.

One option presented itself so, with reluctance, he took it. Lashed to the stanchions on the leeward side of a fifty-foot ketch, was a broad stand-up paddleboard. The long stock of its oar was within reach, tied to the toe rail. He didn't dare stand up on it as he left the marina, shoving it instead like a learner swimmer might push a float. Once out of immediate sight of the revellers, he clambered on top. It wasn't until he dipped the blade in the water that his stupidity revealed itself: feet together, with the water gently lapping over his toes, he realised how the intruder had got on board their boat. It clicked together as he drew the blade down the side of the board all but silently. There was no way his radar would pick up the polystyrene core of a surfboard like the one beneath his feet or indeed the plastic paddle. He had seen SUPs being used a thousand times and many of them were inflatable. Why it hadn't occurred to him before was a total mystery.

He ducked under the shelf as he entered the cove, but he could see nothing. He made his way to where he knew he'd left the counsellor, crucifixional in the depth of the half cave. Now crouching on the board, he dropped to his knees, the blade under his groin, and paddled instead like a dog, hands immersed on either side of the board. His vessel butted against something and Sam reached out to feel along the edges of the rocks, doubting himself in the disorientation of the darkness. But, no, the counsellor was gone.

Sam almost panicked. Worst-case scenario was that the man had fallen forwards and drowned. He dropped into the water and the frigidity took his breath away. He thrashed about beneath the surface but it was pointless – he couldn't see anything. His head swam with the adverse scenarios the death posed: an Irishman, stabbed; another Irishman washed up close by with serious head wounds; a third Irishman, with a colourful career history, flies in before – not after – the stabbing but claims to have arrived because of it. And that was only the start of Sam's issues. He had to find the body.

Sam got back on the board and paddled out of the cove trying to work out how and where the body might have drifted. He knew that it may not have sunk in the time he'd been away, and he could see no reason why the gentle swell would prevent a carcass turning either right towards the marina, or left towards the scene of the stabbing. What would not happen, though, he was sure, was that it would be drawn out to sea. He knew that the body could have slipped just beneath the surface but hoped against hope that it hadn't.

He reckoned the worst outcome was that the body would wash up on the beach beside the marina, which would mean immediate discovery and therefore exposure for Sam, so he drove the paddle into the water and forged forward the way he'd just come, this time paying attention to the sea's surface. He was pleasantly surprised at the speed of the board and the reflection and illumination of the town's lights helped him scour the sea ahead for signs of a floater. The paddle's displacement made a plunge and ripple sound as it cut through the surface, gliding the board like a skimming stone, straight as an arrow. The noise helped him catch a break.

"Help, please!"

He heard a weak call to his right. There was still a mile between the town and him and he couldn't see anyone, but the voice seemed to come from the rock face.

Bloody hell, thought Sam. The voice was unmistakably Irish.

"*Hola?*" Sam called, hoping the voice would guide him in.

"Over here," the counsellor called.

Sam edged in, hunting the rock face for an outline. He was upon the man long before the counsellor understood who his saviour was. The man was hanging like a gymnast from a rock, faced into the cliff, unable to glance behind.

"Here, please, *por favour*, over here."

The logistics of the extraction were far from ideal. Sam needed the man compliant but alive. He also needed to get the man onto the board. There would be nothing easy about any of that, particularly given that the counsellor was likely to go boogaloo when he saw who had come to the rescue.

Sam sat on his arse, shins dangling in the water for stability, and manoeuvred the board parallel to the rock face. Then he placed his hand upon the counsellor's hip.

"Ok, ok, ok," he said reassuringly, drawing the man off the rock face to step back onto the board to squat. Sam then crooked his elbow around the counsellor's throat and began to choke him. The thrashing didn't begin immediately – the victim maybe thinking it was some elaborate rescue manoeuvre, but when reality dawned the counsellor nearly capsized the board with his kicking.

It took three minutes of careful squeezing and release.

Sam had to make sure the pressure was even and just enough to knock the counsellor out without causing brain damage. It was the second time the counsellor had been rendered unconscious that day and Sam knew he was very lucky not to have killed him on the previous occasion.

He arranged the body on the board, face down in a jury-rigged recovery position. Placing one foot either side of the counsellor's hips, he dug deep with the paddle. The weight of the body made the board less predictable and it wobbled beneath him. Sam had a long way to go and he just had to live with it.

Sam estimated the Îlles Medes to be about one mile offshore. He didn't know much about them – everything he did know came from an article he'd read in the in-flight magazine. He'd been so distracted that he didn't remember much but he knew the Medes Islands had been fortified at different times. He recalled mention of Napoleon and that the isles were now part of a protected nature reserve, which suited him just fine. What really interested him, though, was the underwater caves the article had mentioned.

Almost an hour later he sculled around to the south-east side of the rocks, the sheer height of which offered few opportunities for landing. He'd seen an image in the article of divers bobbing just off an outcrop, but in the dark it took a bit of finding. Once there he dragged the board and the counsellor up onto the hard ground and laid him face down. Then he placed his head on the small of the counsellor's back and fell asleep, assured that the man couldn't get away again without him knowing.

Chapter 40

He had no idea how long he'd slept, but it was still dark when the counsellor began to shift. Sam lifted his head and regarded the man's pathetic progress. First came a scared moan, then panting as the damaged body shuffled around the rock face, reaching around, trying to work out what was going on. Sam let the scrabbling continue for a while, deliberating how to get what he needed. The counsellor wasn't even aware of his presence until he spoke.

"Scream if you want to, nobody can hear you. Might be best to get it out."

The man halted, stock-still, like a lizard, senses sharpened. Sam waited, imagining the counsellor's mind reeling.

"Sam?" he said eventually.

"Yes," Sam sighed, "although you're not supposed to know my name, are you?"

The counsellor grunted. "Where is this?"

Sam ignored the question. "I know about the circle, the Harvard professor, the heir, your relationship with her."

The counsellor paused. "How?"

"The mirror. In your bathroom."

"What?"

"When we spoke in there I ran the shower to distort any listening devices."

"You bugged me?"

"No, do try and keep up," Sam said, piling on the confusion to consolidate control. "The steam clung to the mirror. It showed me that her face had been pressed against it. Her scar, all down her face."

The counsellor held his breath before speaking again. "You've met her?"

"Not yet."

"But the scar?"

Sam had the counsellor where he wanted him, confused and afraid. "You told me about it."

"No."

"You didn't mean to, but you're not as smart as you think you are. You touched your face when you talked about her being cut."

"I didn't say her face."

"The steamed mirror showed me. Your hand beside her head. Your other one probably pressed against her skull. You behind her. All to yourself. No sick circle looking on. Just you raping her, abusing her."

"Not rape!" he spat angrily, rising on his knees.

Sam was thinking about how he'd forced the Belgian's face against a glass door, his breath condensing on the glass. "Yes. You drove her face into that glass with force. The mirror never lies."

"Not rape," the counsellor repeated.

"You can call it what you like," Sam poured scorn into

his delivery. "You probably think you're in a relationship. Next thing, you'll be telling me you love her."

"I *do* love her. She and I, we are together."

"That," Sam said, "I do believe. You wanted to get her away from the others. You wanted them to stop raping her. You were jealous."

"No, I was protecting her."

"You're not her counsellor, you're her keeper," Sam said. "You're one of the circle. You are its master of hounds. But you got jealous of them having their twisted way with her."

"Who's been speaking to you?"

"You're just one of the twisted bastards who skinned her."

"She loves me," the counsellor hacked. "I'm not like—"

"It's just Stockholm syndrome," Sam goaded the man, happier with the information flowing his way.

"She loves me. I was getting her out of it."

"After how many years of abusing her?" he asked. "You were her jailer – her jealous jailer. You saw a way to get her out for yourself – through me." Sam heard rather than saw the man roll off his knees and onto his arse.

"You don't understand."

"You needn't start that pompous condescension shit with me, you piece of shit."

"You think you have it all worked out." The counsellor couldn't help himself and Sam knew he would soon start to spout like a cracked drainpipe.

"It took a while to work out what you were up to. Why would one of the circle bring in someone like me and tell me about their sick abuse ring?"

"I love her," the counsellor repeated. "You make it sound like I'm as bad as them."

"There's no way to rank people like you lot."

The counsellor strove to defend himself. "I was trying to free her."

"You incarcerated her. You kept her for them."

"No, I thought—"

"Did you keep her like a dog? In a coal bunker? Under the stairs?"

"No! I wanted better for her. I thought bringing you in would … that you could—"

"Kill them?"

"Yes," the counsellor muttered.

"You thought you could play me against them, didn't you? You thought you could persuade me that you were her shrink."

"I am her counsellor. I have been purging—"

"You talk shit from sunrise."

"We just wanted to break free of them."

"And you were happy to get me to do your wet work."

"That's what people like you are for, isn't it?"

"There you go again. You're a sleekit, self-absorbed weirdo who thinks he's cleverer than everyone else. Yet here you are – you have no idea where – and things aren't looking amazing for you, to be frank."

"You must see that I wanted to get her away from them."

"You're no better than any of them. You fed me just enough information, you calculating prick.

Sam took his silence as acceptance.

"But you didn't have the courage to take on anyone yourself."

"I was trying to do the right thing."

Sam scoffed and spat.

The counsellor continued. "I needed someone like you

– I needed a threat. I needed them to think someone was coming after them so they'd give me permission to move the heir away."

"You wanted their *permission*?" Sam growled. "You really are a pathetic, weak little man. You didn't even have the balls to take her away from that evil by yourself."

"But you don't understand what you're dealing with here. You—"

"There you go again – riddles and nonsense. Do you know how mental you sound? You came for my kid, you stabbed my dad!"

"You have no possible concept..."

"She was going to start a new life with you? Poor bloody woman."

"She needed someone to free her – there was no other way. Just no other way."

"But you were one of them from the start. You were an abuser, a rapist, a sick fanatic. Did you really think you'd be able to sail off into the sunset with her – your victim?"

"I was trying to save her."

"Were you trying to save her when you came for my family?" he asked.

"It's not that simple."

"I know. You're afraid of someone – someone who has played you, who knows who all of you are, who can destroy your fantasy life with the heir. Did you cut her too? Did you put that scar on her face? Did you skin her feet when she was small? Did you rape her as a child?"

The counsellor began to sob.

Sam suppressed the urge to strike the man. He waited for a long time for them both to calm down. "There is only one way you will ever see her again."

"How?" the counsellor asked.

"I need to know about the others – the Brit who has you so terrified, the hierarchy, the arrangements. I need to finish what you started."

The counsellor said nothing for a few minutes, and then he talked and talked. When he finished light was dawning. He looked up, holding Sam's eye for the first time.

"And where is the heir?"

"No."

"She'll be looked after."

"You said…"

"Wise up."

"I'll not tell you where she is."

"You will," Sam said, readying to go to work on him again. "And I need to know how you found me."

"You let me go, I'll look after her. And I will tell you how I found you."

But there was no getting away from the fact that the counsellor had been prepared to take Sam's child.

In the event Sam only managed to get one element of the information he'd demanded before the keeper succumbed to fresh injuries. There had only ever been one possible conclusion, and his remains were deposited in an underwater cave.

Sam paddled ashore to see his dad.

Chapter 41

The going wasn't easy. The key to Sam's hire car had been saturated, so he took out the small rear triangular window to unlock the back door manually, which triggered the alarm, which woke the locals at 7 a.m. The key – when he belatedly found it inserted in a ridiculously inconspicuous part of the key fob, once inserted into the ignition eventually stopped the siren. Three notices crammed behind the windshield wipers appeared to be parking fines. He was just grateful that a wheel hadn't been clamped.

Contrary to what his mother had said, the map in the glovebox suggested that there were about a dozen hospitals in the area, most small and privately owned. It took far too long for him to realise that his definition of a hospital and the Spanish definition were totally different. He spotted an elderly man clutching a freshly baked baguette who not only spoke English but *was* English. The man explained that the nearest hospital with an emergency department was in Palamós, half an hour's drive from L'Estartit.

There, a nurse eyed him with suspicion. He was still damp in places from the paddle, but at least the blood had been washed away. He was salty for sure, and realised he must have looked pretty haggard. The nurse may have put it down to a long flight at short notice – he didn't really care, he just needed to see Isla and his mum.

His daughter's little feet were very brown save for the spaces left by straps of some beach shoes she must have been given. They were sticking out of one blanket and another blanket lay under her on a chair. Her little legs were curled up towards her chest and her head lay across her granny's lap. His mum was dozing upright in a chair, not really asleep but not awake either. Two feet away, his dad was propped up on pillows upon the ramp of a bed. A tube was in his arm, there was packing around his chest and a ventilator billowed at his side. His heart was being monitored; it looked steady to Sam's untrained eye.

The room was private and even had its own shower and toilet. His mother and Isla were dressed – the police had evidently retrieved their bag. Sam put one hand on his dad's shoulder and took an enormous paw in his own. His father stirred and Sam watched his crusty eyes crack open, the drawing of a faint smile, then his eyes closing in peace again.

They opened after a while. His chest heaved with effort. "Ok, son," was all his dad managed, the plastic mask steaming up as he spoke.

"Hi, Dad."

There was no point asking how he was doing; Sam could see it all.

"She's been so good," his mum spoke from behind him. "Isla held his hand all night."

Sam turned to look at her, and saw her eyes welling up.

"What does the doctor say?" He nodded towards his dad.

"Punctured lung," she said. "There was a cardiac arrest last night, which was terrifying, but they got him back and he's been stable since."

The guilt was enormous, but his mum didn't have time for recrimination. Everyone, including Sam, was ok, and that seemed good enough for her.

"I'm so sorry."

"I'm not going to ask what this is all about," she said, "but is it over?"

Sam walked over and scooped up his daughter. He hugged her in tight as she stirred awake.

"Almost," he said, "almost."

Chapter 42

S am looked up and despite having little regard for what happened inside, Westminster, he conceded, was stunning. Much too beautiful for the baying mob of suited buffoons that occupied its green and red benches. Sam loathed their carry-on, hollering like school-boys at one another, scoring small points while his friends, deployed because of the decisions made by such fools, died in the dirt and the dust of distant lands. He knew there had to be good among the bad, but he'd come for the latter.

He'd run through the scenarios time and again: the recce, the surveillance, the approach, the ending. In the event, none of it proved necessary.

Sam saw the Brit emerge from the palace – no doubt having signed in for the day to claim his cash. Peers, he knew, could take a daily allowance – money for nothing, if they so chose. The Brit hadn't spent more than an hour inside and certainly couldn't have taken a seat in the House of Lords. A private car drew up, collected Sam's mark and took off.

"Where's he going?" Sam snapped into a burner.

"Lemme see," said the Belgian.

The investigator was bent over a barrel. Áine, ever aggressive, had liberated many of the Belgian's computer drives and assured Sam they could provide useful leverage if he so required. Sam reckoned the Belgian would probably have complied regardless. Having spilled his guts to Sam, the man suddenly had a vested interest in the circle ending. Both men knew that the keeper's disappearance would eventually lead the Brit back to the investigator, and when the circle discovered the source of the leak it would be bye-bye, Belgian. Between the compromised man and Charity's bolshie twin, Sam had some pretty savvy tech support.

He listened down the line to thumping on a keyboard – the man accessing and searching the Brit's diary. Sam imagined it was held on a server inside the building he was staring at.

"Is good news."

"Hurry up."

"He is going to Belfast."

Which came as a surprise.

So Sam went too.

———

SAM ARRIVED in Belfast with no small amount of curiosity and irritation. He'd wasted time travelling to London only to turn tail, but what annoyed him more was the unexplained nature of the Brit's presence in his home city. Sam had mentally prepared for a showdown outside some exclusive London gentleman's club. He'd plotted a long wait outside for the Brit to emerge full of brandy and bravado.

Belfast wasn't London. He had no idea what was going

on and it made him irritable. He felt the tension in his body as he waited for the plane to empty and used his phone long before he reached the terminal.

"Do you know where he's going yet?"

"He is booked in Culloden Hotel."

"How many nights?"

"Just one."

"That all?"

"He has taxi arranged for tomorrow."

"Can you tell where it's going?"

"Is Rae-form Club," the Belgian said.

Sam suppressed his frustration at the pronunciation. "The what?"

"Rae-form. Is not correct?"

"Spell it," Sam snapped. The Belgian duly spelled out the name of a place Sam had never heard of. "Look it up. Where is it?"

Tapping resumed. "The Ulster Reform Club, 4 Royal Avenue. Very nice," the Belgian muttered.

"What is it?"

"Ehm, is like a ... eh ... I do not know."

Sam didn't want to add it to his search history, given his plans for the Brit. "Read what it says on the website."

"Is private. There are sitting chairs, bar, restaurant, billiards," the Belgian cooed. "Snooker."

"A snooker hall?"

"Nooo," the Belgian said. "Is bourgeois. This website says there are partner organisation all over the world – military, navy. Perhaps you will be welcome."

"Don't be smart. What does it look like?"

"Is old. Dark, wood and leather. Table lamps."

"Ok."

Sam closed the phone. He debated taking the Brit at the

hotel but opted instead to use the hacked information to his advantage. He decided to wait and see whether the Brit's unexplained visit might lead him to others in the circle.

———

AS A SCHOOLBOY SAM had been up and down Royal Avenue in Belfast's city centre probably a thousand times. Memory took him to the road, but when he located the address he could only stare up at the building, baffled as to how he'd never noticed its use before. The doorway was old but well preserved, and there was nothing to betray what lay inside. Little wonder, Sam thought. Anywhere with military connections would have become a target for the IRA during the decades of conflict.

Posh as the Reform Club undoubtedly was, Sam couldn't imagine it comparing well to the plush establishments the Brit was used to in London – the old boys' clubs with deep seats and long pours. There wasn't much to recce, unfortunately. There wasn't much he could see from the street. Sam was tired of racking his mind for a scenario that fitted, so he kept his distance and waited for his next move to reveal itself. He tried to stretch the tension out of his mind and body while he mooched around, observing discreetly.

Until he caught sight of a man he knew well and realised what was going on.

Sam stood in his suit, in his sweat, in astonishment as his old major walked down Royal Avenue. The man stood out like a sore thumb: straight back, garish green tie, matching pocket handkerchief. He looked every inch the English officer, parading down the street like he owned it, in his hand-stitched shoes. Of all the eventualities he might have predicted, this was not one. He drew the phone and hit redial.

"Hallo?"

"What correspondence can you find between my mark and a man in the military?"

"What is the name?"

"I don't want to get into names on the phone. It's a military person – or former military."

The Belgian sighed into the long silence. "I cannot tell who is perhaps military and who is not."

"Check emails for auto signatures. This prick will probably still describe himself by rank."

Sam watched the major pause to admire himself in the tall windows of CastleCourt. Sam remembered how incandescent his boss had been at his refusal to tell him why he'd gone AWOL in the Middle East. He recalled the glee with which the major has busted him from special forces back to the Marines. To Sam, the man in his eyeline was worthy of only hatred, but that didn't explain why he was in Belfast to meet the Brit.

"Is this person one of the circle?" inquired the Belgian.

"No, that would be a coincidence too far."

"Is there anything else you can tell me? There is nothing."

"Look at very brief messages or emails. Anything that confirms the location. Search for Belfast."

"Ah, here is one. It says … ah, ok, it says Reform Club, fourteen hundred."

"Is there anything else?"

"There is a chain. It is saying, 'A job perhaps you will be interested in'. That is all that is here."

Sam had to move. He had a fair idea what kind of job the Brit had in mind for the major and it was the kind of thing that couldn't be discussed in advance. Sam had no doubt, though, that as soon as the major found out what the job entailed, he would accept and enjoy fulfilling the role.

———

SAM STRODE ACROSS THE STREET, sure that the Brit had done his research and found the man capable and content to remove the thorn in his side. But the belief that the Brit intended to engage the major to take Sam out brought with it an opportunity. Perhaps he could take his old boss's place in the posh seats.

The chance of achieving that was minute. Unlike most UK or Irish cities, Sam knew Belfast people were less inclined to take a wide berth. If there was a scrap on the street, he'd bet that strangers would back the underdog and wade in with the boots. Plus, the police were armed. Besides all that, brass or not, the man he was approaching had been a major in the special forces and knew how to handle himself.

Sam glanced down the alleyway between Primark and Tesco, right beside the Reform Club. There was a pub fifty metres away but the laneway was busy. He knew where it led, though, so in the final few steps Sam tried to suppress his temper and go for smarts.

Recognition scudded across the major's face like sunshine from under a cloud. Sam approached, smiling, his face as open as he could make it, hand extended. Confusion and alarm was all that was held in the major's face.

"Thanks for coming, major," Sam said. "Sorry for all the cloak and dagger. Necessary, I'm afraid."

The major stared at him. "What the bloody hell is going on, Ireland?" he managed.

"It's sensitive, major. Our mutual friend has had to change the venue. Press, I'm afraid," he said. "Reporters inside. Coincidental, of course – they're there for another event. Nonetheless, not ideal."

"What?" the major struggled.

Sam couldn't work out whether the major had been briefed and knew in advance what would be asked of him, so he played all bases.

"Look, sir, our mutual friend wasn't able to discuss this on the telephone, so I suggested he mention my name as a bit of a ruse, as it were, to persuade you to pop over from London. I don't know whether you were factoring my presence into the equation or not." Sam didn't pose it as a question but hoped for an acknowledgement or otherwise. None came. He pressed on. "We had no way of knowing there would be another event inside, so our friend has asked me to fetch you, sir, and to take you to an alternative venue."

The major stared at him, bewildered. Sam wondered whether he was going to have to revert to his original plan of choking the bastard.

"I'm not going anywhere with you," the major blurted.

"All I can do is explain to you what's going on, sir. The gentleman from the Lords, whom I now provide security for, was due to meet you here. He got in touch with you in the hope of engaging you to provide a service for him. Because of the phone tapping situation, he may have intimated that it was in relation to an innocuous matter, or he may not have. I am not privy to that information. But he did suggest that because you and I were acquainted," Sam gestured between them, "he should tell you that it concerned me. Two birds, as it were – Belfast and a colleague whom you dismissed, sir."

Sam had no idea how that would land. It had been a

long time since he'd had to adopt his England voice, his more reserved voice, to make dialogue with the brass more easily understood.

The major grunted in disapproval.

"If you would follow me, sir, the gentleman would like to talk to you at a different location because of the media presence at this one."

The major continued to eye him with deep suspicion but Sam didn't want to give him any more thinking time, so turned on his heel and began walking. In his bafflement the major followed. Not a word thereafter was spoken. Sam was the servant, the major, the master. He could hear his old boss remain at his heel as he turned down the wide entry, past the pub and to the door of a church. He stepped into a cold but decent-sized porch, dark and tiled. Sam moved a little further into the gloom and stood aside, waiting for the major's steps to fall in beside his. The major obliged and stood staring at the Marian devotion. Sam waited and watched until he finally decided he'd had enough. Peace process or no peace process, a Catholic chapel in Belfast was no place for a British naval officer. The major fumbled in his pocket for a mobile phone and Sam stepped forward and struck him, full force, in the Adam's apple.

It would take at least three minutes, Sam reckoned, possibly more. The major was a man with diver's lungs and fit as a trout. His arms lashed, flinging Sam aside, and they battled for thirty seconds in the tiny porch; tight, close blows aiming for the soft, painful parts as they had been trained to do. Amateurs fought hard, knuckles on skulls, busted hands and eye sockets. Professionals fought dirty, gouging eyes, ripping bollocks, disabling quickly, cutting off air, vision, sound, touch.

The major didn't stand a chance. His airway was

blocked and the energy he wasted fighting only hastened his suffocation. Sam caught him as his knees gave way, gripping his shoulder and hugging him in tight. There were half-a-dozen silent people scattered throughout the beautiful church as he manoeuvred him through the swinging door. None of the worshippers looked around as he placed the major at one of the rearmost pews, on his knees, head forward in prayer. No one would disturb the devout. His body could rest there for hours before anyone thought to check. Sam hijacked the major's phone and wallet to further delay any identification, and left to meet the man's lunch date.

Chapter 43

He was lurking behind the floppy pages of *The Daily Telegraph*. A waist-coated waiter had shown Sam to his table. All that had been required was a name, with title, naturally. When the Brit saw Sam, his jaw dropped along with the broadsheet, but he did his best to gain composure.

"M'lud," Sam said, sitting in the armchair opposite and drawing it in close. "The major apologises that he will not be able to join you for luncheon." The Brit could only stare open-mouthed. Sam drew out his new phone, stroked it to life and fired up a video the twin had placed on its memory. Leaning in so that the man could hear it, he turned the screen towards the stunned Brit, who pitched forward, naturally, inquisitiveness etched across his forehead and confusion evident in his open mouth and wobbly jowls. He shifted momentarily, looking around, afraid of being overheard. Sam tapped the little arrow to begin the entertainment.

"Look, you little Belgian bastard," it began. The Brit watched himself on a split screen for less than two seconds before he closed his eyes and fell back into his chair. His head tilted back and his neck arched to the ceiling. His eyes reopened and he stared at the beams above him.

"They're all there," Sam said, wagging the phone at him. "We've even got your meeting with the professor while he was in New York. The keeper is gone, but you probably know that by now."

The Brit flinched. That was evidently news to him.

Eventually he spoke softly. "People like you will never understand that there are times when things like this are required to bring about a better outcome for everyone." His delivery was slow, almost sad.

Sam sighed. "Is this where you tell me that your rape and abuse are justified for the greater good?"

"Oh, I'm not an abuser – never was."

"Bullshit."

"No, no, Sam. I simply pull the strings."

The Brit's pompous tone grated with Sam. It was as if he were explaining a complicated proposition to an idiot. Sam listened nonetheless; he still hadn't put the story fully together yet.

"That way we can get people to move in the correct direction."

"What direction? What direction warrants this sick nonsense?"

"Peace, perhaps?" The Brit paused, hoping to land some justification.

Sam stared blankly back.

"Or to persuade influential figures to do the right thing. You see, the public doesn't always vote for what is good for them. They are emotional, they are volatile, they give in to their urges, their angers, their fears. You know all about that, don't you, Sam? You know what it is to give in to violence, to allow your impulses to take over."

Sam ignored the goading. "So your circle of abuse is the fault of the general public, for voting for the wrong people?"

The Brit sighed as if Sam were more to be pitied than scolded. "I was responsible for delivering certain things, certain outcomes. I had to achieve my targets, just like anyone else, and it was left to me to determine how I achieved those ends."

"And your target was?"

"To make important people compliant, of course. If you compromise somebody, in a salacious way, then you have that chap at your mercy. This is not a new concept, Sam. It was always thus."

"So the heir was skinned and raped and imprisoned to what end?"

"Well, peace in Ireland was achieved, Sam, and every element contributed. There was your lot, of course – the military and what have you. There was influence from America and elsewhere. But there was also a certain amount of manipulation to get politicians to do what was required, to change their minds. To subtly alter their positions on certain matters. Politicians in Northern Ireland are particularly belligerent, as you know, so they required what the Americans might call leverage – pressure, persuasion. The truth is that the heir was being abused long before we ever came across the Visitors and their ghastly little ring."

Sam bristled at the use of "visitors". He thought of the professor's computer password and shook his head. "But you led the visitors, that's clear from all the recordings."

"Ultimately, perhaps, but not the abuse. Rather, I insinuated control, which is removed from participation. It took quite some time, Sam – almost two decades, as a matter of fact, but I assure you, the results were really very pleasing."

"So your story is that you came across the abuse group, somehow joined it and then became the boss? To achieve what – blackmail its members to bring about peace?"

"As part of the effort." He shrugged, proud but humble to have done his bit.

"That means you allowed the rape and abuse to continue when you could have stopped it."

"You're not appreciating the complexity of this, Sam, really. This was just one string to a very broad bow. But you can't be expected to understand those who serve in more imaginative ways, you who served your country well as an oily rag. And in your miscomprehension, you have rather got in the way."

"I don't think *The Guardian* newspaper or *The New York Times* will understand it either when they receive these videos."

"No doubt they're ready to go," the Brit was casually dismissive with a wave of his hand, "from your friend's twin sister or that money-grabbing little foreigner. But it is of little consequence now."

And with that he reached forward and popped a pill into his glass of white wine. Alarm shot through Sam's spine as he anticipated the arrival of others to pin him back and force the liquid down his throat. The Brit read him like a book.

"Oh, no, Sam, this is not for you. I'm aware I've made a few faux pas, as it were. Allowing myself to be recorded was a touch of naivety from an old dog in a new world. I often wonder why we go to such lengths to gain access to encrypted media when, in fact, a twelve-year-old can work out how to record it. Easier than setting a tape for the *Antiques Roadshow.*"

"Who do you work for?" Sam asked with more urgency than he would have liked.

"Nobody, any more. But there are always loose ends when one has dabbled in the things I've been involved in. Few are quite as convoluted as this, granted, but nonetheless I had hoped to tidy up and end my retirement in the Lords. You've become a spoke in the works."

"How do you do it? How do you just carry on when you know there are children being raped?"

"Bit rich, is it not, Sam, with your extrajudicial existence? How many people have you made disappear in the past year?"

Sam didn't really want to start counting.

"Of course, you're quite right. The shame for me," he shook his head, "latterly it builds in my more contemplative years. One makes decisions when young that are impulsive. You of all people will come to understand that if you live long enough. But for me it has become," he paused, looking toward a distant window to the side, "too much. Much too much." He snapped up the wine glass and drank back the golden fluid. "Rather unpleasant drop, that," he looked at his glass, "to finish with, which is a shame."

The Brit looked into Sam's eyes for a hint of what was to come. "I don't expect compassion from a brute like you," he said, "but if there were any means by which I could be kept out of the picture, it would rather serve you well."

Sam almost laughed at him. "I intend to stop this ring – these visitors, this circle."

"Yes, I quite follow. If you are prepared to do that without going to the newspapers, I shall agree to help you.

But it will require a gentleman's agreement, and time is really quite tight."

Sam snorted at him. "Are you for real?"

"Quite real, as you put it, Sam. Now, if you deal with these people without exposing the whole saga, I shall entrust to you the job I had intended to pass to your former boss, the major."

"What?"

"I shall give you the information you will require to close down the circle. Of course, I had intended that the major see to you as well, but that plan has rather gone awry."

"You wanted the major to kill me and then the members of the circle?"

"Exactly," he said. "You have proven so difficult to contain I considered it prudent to deploy someone with similar skills to yours but perhaps with better breeding and intelligence to put an end to your prying. And I chose the major because, like the rest of us, the major is not squeaky clean either."

"And this is supposed to persuade me to protect your legacy?"

"As I say, time is tight. You have moments to make up your mind. Agree to deal with these people quietly and live with your child in blissful abandon upon the ocean wave—"

"Or what?"

"Or forever look over your shoulder. You see, Sam, you're not the only one with contingencies."

Sam's shook his head as the Brit pressed on. "I need an answer. Now."

"Ok," Sam said.

The Brit nodded, took out his own phone, selected a contact and spoke.

"You can stand down. No further action is necessary on the continent, understood?"

Sam couldn't hear the answer, but he could hear someone on the other end of the call. The man set the phone down and reached around his back. Sam tensed to pounce but the Brit remained astonishingly calm.

"It's quite alright, Sam," he said in his consistently condescending tone. "It's merely a gift."

He handed over a hanging file folder from a filing cabinet. The tab on the top was handwritten: VISITORS.

Sam watched as the Brit began to shake, then shudder, whatever he'd swallowed hitting its mark.

"They'll all go quietly, just like me, if you manage it correctly."

Final words before the induced stroke erupted inside his head.

———

SAM LIFTED the wine glass and dropped it into the cardboard file folder. The Brit looked as if he was asleep. Sam imagined such a state was not uncommon in gentlemen's clubs, so he walked quietly out, noting the absence of CCTV cameras. He took some comfort that anyone inquiring after the Brit's lunch companion would consult the guest list and begin a search for someone else – a major in the Royal Navy, no less, who was in fact dead in a nearby church. All of that would pose quite a conundrum for any investigator, Sam reckoned, but if they ever worked it out, he would be well offshore.

Sam didn't open the file until he got back to the boat. Inside were the images and profiles of a dozen people. Taped to a piece of paper was a tiny computer memory drive, smaller than an SD card. Beside it was a scrawl: *All sorts of compromising behaviour. Enough to achieve the goal.*

Sam took the note to be from the Brit – some sort of establishment-sponsored manipulator, to his former major.

There was a separate A4 sheet with different images of the twelve people with profiles in the file. Sam gave it a glance. At least two he knew to be influential figures in Irish politics, back roomers, the powerful ones. He imagined them to have the clout to manipulate big decisions. Sam assumed the Brit had used his leverage to employ them to do his bidding, but he'd heard enough about the brutality involved to give the rest of the file a miss, for now. He had already decided what he would do with the information, but that could wait too.

The idea of sending the videos to the press vanished. He felt, for the first time, that Isla and he had an opportunity. He feared being drawn in further, having their privacy compromised, disrupting the peace he needed to build around her.

He layered up for a long haul. The windlass ground the anchor aboard, the donkey fired and the impeller hove water in to cool the engine. He set the autohelm and skipped on deck to unleash the sails. Then he sat at the navigation table and pulled out the almanac for information on the tides heading south. Biscay, Lisbon, Gibraltar, Valencia, he reckoned. If he didn't stop, and with good breeze, he might make it in eight days.

Chapter 44

S am gave Charity the heir's address, as involuntarily imparted by the keeper in his final breaths. He outlined what he knew of the woman's circumstances, her vulnerabilities and left it to the expert in the knowledge that the victim was finally in good hands. He had others to care for.

Sam sailed into a small marina in Palamós on the east coast of Spain. His father wouldn't be hauling any ropes, but for a seventy-something with a freshly punctured chest he was in astonishing shape.

Isla's little arms wrapped around his neck and they hugged for five solid minutes before he swung her aboard and gave her her orders. Like a salty little seabird she fell into line, busying herself with the warps. Brown as a berry and steady as a rock, she leaned into him as the breeze took the cutter and heeled her to lee. With the warm breeze on their necks and a glass in their paws, they left the coast of one country and headed to another.

Sam never asked what was on the memory card. The

twin made copies and the Belgian tracked down the addresses. Each of the twelve was posted a copy of their compromising behaviour.

He read the obituaries in the online sections of various newspapers. Nine of the Visitors appeared to have perished at their own instigation. The keeper made ten and the professor had taken a nose dive off his own balcony. Which left one.

Sam filed it away. He'd get to it, and he would work to find out how the keeper had found Sam's contact. It would vex him until dealt with, but it would have to wait. Isla fell asleep against him. That would do for now.

Next in the Sam Ireland series

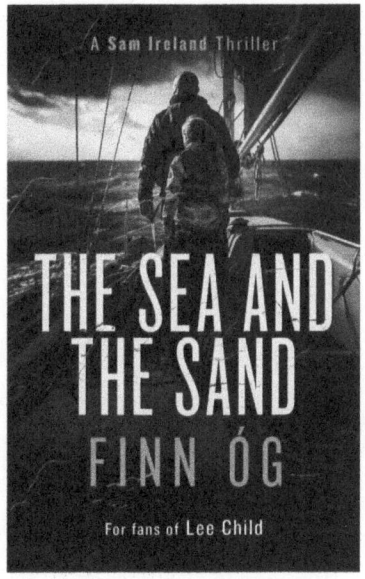

vinci-books.com/sand

Sam Ireland wants to raise his daughter in peace, but when he saves a woman and child from drowning, he's drawn into a dangerous web of human trafficking.

Turn the page for a free preview.

The Sea and the Sand - Preview

CHAPTER ONE

The world is irritatingly small.

Sam stood on Grafton Street, watched the man go up in flames and cursed how approximate people have become. He sighed for a moment and watched the crowd part like a sea of red, the glow of the inferno flickering off their faces, horrifying and beguiling in almost equal measure. Sam shook his head, looked to the sky and stepped forward to douse the screams.

He'd grow to wish he'd let the man burn.

———

"Snap!"

Isla was cheating, as usual, in part due to a misunderstanding of the rules. At six years old the fun was more in beating her father to the draw than in stockpiling cards, and so she shouted before the face had even been flipped. It delighted Sam to watch how her little mind anticipated his hand movements, to see her excitement. It seemed like a normal, wholesome thing to do of an evening after all the wee woman had been through.

They were drifting, alone, across the Mediterranean in their fifty-four-foot home. Progress was deliberately slow, there'd been a lot of rebuilding to do and the work was far from finished. Sam wasn't sure whether his daughter's scars would ever properly heal but she was gradually becoming less afraid of bedtime and the potential horror that sleep could bring.

He'd made resolutions, starting with how he made a living. He wouldn't take on any more work that could possibly impact his daughter or his family. The last job he'd been embroiled in had done that and more. From here on in, Sam determined, any risks taken would be his alone, and even at that they would be minimal. He had a child to raise and she no longer had a mother to step into the breach.

"Daddy, you can have some of my cards," she told him, sliding a frugal collection to his side of the chart table.

"Thank you, darlin'," said Sam, the salt and the stubble tautening at a gentle reminder of his daughter's provenance. Isla's mother would never have seen anyone stuck; winning had never been Shannon's priority.

"What story do you want tonight?"

"Aw-uh, is it bedtime already?"

"Not yet, little lady, but in a while."

It had become part of the ritual to keep the imagery gentle: stories at night of normal life, of other girls, of school and excitement and toys and boys and the weird and horrible things they do. Sam's plan was to encourage Isla to want such things again, to grow the appeal of ordinariness rather than the nomadic sea-gypsy style they'd become accustomed to. Although the perpetual sailing suited Sam, and for a while it had seemed the best way to make Isla feel safe, he knew the time would come when she would have to swim in the real world again, so their grift when the wind blew them west, was aimed at Ireland once more.

By night Sam plotted the charts and the future and occasionally sailed. It allowed Isla to keep watch while he dozed by day in the cockpit. She'd become quite the little sailor, careful and clipped on at all times above deck, and he trusted her. Mostly they anchored or found a marina at night but they'd ended up further east and south than he'd ever intended and luxuries like safe harbours were thin on the North African coast.

Occasionally, when the notion took him, he stood at the helm and allowed his own healing. The breeze peeled back his grief and the anonymity and privacy of the sea enabled him to let the stream roll down his cheeks. Such moments kept his pain from Isla, avoiding her interrogation and worry. He'd never allow her to see him weep – it would upset her too much. She understood how much he missed his wife, her mother, but it would never be the same as it was for her. Isla hadn't just lost her mam, she'd held her hand as that beautiful life ebbed away. They'd spoken as she bled out. Isla had cuddled her and looked into the face of her killer, convinced she was next. Worse still, she'd believed it was all her fault.

Sam read to her until the flood and fall of her little body slowed, and curled his neck to make sure she was deep enough to extract his arm from under her. Then he waited for two full minutes, watching her eyelids for any sign of disturbance. Placated, he went on deck and indulged his maudlin currents, allowing himself to be swept back to better times and to lament his loss. That's when the tears came. Eventually he'd snap out of it and sail the boat, but for a while he would purge. It brought an odd sort of pleasure – the wallowing, the reminiscence.

He was shocked when Isla's little face appeared in the companionway; the yellow light breaking his night vision as she came up the steps.

"What was that, Daddy?" she said.

"What, wee lamb?" Sam replied, scraping the tears from the crevices in his face.

"The noise – the whistle."

Sam turned his ears from the wind and stood stock-still but could catch nothing.

"There. Can you hear it, Daddy?"

"No, snugs, I think you better go back to sleep," he said, pressing the autohelm into gear and checking the radar screen to make sure their course was clear.

He was lifting her into her bunk when she said it again.

"There it is, Daddy. Why can't you hear that?"

"You're dreaming, wee love. You're still a bit asleep," he told her, tucking her in, keen to get back to the helm.

"I'm not, Daddy. I'm really, really not," she replied.

"Ok, I'll go up and keep an ear out," he said as he hugged her. He was worried she might not sleep now, and was anxious they were sailing with no watch above. "I love you so much," he said, and returned to the cockpit.

And then came the sound: high-pitched – audible to younger ears at a distance, older ones when up close.

And it was close.

Amid one hundred thousand square miles of sea, Sam and Isla were no longer alone, and every resolution he had made went over the side.

CHAPTER TWO

"Wasters," spat Habid, as he watched honest men haul nets out of the sea. The noise behind him was gradually increasing as the bumper-track of a city came to life with a relentless hammering upon horns. Not that Alexandria ever really slept, Habid was struggling to adjust to the relentless commotion.

His life had taken some curious turns in recent months. Habid had been a shepherd, of sorts, herding flocks through the sands of eastern Libya. Now he was amassing money hand over fist, more than he'd ever known. It made him rather pleased with himself – cocky, harder, less pleasant than his usual unpleasant self.

He wrapped up the bits and pieces, keen to get them cleared from the beach before the darkness disappeared entirely. But he afforded himself a few minutes to sneer at the fishermen as they stood thigh deep in their underpants and plucked the occasional wriggler from an otherwise empty net. What a lot of work for absolutely nothing, he thought. There were barely enough fish in their buckets to make a meal for each man's family.

He looked into his little bag – well, it was his now, but a few hours ago it had belonged to someone else. It was filled with pawn, of a sort. For extras. Other travel providers were at it, he thought, so why not? Airlines, rail companies, inter-continental crossings weren't cheap. Nothing was complimentary any more, even the basics came at a cost. Like water. Or sunscreen. Or a life jacket. Of course, his clients didn't have any cash left, so he'd been generous to take alternatives.

Habid hadn't a clue how long it took. He knew nothing about boats. He knew about dust and sand and living like a bloody Bedouin. The disruption in his own failed state had allowed him to abandon his post as a border guard for

Gaddafi, but the sea was a mystery he had no notion of finding out about. That's why he hadn't gone himself. Not yet anyway.

———

"Get dressed and get your life jacket on," Sam barked below at Isla.

"What's wrong?" she shouted, reawakened from her sleep and instantly alarmed.

"I think there might be someone in the water," he shouted back. "Pass me up the flashlight."

Isla emerged from her cabin half dressed, reached for the lamp and handed it up to him as he worked the helm with his other hand.

"Now go and get warm clothes on and your harness and your life jacket."

"Ok, Daddy." She tore off.

Sam held the wheel and leaned as far outboard as he could, straining to hear the sound again, but it was gone on the building breeze. He must have passed it, whatever it was. He debated leaving it in his wake – it wasn't his problem, then he saw Isla coming and she put paid to that.

"We can rescue them," she said, excitement dancing in her eyes, and for a moment Sam saw her mother looking straight at him.

There was no question in Isla's mind about what they ought to do. None. And there shouldn't have been for Sam either, except that he didn't want anyone else on his boat, near his kid, for what would inevitably be days at sea.

Perhaps one day Sam would learn to trust his instincts.

———

Habid fancied a treat. A nice place to put his head down before returning to the dust. It was a risk, he conceded, to check into the Sofitel Cecil but it looked so sumptuous after his filthy journey across the desert. He imagined a beautiful shower, a soft, clean bed, a toilet that flushed. He had enough money, but there was no concealing what he was: a sun-dried Libyan blown with the sand by a Spring that had uprooted countless thousands across North Africa.

Except he wasn't seeking refuge from it – he was making his fortune from it, and he had a fake passport and a bag full of cash, so he strode in and acted like he owned the place.

———

"I can hear someone screaming!" called Isla from her vantage point above the spray hood. She was on tiptoes, peering into the dark, her little ears straining for sounds from the sea. The girth of the waves was increasing and the boat had begun to roll gently into them.

"What direction?" shouted Sam.

"What?" screamed Isla in return.

"Point to it!" he tried instead.

His little girl turned and gestured with absolute confidence. Sam turned the wheel and headed as she directed. Eventually he too heard the noise – a woman, he reckoned, yelling from the surface. He leaned over again, glancing at Isla to make sure she stayed well inboard. He painted the surface of the sea with the LED beam but detected nothing.

"We're not close enough, Daddy. It's over there," shouted Isla above the thunking draw of the diesel's pistons.

They carried forward. A high-pitched wail reached Sam from the starboard side, just as Isla had indicated, and he gently brought the boat around, conscious he could do more harm than good to anyone flailing around beneath them. He was also wary of any stricken vessel languishing in the sea. If he hit something, they would all end up in the water.

His beam caught something and he stroked the torch back to find it again, but it was gone in the swell. His mind reached for the image – a black-clad human with arms in the air. In that position they'd no doubt plummeted beneath the waves and perhaps hadn't come up again. He coated the area again, hunting as much for a boat as a person. As always, his primary concern was his little girl; he wouldn't let their home sink for anyone.

Then there was a slightly different tone coming from the water, a new urgency to attract the beam. Sam jabbed and swiped the torch like a dagger but couldn't find a face, which must surely be turned towards the light. Suddenly two images were revealed and he juddered back to catch a veiled woman and a child. Of all the thoughts he might have mustered, his first was pointless: why hadn't she taken off the niqab? The child was clinging to a pathetic life jacket, half inflated; the sort of useless article found under the seat in a passenger plane.

"Come and take the wheel, Isla," Sam ordered, confident in his little woman's ability to hold the boat steady to a compass bearing. He reached for a line out of the aft locker and tied it around his waist.

"Keep the boat at zero-six-zero, darlin', ok?"

"Ok, Daddy," Isla said, half frightened, half excited.

He kicked off his shoes, tore off his fleece, stepped over the guardrail and dived in.

———

Habid lay between the fragrant crisp white linen sheets of the largest bed he'd ever seen and wondered whether the job had been done.

He took comfort from his surroundings as the wind rattled the shutters outside. He imagined the fuel must be close to exhausted as his cheek plunged deep into the spongy pillow. Habid hadn't cared about the outcome of previous trips – he hadn't given them a second thought, but this one was slightly different – if it worked out then a much grander plan could be put into action. So, try as he might, his thoughts prevented him from dozing off.

————

Sam pulled fifteen hard strokes before the line snagged at his waist. His strength in the water had been hewn long before his years in the Special Boat Service but that had its drawbacks: he swam face down. It had been drilled into him in childhood, during the 6 a.m. training lengths he'd hammered out every morning in a Belfast pool as one of his bleary-eyed parents gazed on from the gallery. Because of that he'd taken his eyes off the woman in the water and now had to relocate her in the moonlight. He needn't have worried.

Treading hard and breathing fast, he kicked round to confirm his bearings and find Isla but was gripped from the sea by a birdlike claw. He span in shock and was confronted with the menacing mask of the niqab and rabid eyes cutting through even the blackness of the garb. How the woman managed to remain afloat in the sodden shroud baffled Sam, but he barely had a second to ingest the image of the frightening figure before a girl of similar age to Isla was thrust towards him, unconscious, her head lolling back into the sea.

It took all the power in his legs to remain afloat in the waves as he extended the child, unfolding her like a tripod. He raised her head and rolled her slightly towards him. With his left arm curled all the way round her neck and over her face, he managed to pinch her nose and place his mouth over hers, forcing it open with his chin.

The woman immediately started screaming, slapping and grabbing at him in protest and Sam wished she would just succumb to the deep. He breathed hard into the tiny lungs and used his right forearm to bellow the child's stomach as if playing the pipes. All the time he was being scrabbed and punched by the woman, and it was after he'd exhausted his second lungful that he turned and pushed her back, lifting his legs to give her as hard a kick off as he could. But she had somehow caught the life jacket and the rope between him and the boat, so wasn't going anywhere. He'd no choice but to keep kicking and breathing for two. Every exhale was matched with a glance up towards the boat and Isla and at least two slaps or punches from the woman to his rear. He was about to give the effort up as hopeless when the child's body started to gently convulse in his arms. He raised her further from the sea and she vomited heartily all over his half-submerged face. The result quieted the mother and placated Sam until he became aware of an entirely more frightening risk.

He looked up at their boat, now thirty feet away, and saw another woman emerging from the water, up the bathing ladder towards where Isla stood, alone.

vinci-books.com/sand

About the Author

Finn Óg lives in Ireland and is surrounded by rogues and the sea. He writes when not afloat or when everyone else is asleep. His work includes drama and comedy under other pen names for multiple outlets.

Charlie, his first book, was originally published in 2018. It was followed by the *The Sea and the Sand* in 2019 and *Too Close to Home* in 2020.

Originally planned as a trilogy, a fourth book, *Before*, was published in 2021. *Charlie* was also rewritten that year. Each book features Sam Ireland and his daughter Isla.

The series can be read in any order.

vinci-books.com/samireland

For more information, or to sign up and receive new releases and short stories, you can visit Finn's website at: www.finnog.com

Acknowledgments

Thanks to the ladies, always. To my family and close friends who have kept secrets and a hawk eye. To those who left reviews and to my pal up north for first eyes. To those who edited and published – most recently Victoria Woodside, and to my crackin' wee curly crew for keeping us at sea. To the big one for her uncompromising sense of fairness and justice. Most of all, thank you to the real Isla for the laughing, the roguery, the questions and the creativity with which you approach everything. May your pencil and bow never rest. I luff you with all my heart.